ELSIE'S
KITH ⚜ KIN

Elsie's Kith and Kin
A Sequel to The Two Elsies
Book 12 of The Elsie Books

by Martha Finley

Any revisions or special features in this edition are
©2000 Hibbard Publications
ISBN 1-931343-03-9

Hibbard Publications Inc.
P. O. Box 3091
Wilmington, DE 19804

For information on all the quality books from Hibbard
Publications, email them at drabbihp@aol.com

Original Cover Design, ©Mark Dinsmore, Arkworks
Cover Concept & Production, ©Pneuma Books
Cover Illustration and page "x", ©Alicia Baker
Original Interior Design, ©Mark Dinsmore, Arkworks
Interior Production & Flourishes, ©Pneuma Books

Body typeset in Dutch 10 | 11
Titling in Seagull with Quotations in Shelley Volante

Printed in the United States of America by Lithocolor
07 06 05 04 03 02 01 00   7 6 5 4 3 2 1

ELSIE'S
KITH ✤ KIN

A Sequel to The Two Elsies

BOOK TWELVE IN THE ORIGINAL SERIES OF
THE ELSIE BOOKS

BY

MARTHA FINLEY

PUBLISHED BY HIBBARD PUBLICATIONS

Martha Finley

ABOUT MARTHA FINLEY

Faces We Seldom See:
The Author of the Elsie Books

BY FLORENCE WILSON FOR THE
LADIES HOME JOURNAL, 1893

THE AUTHOR of the famous "Elsie" books has succeeded in keeping her personality hidden so completely from a curious public that it is almost as an entire stranger to her readers that *The Ladies Home Journal* is able to present Miss Martha Finley.

She was born at Chillicothe, Ohio, in 1828, and for her first score or so of years, lived in different towns of Ohio and Indiana with her parents, Dr. James Brown Finley and Maria Theresa Brown. She was educated, for the most part, at home and in private schools in these different cities.

Soon after the death of her parents, about 1853, Miss Finley removed to New York, and a little later to Philadelphia, which she in turn left for Phoenixville, in the same State, and where she taught school for a number of years. During the war, and until 1874, her time was spent in either the one or the other of those places, and in the early part of 1874 — her school having been destroyed by the war — she removed to Bedford, Pennsylvania, where she made her home with an aunt and a sister. While in Philadelphia in 1876, at the Centennial Exposition, she visited relatives at Elkton, Maryland, and being in very poor health, and the surgeon whom she had selected as her physician residing there, she decided to make her home in that delightful town.

When about twenty-six years of age Miss Finley began her career as a writer, by contributing short stories to the children's departments of various Sunday school papers. Writing at first anonymously, the success of her stories induced her publishers to ask her to sign them; and as her family objected to the publishing of her own name, "Martha Farquharson" was chosen as her nom de plume. Farquharson is the clan name, the Gaelic of Finley, the family being of Scotch Irish ancestry.

Miss Finley's first successful Sunday school book was called "Jennie White." "Elsie Dinsmore," the idea of which, Miss Finley says, was given her as answer to a prayer for something which would yield her an income, was begun during the war, and with no intention of ever being continued in sequels, but the requests for the continuation have been so numerous and the demands of both public and publisher so imperative that it has never seemed possible to bring the series to a conclusion. In addition to Miss Finley's stories for children she has published several novels.

Miss Finley has been an invalid for a number of years and has done much of her writing while prostrated by illness. Despite this she keeps a bright and cheerful disposition, and is loved by all who know her.

In appearance Miss Finley is very pleasant. She is of average height with a figure inclined to plumpness. Her hair is snow white and forms a lovely setting to the delicate features and beautiful eyes beneath it. She dresses in the simplest taste, her favorite colors for her own wear being navy blue and gray.

Although the dogs of criticism have been let loose upon "Martha Farquharson" and her series of "Elsie," there has been almost no character in American juvenile fiction which has attained more widespread interest and affection. And for the author of this children's heroine there can be nothing but the kindliest feeling. In her simple womanliness and Christianity she is a type of the best in American spinsterhood.

—*Ladies' Home Journal* April 1893

Elsie's Kith & Kin

PREFACE
Publisher's Note

Hibbard Publications is the new publishing imprint dedicated to bringing you all of Martha Finley's 28 books in Dodd Mead's original published series of *The Elsie Books*.

Spanning over 38 years, Martha Finley penned the adventures of Elsie Dinsmore, often using members of her own family for characterization. Certainly, the socio-political climate of her time is evident in her storytelling, in addition to currents of Christian denominational debate. Truth, faith, religion, morality, and humanity are all underlying virtues in this extraordinary series of children's fiction.

As Miss Finley's stories evolve, Elsie Dinsmore is faced with a myriad of trials and tribulations. Elsie's devout faith and clear knowledge of Scripture enable her to persevere through each troublesome circumstance. As Elsie matures into a godly woman, so her unique family grows, adding to the lovable — and sometimes not so likeable — cast of Miss Finley's interesting characters.

In 1868, the New York firm of Dodd Mead released the first "Elsie" book, *Elsie Dinsmore*. Quickly becoming a bestseller for the publisher, it launched the succesful series, *The Elsie Books*. Martha Finley became one of the most renowned children's writers of her time, with book sales second only to Louisa May Alcott. By 1945, an estimated 5 million copies of volumes 1-12 alone had been sold.

Hibbard Publications is honored to continue this heartwarming series, bringing back values and faith that are jeopardized in today's society. We hope you enjoy *The Elsie Books*.

—The Publisher

CHAPTER ONE

O married love! Each heart shall own,
Where two congenial souls unite,
Thy golden chains inlaid with down,
Thy lamp with heaven's own splendor bright.

—LANGHORNE

"THERE, THERE, little woman! Light of my eyes and core of my heart! If you don't stop this pretty soon, I very much fear I shall be compelled to join you," Edward Travilla said, between a laugh and a sigh, drawing Zoe closer to him, laying her head against his chest, and kissing her tenderly on lip and cheek and brow. "I shall begin to think you already regret having stayed behind with me."

"No, no, no!" she cried, dashing away her tears, then putting her arms about his neck, and returning his caresses with ardor of affection. "Dear Ned, you know you're more than all the rest of the world to your silly little wife. But it seems lonely just at first, to have them all gone at once, especially mamma — and to think we'll not see her again for months! I do believe you'd cry yourself if you were a girl."

"Altogether likely," he said, laughing and giving her another hug. "But, being a man, it wouldn't do at all to allow my feelings to overcome me in that manner. Besides, with my darling little wife still left me, I'd be an ungrateful wretch to repine at the absence of other dear ones."

"What a neat little speech, Ned!" she exclaimed, lifting her head to look up into his face and laughing through her tears — for her eyes had filled again. "Well, you know I can't help feeling a little lonely and sad just at first. But, for all that, I wouldn't for the world be anywhere else than here in your arms." And with a sigh of content and thankfulness, she let her pretty head drop upon his shoulder again.

"My darling! May it ever be to you the happiest place on earth! God helping me, I shall always try to make it so," he said with a sudden change to gravity and in low, moved tones.

"My dear, dear husband!" she murmured, clinging closer to him.

Then, wiping her eyes, "I sha'n't cry any more; for, if I'm not the happiest woman in the world, I ought to be. And what a nice time we shall have together, dear Ned! Each wholly devoted to the other all winter long. I have it all planned out. While you are out about the plantation in the mornings, I'll attend to my housekeeping and my studies and in the afternoons and evenings — after I've recited — we can write our letters, or entertain ourselves and each other with music and books. You can read to me while I work, you know."

"Yes, a book is twice as enjoyable read in that way — sharing the pleasure with you," he said, softly stroking her hair and smiling down into her eyes.

"Especially if it is a good story or a bit of lovely poetry," she added.

"Yes," he said, "we'll have both those in turn, and some solid reading besides."

"I don't like solid reading," she returned, with a charming pout.

"One may cultivate a taste for it, I think,' he answered pleasantly.

"But you can't cultivate what you haven't got,' she objected.

"True enough," he said laughingly. "Well, then, we'll try to get a little first and cultivate it carefully afterward. I must go now, love," he added, releasing her. "The men need some directions from me in regard to their work."

"And the women need some from me," said Zoe. "Oh! You needn't laugh, Ned," shaking her finger at him as he turned in the doorway to give her an amused glance. "Perhaps some of these days you'll find out that I am really an accomplished housewife, capable of giving orders and directions, too."

"No doubt, my dear, for I am already proud of you in that capacity," he said, throwing her a smiling kiss, then hurrying away.

Zoe summoned Aunt Dicey, the housekeeper, gave her orders for the day, and the needed supplies from pantry and storeroom. Then she went to the sewing room to give some directions to Christine and Alma.

She lingered there for a little, trying on a morning dress they were making for her. Then she repaired to her boudoir, intent upon beginning her studies, which had been rather neglected of late in the excitement of the preparations for the departure of the greater part of the family for a winter at Viamede.

BUT SHE HAD scarcely taken out her books when the sound of wheels on the avenue attracted her attention, and glancing from the window, she saw the Roselands carriage draw up at the front entrance, and Ella Conly alight from it and run up the veranda steps.

"There, I'll not do much studying today, I'm afraid," said Zoe, half aloud, "for even if it's only a call she has come for, she'll not leave under an hour."

She hastily replaced the books in the drawer from which she had taken them. She had a feeling, only half acknowledged even to herself, of repugnance to having Ella know of her studies — Ella, who had graduated from boarding school and evidently felt herself thoroughly educated. Then she hurried down to meet and welcome her guest.

"I told Cal and Art I thought you'd be sure to feel dreadfully lonely today after seeing everybody but Ned start off on a long journey, and so I'd come and spend the day with you," said Ella when the two had exchanged kisses and inquiries after each other's health.

"It was very kind and thoughtful of you," returned Zoe, leading the way into the parlor usually occupied by the family, where an open wood fire blazed cheerily on the hearth.

"Take this easy chair, won't you?" she said, wheeling it a little nearer the grate, "and Dinah shall carry away your wraps when it suits you to doff them. I wish cousins Cal and Art would invite themselves to dine with us too."

"Art's very busy just now," said Ella. "There's a great deal of sickness and I don't believe he's spent a whole night at home for the last week or more."

"Dear me! I wouldn't be a doctor for anything — nor a doctor's wife!" exclaimed Zoe.

"Well, I don't know. There's something to be said on both sides of that question," laughed Ella. "I can tell you, Art would make a mighty good husband, and it's very handy, in case of sickness, to have the doctor in the house."

"Yes, but, according to your account, he's generally somewhere else than in his own house," returned Zoe playfully.

Ella laughed. "Yes," she said, "doctors do have a hard life, but, if you say so to Art, he always says he has never regretted having chosen the medical profession, because it affords so many opportunities for doing good. It's plain he makes that the business of his life. I'm proud of Art. I don't believe there's a better man anywhere. I was sick last summer and you wouldn't believe how kindly he nursed me."

"You can't tell me anything about him that I should think too good to believe," said Zoe. "He's our family doctor, you remember, and, of course, we are attached to him on that account, as well as because of the relationship."

"Yes, to be sure. There, Dinah, you may carry away my hat and cloak," Ella said, divesting herself of them as she spoke, "but leave the satchel. I brought my fancywork, Zoe. One has to be industrious now, as Christmas is coming. I decided to embroider a pair of slippers for each of my three brothers. Walter does not expect to get home, so I made his first, as they had to travel so far. I'm nearly done with Art's, and then I have Cal's to do."

"Oh, how pretty!" exclaimed Zoe, examining the work, "and that's a new stitch. Won't you teach it to me?"

"Yes, indeed, with pleasure. And I want you to teach me how to crochet that lace I saw you making the other day. I thought it so pretty."

The two spent a pleasant morning chatting together over their fancywork, saying nothing very wise, perhaps, but neither did they say anything harmful. An innocent jest now and again, something — usually laudatory — about some member of the family connection, and remarks and directions about their work, formed the staple of their talk.

"Oh! How did it come that you and Ned stayed behind when all the rest went to Viamede for the winter?" asked Ella.

"Business kept my husband, and love for him and his company kept me," returned Zoe, with a look and smile that altogether belied any suspicion Ella might have had that she was fretting over the disappointment.

"Didn't you want to go?"

"Yes, indeed, if Edward could have gone with me, but my place with him is better than any other without him."

"Well, I don't believe I should have been willing to stay behind, even in your place. I've always had a longing to spend a winter there visiting my sister Isa, and my cousins Elsie and Molly. Cal and Art say, perhaps one or both of them may go on to spend two or three weeks this winter, and in that case I shall go along."

"Perhaps we may go at the same time. What a nice party we will make!" said Zoe. "There," glancing from the window, "I see my husband coming, and I want to run out and speak to him. Will you excuse me a moment?" and scarcely waiting for a reply, she ran happily away.

Meeting Edward on the threshold, "I have no lessons to recite this time," she said, "but you are not to scold, because I've been prevented from studying by company. Ella is spending the day with me."

"Ah! I hope you have had a pleasant time together — not

too much troubled by fear of a lecture from the old tyrant who hears your lessons," he said laughingly, as he bent his head to press a kiss of ardent affection upon the rosy lips she held up to him.

"No," she laughed in return. "I'm not a bit afraid of him."

Zoe had feared the hours when Edward was unavoidably absent from her side would be very lonely now while the other members of the Ion family were away, but she did not find it so. Her studies and the work of making various pretty things for Christmas gifts kept her very busy.

And when he was with her, time flew on very rapid wings. She had grown quite industrious and generally plied her needle in the evenings while he read or talked to her. But occasionally he would take the embroidery or whatever it was out of her hands and toss it aside, saying she was trying her eyes by such constant use. And, besides, he wanted her undivided attention.

And she would resign herself to her fate, nothing loath to be drawn close to his side or to a seat upon his knee, to be hugged and caressed like a child, which, indeed, he persisted in calling her.

This was when they were alone, but very frequently they had company to spend the day, afternoon or evening. Ion had always been noted for its hospitality, and scarcely a week passed in which they did not pay a visit to the Oaks, the Laurels, the Pines, or Roselands.

Also, a brisk correspondence was carried on with the absent members of the family. And Zoe's housekeeping cares and duties were just enough to be an agreeable variety in her occupations. Every day, too, when the weather permitted, she walked or rode out with her husband.

And so the time passed quite delightfully for the first two months after the departure of the Viamede party.

It was a disappointment that Edward found himself too busy to make the hoped-for trip to Viamede at Christmas time, yet Zoe did not fret over it and really enjoyed the holidays extremely — giving and receiving numerous handsome presents, and, with Edward's assistance, making it a merry and happy time for the servants and other dependants, as well as for the relatives and friends still in the neighborhood.

The necessary shopping, with Edward to help her, and the packing and sending off of the Christmas boxes to Viamede, to the college boys — Herbert and Harold, and numerous other relatives and friends far and near, Zoe thought altogether the most delightful business she had ever taken in hand.

A very merry, happy little woman she was through all those weeks and months, Edward as devoted as any lover, and as happy and lighthearted as herself.

"Zoe, darling," Edward said one day at dinner, "I must drive over into our little village of Union — by the way, do you know that we have more than a hundred towns of that name in these United States?"

"No, I did not know, or suspect, that we had nearly so many," she interrupted, laughing. "No wonder letters go astray when people are not particular to give the names of both county and state. But what were you going to say about driving over there?"

"I must see a gentleman on business who will be there to meet the five o'clock train and leave on it. In order to be certain of seeing him, I must be there at least fifteen or twenty minutes before it is due. Shall I have the pleasure of my wife's company in the carriage? I have ordered it to be at the door by fifteen or twenty minutes past four, which will give us plenty of time, as it is an easy matter to drive from here to Union in ten minutes."

"Thank you," she said. "I accept the invitation with pleasure and promise to be ready at the minute."

"You are the best little woman about that," he returned with an appreciative look and smile. "I don't remember that you have ever yet kept me waiting when told beforehand at what time I intended to start."

"Of course not," she said with a pleased laugh, "because I was afraid if I did, I shouldn't be invited so often. And I'm always so glad to go with you."

"Not happier than I am to have you," he said with a very

lover-like glance and smile. "I always enjoy your society and am always proud to show my friends and acquaintances what a dear little wife I have. I dare say I'm looked upon as a very fortunate fellow in that respect, and sometimes envied on account of having drawn such a prize in the matrimonial lottery."

They had left the table while he spoke, and with the last words he passed his arm round her waist.

"Dear me, Ned, what a gallant speech!" she said, flushing with delight. "You deserve a reward," and she held up her face for a kiss.

"I am overpaid,' he said when he had bestowed it.

"In spite of the coin being such as you have right to help yourself to whenever you will?" she returned with a merry laugh. "Oh, Ned, my lover-husband!" she added, laying her head on his shoulder, "I am so happy in belonging to you, and I can never love you enough for all your goodness to me!"

"Darling, are you not equally good and loving to me?" he asked in tender tones and holding her close.

"But I owe everything to you," she responded with emotion. "If you had not come to my aid when my dear father was taken from me, what would have become of me, a mere child, without a near relative in the world, alone and destitute in a foreign land?"

"But I loved you, dearest. I sought my own happiness, as well as yours, in asking you to be my wife. So you need never feel burdened by the idea that you are under special obligation to me, to whom you are the very sunshine of life."

"Dear Ned, how very kind of you to say so," she responded, gazing with ardent affection into his eyes, "but it isn't burdensome to be under obligation to you, anymore than it is a trial to be ruled by you," she added with playful tenderness. "And I love to think of your goodness to me."

It was five minutes past four by Zoe's watch and she was just about to go to her dressing room to put on her hat and cloak, when visitors were announced — some ladies who always made a lengthy call at Ion, so she at once resigned herself to the loss of her anticipated drive with her husband.

"Oh, Ned!" she whispered in a hasty, vexed aside, "you'll have to go alone."

"Yes, dear," he returned, "but I'll try to get back in time to take you for a drive in the other direction."

They stepped forward, and greeted their guests with hospitable cordiality.

They were friends whose visits were prized and enjoyed, though their coming just at this time was causing Zoe a real disappointment. However, Edward's promise of a drive with him at a later hour so far made amends for it that she could truthfully express pleasure in seeing her guests.

Edward chatted with them for a few moments, then, excusing himself on the plea of business that could not be deferred, left them to be entertained by Zoe, while he entered his waiting carriage and went on his way to the village where he expected to meet his business acquaintance.

CHAPTER SECOND

The truth you speak doth lack some gentleness.

— SHAKESPEARE

EDWARD HAD MET and held his desired interview with his business acquaintance, seen him aboard his train, and was standing watching it as it steamed away and disappeared in the distance, when a feminine voice, close at hand, suddenly accosted him.

"Oh, Mr. Travilla! How are you? I consider myself very fortunate in finding you here."

He turned toward the speaker, and was not too greatly pleased at sight of her.

"Ah! Good evening, Miss Deane," he said, taking her offered hand and speaking with gentlemanly courtesy. "In what can I be of service to you?"

"By inviting me to Ion to spend the night," she returned laughingly. "I've missed my train and was quite in despair at the thought of staying alone overnight in one of the miserable little hotels of this miserable little village. So I was delighted to see your carriage standing there and you yourself beside it. For, knowing you to be one of the most hospitable of men, I am sure you will be moved to pity, and take me home with you."

Edward's heart sank at the thought of Zoe, but, seeing no way out of the dilemma, "Certainly," he said and helped his self-invited guest to a seat in his carriage, placed himself by her side, and bade the coachman drive on to Ion.

"Now, really, this is very good of you, Mr. Travilla," remarked Miss Deane. "There is no place I like better to visit than Ion, and I begin to think it was a rather fortunate mishap — missing my train."

"Very unfortunate for me, I fear," sighed Edward to himself. "The loss of her drive will be a great disappointment to Zoe and the sight of such a guest far from making it up to her. I am thankful the visit is to be for only a night."

Aloud he said, "I fear you will find it less pleasant than on former occasions — in fact, rather lonely, as all the family are absent — spending the winter at Viamede, my mother's Louisiana plantation — except my wife and myself."

"Ah! But your wife is a charming little girl — I never can think of her as a woman, you know — and you are a host in yourself," returned the lady laughingly.

Zoe's callers had left, and she, having donned her hat and cloak, not to keep her husband waiting a single moment, was at the window watching for his coming, when the carriage came driving up the avenue and drew up at the door.

She hurried out, expecting to find no one there but him, and to be at once handed to a seat in the vehicle — the next minute be speeding away with him, enjoying her drive all the more for the little disappointment that had preceded it.

What then was her chagrin to see a visitor handed out, and that visitor the woman for whom she had conceived the most violent antipathy!

"Miss Deane, my dear," Edward said with an entreating look at Zoe, which she did not see, her eyes being at that instant fixed upon the face of her uninvited and unwelcome guest.

"How do you do, my dear Mrs. Travilla? I hope you are glad to see me?" laughed the intruder, holding out a delicately gloved hand. "Your husband has played the Good Samaritan to me tonight — saving me from having to stay in one of those wretched little hotels in the village till two o'clock tomorrow morning."

"I am in usual health, thank you. Will you walk in?"

returned Zoe in a freezing tone, and utterly ignoring the offered hand. "Will you step into the parlor? Or would you prefer being shown to your room first?"

"The latter, if you please," Miss Deane answered sweetly, apparently quite unaware that Zoe's manner was in the least ungracious.

"Dinah," said Zoe, to a maid-in-waiting, "show Miss Deane to the room she occupied on her last visit. Carry up her satchel, and see that she has everything she wants."

Having given the order, Zoe stepped out to the veranda where Edward still was, having stayed behind to give directions in regard to the horses.

"Zoe, love, I am very sorry," he said, as the man turned his horses' heads and drove away toward the stables.

"Oh, Edward! How could you?" she exclaimed reproachfully, tears of disappointment and vexation springing to her eyes.

"Darling, I really could not help it," he replied soothingly, drawing her to him with a caress, and went on to tell exactly what had occurred.

"She is not a real lady," said Zoe, "or she never would have done a thing like that."

"I agree with you, love," he said, "but I was sorry your reception of her was so extremely ungracious and cold."

"Would you have me play the hypocrite, Ned?" she asked indignantly.

"No, Zoe, I should be very far from approving of that," he answered gravely, "but while it was right and truthful not to express pleasure which you did not feel at her coming, you might on the other hand have avoided absolute rudeness. You might have shaken hands with her, and asked after her health and that of her father's family."

"I treated her as well as she deserved. And it does not make her any the more welcome to me, that she has already been the means of drawing down upon me a reproof from my husband's lips," Zoe said in tremulous tones, and turning away from him with her eyes full of tears.

"My words were hardly intended as that, little wife,"

Edward responded in a kindly tone, following her into the hall, catching her in his arms, and imprinting a kiss on her ruby lips.

"And I wanted my drive with you so badly," she murmured, half hiding her face in his chest, "but she has robbed us of that, and — oh, Ned! Is she to come between us again, and make us quarrel, and be so dreadfully unhappy?" Her voice was full of tears and sobs before she had ended.

"No, no, I could not endure that any more than you," he said with emotion, and clasping her very close, "and it is only for tonight you will have to bear the annoyance of her presence. She is to leave in the morning."

"Is she? That is some comfort. I hope somebody will come in for the evening and share with us the infliction of her society," Zoe said, concluding with a forlorn attempt at a laugh.

"Won't you take off that very becoming hat and cloak, Mrs. Travilla, and spend the evening?" asked Edward playfully.

"Thank you. I believe I will, if you will accompany me to the dressing room," she returned, with a smiling look up into his face.

"That I will with pleasure," he said, "provided you will reward me with some assistance with my grooming."

"Such as brushing your hair and tying your cravat? Yes, sir, I will. It's a bargain."

And so, laughing and chatting, they went up to their own private apartments.

Half an hour later they came down again together to find Miss Deane in the parlor, seated by the window overlooking the avenue.

"There's a carriage just drawing up before your front entrance," she remarked. "The Roselands family carriage, I think it is."

Zoe gave her husband a bright, pleased look. It seemed her wish for an addition to their party for the evening had been granted.

The next moment the drawing room door was thrown open and Dr. Conly and Miss Ella were announced.

They were cordially welcomed, asked to tea, and stayed the evening, greatly relieving Zoe in the matter of entertaining her unwelcome guest, who devoted herself to the doctor and left Edward to his wife and cousin, a condition of things decidedly agreeable to Zoe.

A little after nine the Roselands carriage was announced and the doctor and Ella took their departure, Edward and Zoe accompanying them to the outer door.

The sky was black with clouds and the wind roaring through the trees on the lawn.

"We are going to have a heavy storm, I think," remarked Arthur, glancing upward. "There is not a star to be seen, and the wind blows almost a gale. I hope no patient of mine will want the doctor very badly tonight," he added with a slight laugh. "Step in out of the wind, Cousin Zoe, or you will be the very one to send for me."

Doing as directed, "No, indeed," she said. "I'm sure I couldn't have the heart to call anybody up out of a warm bed to face a cutting wind as this."

"No, no, never hesitate when there is a real necessity," he returned, speaking from his seat in the carriage, where he had already taken his place beside his sister, whom Edward had handed in. "Good night, and hurry in, both of you, for my sake if not for your own."

But they lingered a moment till the carriage turned and drove swiftly down the avenue.

"I am so glad they came," remarked Zoe, as Edward shut the door and locked it for the night.

"Yes," he said, "they added a good deal to the pleasure of the evening. As we couldn't be alone together, three guests were more acceptable than one.'

"Decidedly, and that one was delighted, I'm sure, to have an opportunity to exercise her conversational gifts for the benefit of a single man instead of a married one."

"Zoe, love, don't allow yourself to grow bitter and sarcastic," Edward said, turning toward her, laying a hand lightly, affectionately, upon her shoulder, and gazing down into her eyes with a look of grave concern.

She colored under it, and turned away with a pout that almost spoiled the beauty of her fair face. She was more than ever impatient to be rid of their self-invited guest.

"She always sets Ned to scolding me," was the bitter thought in her heart as she went slowly back to the parlor, where they had left Miss Deane, Edward following, sighing inwardly at the change in his darling always wrought by that unwelcome presence in the house.

"How the wind roars down the chimney!" Miss Deane remarked as her host and hostess re-entered the room where she was comfortably seated in an easy chair beside the glowing grate. "I fear tomorrow will prove a stormy day, but in that case I shall feel all the more delighted with my comfortable quarters here — all the more grateful to you, Mr. Travilla, for saving me from a long detention in one of those miserable little country taverns, where I should have died of ennui."

"You seem kindly disposed, my dear madam, to make a great deal of a small service," returned Edward gallantly.

But Zoe said not a word. She stood gazing into the fire, apparently lost in thought, but the color deepened on her cheek and a slight frown contracted her brows.

Presently she turned to her guest, saying courteously, "You must be weary with your journey, Miss Deane. Would you like to retire?"

"Thank you, I should," was the reply, and thereupon the goodnights were said and they sought their respective rooms.

"You are not displeased with me, dear?" Zoe asked, lifting her eyes inquiringly to her husband's face as she stood before their dressing room fire with his arm about her waist. "You are looking so very grave."

"No, dearest, I am not disposed to find fault with you," he said, softly caressing her hair and cheek with his free hand, "though I should be glad if you could be a trifle more cordial to our uninvited guest."

"It's my nature to act just as I feel, and, if there's a creature on earth I thoroughly detest, it is she!" returned the child-wife with almost passionate vehemence. "I know she hates me, for all her purring manner and sweet tones and words, and that she likes nothing better than to make trouble between my husband and me."

"My dear child, you really must try not to be so uncharitable and suspicious," Edward said in a slightly reproving tone. "I do not perceive any such designs or any hypocrisy in her conduct toward you."

"No, men are as blind as a bat in their exchange with such women — never can see through their designs — always take them to be as sweet and amiable as they pretend to be. It takes a woman to understand her own sex."

"Maybe so," he said soothingly, "but we will leave the disagreeable subject for tonight at least, shall we not?"

"Yes, and, oh, I do hope the weather tomorrow will not be such as to afford her an excuse for prolonging her stay!"

"I hope not, indeed, love," he responded, "but let us resolve, that, if it does, we will try to bear the infliction patiently, and give our self-invited guest no right to accuse us of a lack of hospitality toward her. Let us not forget or disobey the Bible injunction to 'use hospitality one to another without grudging,' "

"I'll try not to. I'll be as good to her as I can, without feeling that I am acting insincerely."

"And that is all I ask, love. Your perfect freedom from anything approaching to deceit is one of the greatest charms, in your husband's eyes," he said, tenderly caressing her. "It would, I am sure, be quite impossible for me to love a wife in whose absolute truth and sincerity I had not entire confidence."

"And do you love me, your foolish, faulty little wife?" she said, in a tone that was a mixture of assertion and inquiry, while her lovely eyes gazed searchingly into his.

"Dearly, dearly, my sweet!" he said, smiling fondly down upon her. "And now to bed, lest these bright eyes and rosy cheeks should lose something of their brilliance and beauty."

"Suppose they should," she said, turning slightly pale, as with sudden pain. "Oh, Ned! If I live, I must some day grow old and gray and wrinkled — my eyes dim and sunken. Shall you love me then, darling?"

"Better than ever, love," he whispered, holding her closer to his heart. "For how long we shall have lived and loved together! We shall have come to be as one indeed, each with hardly a thought or feeling unshared by the other."

CHAPTER THIRD

One woman reads another's character, without the tedious trouble of deciphering.

—JONSON

ZOE'S SLEEP that night was profound and refreshing, and she woke in perfect health and vigor of body and mind; but the first sound that smote her ear — the dashing of sleet against the window pane — sent a pang of disappointment and dismay to her heart.

She sprang from her bed, and, running to the window, drew aside the curtain, and looked out.

"Oh, Ned!" she groaned, "the ground is covered with sleet and snow, — about a foot deep, I should think, — and just hear how the wind shrieks and howls round the house!"

"Well, love," he answered in a cherry tone, "we are well sheltered, and supplied with all needful things for comfort and enjoyment."

"And one that will destroy every bit of my enjoyment in any or all the others," she sighed "but," eagerly and half hopefully, "do you think it is quite certain to be too bad for her to go?"

"Quite, I'm afraid. If she should offer to go," he added mischievously, "we will not be more urgent against it than politeness demands, and, if she persists, will not refuse the use of the closed carriage as far as the depot."

"She offer to go!" exclaimed Zoe scornfully. "You may depend, she'll stay as long as she has the least vestige of an excuse for doing so."

"Oh, now, little woman! Don't begin the day with being so hard and uncharitable," Edward said, half seriously, half laughingly.

Zoe was not far wrong in her estimate of her guest. Miss Deane was both insincere and a thoroughly selfish person, caring nothing for the comfort or happiness of others. She had perceived Zoe's antipathy from the first day of their acquaintance, and took a revengeful, malicious delight in tormenting her; and she had sufficient insight to see that the most effectual way to accomplish her end was through Edward. The young wife's ardent and jealous affection for her husband was very evident; plainly it was pain to her to see him show Miss Deane the slightest attention, or seem interested in anything she did or said. Therefore, the intruder put forth every effort to interest him, and monopolize his attention. At the same time she contrived to draw out into exhibition the most unamiable traits in Zoe's character, doing it so adroitly that Edward did not perceive her agency in the matter, and thought Zoe alone to blame. To him Miss Deane's behavior appeared unexceptionable, her manner most polite and courteous, Zoe's just the reverse.

It was so through all that day and week; for the storm continued, and the uninvited guest never so much as hinted at a wish to leave the shelter of their hospitable roof.

Zoe began each day with heroic resolve to be patient and forbearing, sweet-tempered and polite, toward her tormentor. She ended it with a deep sense of humiliating failure and of having lost something of the high esteem and admiration in which her almost idolized husband had been wont to hold her.

Feeling that, more or less of change in her manner toward him was inevitable; less sure than formerly of his entire approval and ardent affection, a certain timidity and hesitation crept into her manner of approaching him, even when they were quite alone together. She grew sad, silent, and reserved; and he, thinking her sullen and jealous without reason, ceased to lavish endearments upon her, and, more than that, half unconsciously allowed both his looks and tones to express disapprobation and reproof.

That almost broke Zoe's heart, but she strove to hide her wounds from him and especially from her tormentor.

The storm kept Edward in the house. At another time that would have been a joy to Zoe, but now it only added to her troubles, affording constant opportunity to the wily foe to carry out her evil designs.

On the evening of the second day from the setting in of the storm, Miss Deane challenged Edward to a game of chess. He accepted at once, and with an air of quiet satisfaction brought out the board, and placed the men.

He was fond of the game, but Zoe had never fancied it, and he had played but seldom since their marriage.

Miss Deane was a more than ordinarily skillful player and so was he. Indeed, so well matched were they, that neither found it an easy matter to checkmate the other, and that first game proved a long one. It was so long that Zoe, who had watched its progress with some interest in the beginning, eager to see Edward win, at length grew so weary as to find it difficult to keep her eyes open, or refrain from yawning.

But Edward, usually so tenderly careful of her, took no notice — indeed, as she said bitterly to herself, seemed to have forgotten her existence.

Still, it was with a thrill of delight that she at length perceived that he had come off victorious.

Miss Deane took her defeat with very good grace, and smilingly challenged him to another contest.

"Rather late, isn't it?" he said with a glance at the clock, whose hands pointed to half past eleven. "Suppose we sign a truce until tomorrow?"

"Certainly, that will be decidedly better," she promptly replied, following the direction of his glance. "I feel so fresh, and have enjoyed myself so much, that I had no idea of the hour, and am quite ashamed of having kept my youthful hostess up so late," she added, looking sweetly at Zoe. "Very young people need a large amount of sleep, and can't keep up health and strength without it."

"You are most kind," said Zoe, a touch of sarcasm in her tones. "It must be a very sympathetic nature that has enabled you to remember so long how young people feel."

A twinkle of fun shone in Edward's eyes at that.

Miss Deane colored furiously, bade a hasty goodnight and departed to her own room.

"That was a rather hard thrust, my dear," remarked Edward, laughing, as he led the way into their dressing room, "not quite polite, I'm afraid."

"I don't care if I wasn't!" said Zoe. "She is always twitting me on my extreme youth."

"Sour grapes," he said lightly. "She will never see twenty-five again, and would give a great deal for your youth. And since you are exactly the age to suit me, why should you care a fig for her sneers?"

"I don't, when I seem to suit you in all respects," returned Zoe with tears in her voice.

Her back was toward him, but he caught sight of her face in a mirror, and saw that tears were also glistening in her eyes.

Putting his arms round her waist and drawing her to him, "I don't want a piece of perfection for my wife," he said. "She would be decidedly too great a contrast to her husband; and I have never seen the woman or girl I should be willing to take in exchange for the one belonging to me. And I'm very sure such a one doesn't exist."

"How good of you to say it!" she said, clinging about his neck, and lifting to his, eyes shining with joy and love. "Oh, Ned, we were so happy by ourselves!"

"So we were," he assented, "and so we may hope to be again very soon."

"Not so very, I'm afraid," she answered with a rueful shake of her head, "for just hark how it is storming still!"

"Yes, but it may be all over by morning. How weary you look, love! Get to bed as fast as you can. You should not have waited for the conclusion of that long game, that, I know, did not interest you."

"I was interested for your sake," she said, "and so glad to see you win."

"Wife-like," he returned with a smile, adding, "it was a

very close game and you needn't be surprised to see me beaten in the next battle."

"I'm afraid she will stay for that, even if the storm is over," sighed Zoe. "Dear me! I don't see how anybody can have the face to stay where she is self-invited, and must know she isn't a welcome guest to the lady of the house. I'd go through any storm rather than prolong a visit under such circumstances."

"You would never have put yourself in such a position," Edward said. "But I wish you could manage to treat her with a little more cordiality. I should feel more comfortable. I could not avoid bringing her here, as you know; nor can I send her away in such inclement weather, or, indeed, at all, till she offers to go. And your want of courtesy toward her — to put it mildly — is a constant mortification to me."

"Why don't you say at once that you are ashamed of me?" she exclaimed, tears starting to her eyes again, as with a determined effort she freed herself from his grasp and moved away to the father side of the room.

"I am usually very proud of you," he answered in a quiet tone, "but this woman seems to exert a strangely malign influence over you."

To that Zoe made no response; she could not trust herself to speak, so prepared for bed and laid herself down there in silence, wiped away a tear or two, and presently fell asleep.

Morning brought no abatement of the storm and consequently no relief to Zoe from the annoyance of Miss Deane's presence in the house.

On waking, she found that Edward had risen before her. She heard him moving about in the dressing room, then he came to the door, looked in, and seeing her eyes open, said, "Ah, so you are awake! I hope you slept well? I'm sorry for your sake that it is still storming."

"Yes, I slept soundly, thank you; and, as for the storm, I'll just have to try to bear with it and its consequences as patiently as possible," she sighed.

"A wise resolve, my dear. I hope you will try to carry it

out," he returned. "Now I must run away and leave you to your dressing, as I have some little matters to attend to before breakfast."

She made no reply, and he passed out of the room and down the stairs.

"Poor little woman!" he said to himself, "she looks depressed, though usually she is so bright and cheery. I hope, from my heart, Miss Deane may never darken these doors again."

Zoe was feeling quite out of spirits over the prospect of another day to be spent in society so distasteful. She lay for a moment contemplating it ruefully.

"The worst of it is that she manages to make me appear so unamiable and unattractive in my husband's eyes," she sighed to herself. "But I'll foil her efforts," she added between her shut teeth, springing up and beginning to get dressed as she spoke, "He likes to have me bright and cheery, and well and becomingly dressed, and so I will be."

She made haste to arrange her hair in the style he considered most becoming, and to don the morning dress he most admired.

As she put the finishing touches to her attire, she thought she heard his step on the stairs, and ran out eagerly to meet him, and claim a morning kiss.

But the bright, joyous expression on her face suddenly changed to one of anger and chagrin as she caught the sound of his and Miss Deane's voices in the hall below, and looking over the balustrade, saw them go into the library together.

"She begins early! It's a pity if I can't have my own husband to myself even before breakfast," Zoe muttered, stepping back into the dressing room.

Her first impulse was to remain where she was; the second, to go down at once, and join them.

She hastened to do so, but, before she reached the foot of the stairway, the breakfast bell rang; and, instead of going to the library, she passed on directly to the dining room. As the other two entered a moment later, gave Miss Deane a cold "Good morning" and Edward a half-reproachful, half-pleading look. He, however, returned it with one so kind and reassuring that she immediately recovered her spirits, and was able to do the honors of the table with ease and grace.

Coming upon her in that room alone, an hour later, just as she had dismissed Aunt Dicey with her orders for the day, "Little wife," he said, bending down to give her the coveted caress, "I owe you an explanation."

"No, Ned, dear, I don't ask it of you. I know it is all right," she answered, flushing with happiness and her eyes smiling up into his.

"Still, I think it best to explain," he said. "I had finished attending to the little matters I spoke of — writing a note, giving some direction to Uncle Ben — and was on my way back to our apartments, when Miss Deane met me on the stairway and asked if I would go into the library with her and help her to look up a certain passage in one of Shakespeare' plays, which she wished to quote in a letter she was writing. She was anxious to have it perfectly correct she said, and would be extremely obliged for my assistance in finding it."

"And you could not in politeness refuse. I know that, Ned, and please don't think me jealous."

"I know, dear, that you try not to be, and it shall be my care to avoid giving you the least occasion. And I do again earnestly assure you, you need have no fear that the first place in my heart will not always be yours."

"I don't fear it," she said, "and yet — oh, Ned, it is misery to me to have to share your company with that woman, even for a day or two!"

"I don't know how I can help you out of it," he said, after a moment's consideration, "unless by shutting myself up alone — to attend to correspondence or something — and leaving you to entertain her by yourself. Shall I do that?"

"Oh, no! Unless you much prefer it. I think it would set me wild to have her whole attention concentrated upon me," Zoe answered with an uneasy laugh.

So they went together to the parlor, where Miss Deane sat waiting for them, or rather for Edward.

She had the chessboard out, the men placed, and at once challenged him to a renewal of last night's contest.

He accepted, of course, and they played without intermission till lunch time, Zoe sitting by, for the most part silent, and wishing Miss Deane miles away from Ion.

This proved a worse day to her than either of the preceding ones. Miss Deane succeeded several times in rousing her to an exhibition of temper that very much mortified and displeased Edward; and his manner, when they retired that night to their private apartments, was many degrees colder than it had been in the morning. He considered himself forbearing in refraining from remark to Zoe on her behavior — while she said to herself, she would rather he would scold her, and have done with it, than keep on looking like a thundercloud, and not speaking at all. He was not more disgusted with her conduct than she was herself, and she would own it in a minute if he would but say a kind word to open the way.

But he did not, and they made their preparations for the night and sought their pillows in uncomfortable silence, Zoe wetting hers with tears before she slept.

Chapter Fourth

Forbear sharp speeches to her. She's a lady
So tender of rebukes, that words are strokes,
And strokes death to her.

— Shakespeare

THE STORM LASTED a week, and all that time Edward and Zoe were slowly drifting farther and farther apart.

But at last the clouds broke and the sun shone out cheerily. It was about the middle of the forenoon when this occurred.

"Oh," cried Miss Deane, "I do see the sun! Now I shall no longer need to encroach upon your hospitality, my kind entertainers. I can go home by this afternoon's train, if you, Mr. Travilla, will be so very good as to take or send me to the depot."

"The Ion carriage is quite at your service," he responded politely.

"Thanks," she said, "then I'll just run up to my room, and do my bit of packing."

She hurried out to the hall, then the front door was heard to open; and the next minute a piercing shriek brought master, mistress, and servants running out to the veranda to inquire the cause.

Miss Deane lay there groaning, and crying out that she had sprained her ankle terribly. She had slipped on a bit of ice and fallen, and, oh, when now would she be able to go home?

The question found an echo in Zoe's heart, and she groaned inwardly at the thought of having this most unwelcome guest fastened upon her for weeks longer.

Yet she pitied her pain, and was anxious to do what she

could for her relief. She hastened to the medicine closet in search of remedies, while Edward and Uncle Ben gently lifted the sufferer, carried her in, and laid her on the sofa.

Also a messenger was at once dispatched for Dr. Conly. Zoe stationed herself at a front window of the drawing room to watch for his coming. Presently Edward came to her side. "Zoe," he said, "can't you go to Miss Deane?"

"What for?" she asked, without turning her head to him.

"To show your kind feeling."

"I'm not sure that I have any."

"Zoe! I am shocked! She is in great pain."

"She has plenty of helpers about her — Christine, Aunt Dicey, and a servant or two — who will do all they can to relieve her. If I could do anything more, I would; but I can't, and should only be in the way. You forget what a mere child you have always considered me, and that I have had no experience in nursing."

"It isn't nursing I am asking you to give her, but a little kindly sympathy."

A carriage was coming swiftly up the avenue.

"There's the doctor," said Zoe. "You'd better consult with him about his patient. And if he thinks my presence in the room will hasten her recovery, she shall have all I can give her of it, that we may get her out of the house as soon as possible."

"Zoe! I had no idea you could be so heartless," he said with much displeasure, as he turned and left the room.

Zoe remained where she was, shedding some tears of mingled anger and grief, then hastily endeavoring to remove their traces, for Arthur would be sure to step into the parlor, to see her before leaving, if it were but for a moment.

She had barely recovered her composure when he came in, having found the patient not in need of a lengthened visit.

His face was bright, his tone cheery and kind, as he bade her good morning and asked after her health.

"I'm very well, thank you," she said, giving him her hand. "Is Miss Deane's accident a very bad one?"

"It is a severe sprain," he said. "She will not be able to bear her weight upon that ankle for six weeks." Then seeing Zoe's look of dismay and shrewdly guessing at the cause, he hastened to add, "But she might be sent home in an ambulance a few days hence without the least injury."

Zoe looked greatly relieved, Edward scarcely less so.

"I can't understand how she came to fall," remarked Arthur reflectively.

"Nor I," said Zoe. "Wouldn't it be well for you to advise her never to set foot on that dangerous veranda again?"

Arthur smiled. "That would be a waste of breath," he said, "while Ion is so delightful a place to visit."

"How are they all at Viamede?" he asked, turning to Edward.

"Quite well at last accounts, thank you," Edward replied, adding, with a slight sigh, "I wish they were here — my mother at least, if none of the others."

Zoe colored violently. "Cousin Arthur, do you think I am needed in your patient's room?" she asked.

"Only to cheer and amuse her with your pleasant society," he answered.

"She would find neither pleasure nor amusement in my society," said Zoe, "and hers is most distasteful to me."

"That's a pity," said Arthur, with a look of concern. "Suppose I lend you Ella for a few days? She, I think, would rather enjoy taking the entertainment of your guest off your hands."

"Oh, thank you!" said Zoe, brightening. "That would be a relief, and besides, I should enjoy Ella myself, between times, and after Miss Deane goes home."

"Please tell Ella we will both be greatly obliged if she will come," Edward said.

"I'll do so," said Arthur, rising to go, "but I have a long drive to take in another direction, before returning to Roselands. And you must remember," he added with a smile, "that I lend her for only a few days. Cal and I wouldn't know how to do without her very long."

With that, he took his departure, leaving Edward and Zoe alone together.

"I am sorry, Zoe, that you thought it necessary to let Arthur into the secret of the mutual dislike between Miss Deane and yourself," remarked Edward, in a grave, reproving tone.

Zoe colored angrily. "I don't care who knows it," she retorted, with a little toss of her head. "I did not think it necessary to let Arthur into the secret, as you call it (I don't consider it one), but neither did I see any objection to his knowing about it."

"Then, let me request you to say no more on the subject to anyone," he said, with vexation.

"I sha'n't promise," she muttered, half under her breath. But he heard it.

"Very well, then, I forbid it, and you have promised to obey me."

"And you promised that it should always be love and coaxing," she said in tones trembling with pain and passion. "I'll have to tell Ella something about it."

"Then, say only what is quite necessary," he returned, his tones softening.

Then, after a moment's silence, in which Zoe's face was turned from him so that he could not see its expression, "Won't you go now, and ask if Miss Deane is any easier? Surely, as her hostess, you should do so much."

"No, I won't! I'll do all I can to make her comfortable. I'll provide her with society more agreeable to her than mine. I'll see that she has interesting reading matter, if she wants it. I'll do anything and everything I can, except that, but you needn't ask that of me."

"Oh, Zoe, I had thought you would do a harder thing than that at my request!" he said reproachfully.

Ignoring his remark, she went on, "I just believe she fell and hurt herself purposely, that she might have an excuse for prolonging her visit, and continuing to torment me."

"Zoe, Zoe, how shockingly uncharitable you are!" he exclaimed. "I could never have believed it of you! We are told, 'Charity thinketh no evil.' Do try not to judge so harshly."

He left the room, and Zoe indulged in a hearty cry, but

hastily dried her eyes and turned her back toward the door as she heard his steps approaching again.

He just looked in, saying, "Zoe, I am going to drive over to Roselands for Ella. Will you go along?"

"No, I have been lectured enough for one day," was her ungracious rejoinder, and he closed the door and went away.

He was dumb with astonishment and pain. "What has come over her?" he asked himself. "She has always before been so delighted to go any and everywhere with me. Have I been too ready to reprove her of late? I have thought myself rather forbearing, considering how much ill temper she has shown. She has had provocation, to be sure; but it is high time she learned to exercise some self-control. Yet perhaps I should have been more sympathizing, more forbearing and affectionate."

He had stepped into his carriage and was driving down the avenue. He passed through the great gates and turned into the road, still thinking of Zoe, and mentally reviewing their behavior toward each other since the unfortunate day in which Miss Deane had crossed their threshold.

The conclusion he presently arrived at was that he had not been altogether blameless. If his reproofs had been given in more loving fashion, they would have been received in a better spirit, that he had not been faithful to his promise to try "love and coaxing" with the impulsive, sensitive child-wife, who, he doubted not, loved him with her whole heart. Once convinced of that, he determined to say so on his return, and make it up with her.

True, it seemed to him that she ought to make the first advances toward an adjustment of their slight differences (quarrels they could scarcely be called — a slight coldness, a cessation of accustomed manifestations of conjugal affection, a few sharp or impatient words on each side). But he would be too generous to wait for that. He loved her dearly enough to sacrifice his pride to some extent. He could better afford that than the sight of her unhappiness.

In the meantime Zoe was bitterly repenting of the rebuff she had given him. He had hardly closed the door when she started up and ran to it to call him back, apologize for her curt refusal to go with him, and ask if she might still accept his invitation. But it was too late. He was already beyond hearing.

She could not refrain from another cry, and was very angry with herself for her petulance. She regretted the loss of the drive, too, which would have been a real treat after the week of confinement to the house.

She had refused to comply with her husband's request that she would go to Miss Deane and ask how she was. Now she repented and went as soon as she had removed the traces of her tears.

"Ah! You have come at last!" was the salutation she received on entering the room where Miss Deane lay on a sofa with the injured limb propped upon pillows. "I began to fear," she said sweetly, "that your delicate nerves had given way under the sight of my suffering."

"My nerves are not delicate," returned Zoe coldly. "In fact, I never discovered that I had any, so please do not trouble yourself with anxiety on that account. I trust the applications have relieved you somewhat."

"Very little, thank you. I suppose it was hardly expected that they would take effect so soon. Ah, me!" she added with a profound sigh, "I fear I am tied to this couch for weeks."

"No, do not disturb yourself with that idea," said Zoe. "The doctor told me you could easily be taken home in a few days in an ambulance."

"I shall certainly avail myself of the first opportunity to do so," said Miss Deane, her eyes flashing with anger, "for I plainly perceive that I have worn out my welcome."

"No, not at all," said Zoe, "at least, not so far as I am concerned." Miss Deane looked her with incredulity and surprise, and Zoe explained — "I think I may as well be perfectly frank with you," she said. "You have not worn out your welcome with me, because I had none for you when you came. How could I, knowing that you invariably make trouble between my husband and myself?"

"Truly, a polite speech to make to a guest!" sniffed Miss

Deane. "I hope you pride yourself on your very polished manners."

"I prefer truth and sincerity," said Zoe. "I shall do all I can to make you comfortable while you are here, and, if you choose to avoid the line of conduct I have objected to, we may learn to like each other. I very well know that you do not love me now."

"Since frankness is in fashion at this moment," was the contemptuous retort, "I will own that there is no love lost between us. Stay," she said as Zoe was about to leave the room, "let me give you a piece of disinterested advice. Learn to control your quick temper and show yourself more amiable, or you may find one of these days, when it is too late, that you have lost your husband's heart."

At that Zoe turned away and went swiftly from the room. She was beyond speaking, her whole frame quivering from head to foot with the agitation of her feelings.

Lose the love of her idolized husband? That would be worse than death. But it should never be. He loved her dearly now (it could not be possible that these few wretched days had robbed her quite of the devoted affection she had known beyond a doubt to be hers before). And she would tell him, as soon as he came in, how sorry she was for the conduct that had vexed him, and never, no, never again, would she do or say anything to displease him, or lower herself in his estimation.

As she thought thus, hurrying down the hall, she caught the sound of wheels on the drive and ran out, expecting to see him, as it was about time for his return from Roselands.

It was the Ion carriage she had heard, but only Ella Conly alighted from it.

They exchanged greetings, then Zoe asked half breathlessly, "Where's Edward?"

"Gone," Ella responded, moving on into the hall. "Come, let's go into the parlor and sit down, and I'll tell you all I know about it. Why, Zoe," as she turned and caught sight of her companion's face, "you are as pale as death and look ready to faint! There's nothing to be scared about and you mustn't mind my nonsense."

"Oh, tell me! Tell me quickly!" gasped Zoe, sinking into a chair, her hands clasped beseechingly, her eyes wild with terror, "what, what has happened?"

"Nothing, child, nothing, except that we met Cousin Horace on our way here, and he carried Ned off to Union. They had to hurry to catch a train, in order to be in time for some business matter in the city. I didn't understand what. So Ned couldn't wait to write the least bit of a note to tell you about it. He told me to explain everything to you, and say you were not to fret or worry — not even if he shouldn't get home tonight, for he might not be able to finish up the business in time for even the last train that would bring him."

The color had come back to Zoe's cheek, but her countenance was still distressed. And, as Ella concluded, two scalding tears rolled quickly down her face, and splashed upon the small white hands lying clasped in her lap.

"Dear me!" said Ella, "how fond you are of him!"

"Yes," said Zoe, with a not very successful effort to smile through her tears, "who wouldn't be, in my place?" I owe everything to Ned, and he indulges me to the greatest extent. Besides, he is so good, noble, and true, that any woman might be proud to be his wife."

"Yes, I admit every word of it, but all that doesn't explain your tears," returned Ella, half sympathizingly, half teasingly. "Now, I should have supposed that anybody who could boast of such a piece of perfection for a husband would be very happy."

"But I — we've hardly ever been separated overnight," stammered Zoe, blushing rosy red, "and — and — oh, Ella, I hadn't a chance to say goodbye to him, and — and you know accidents so often happen — "

She broke down with a burst of tears and sobs that quite dismayed her cousin.

"Why, Zoe, I'm afraid you cannot be well," she said. "Come, cheer up and don't borrow trouble."

"I'm afraid I'm very silly and have been making you uncomfortable," said Zoe, hastily wiping away her tears, "and it's a great shame, particularly considering that you have kindly come on purpose to help me through with a disagreeable task.

"I'll show you to your room now, if you like," she added, rising, "and try to behave myself better during the rest of your visit."

"Apologies are quite uncalled for," returned Ella lightly, as they went upstairs together. "I have always had a good time at Ion and don't believe this is going to be an exception to the general rule. But do you know," lowering her voice a little, "I don't propose to spend nearly all my time with that hateful Miss Deane. I never could bear her."

"Then, how good it was of you to come!" exclaimed Zoe gratefully. "But I should never have asked it of you, if I had thought you disliked her as well as I."

They were now in the room Ella was to occupy and she was taking off her hat and cloak. "Oh, never mind! I was delighted to come anyhow," she answered happily as she threw aside the latter garment and took possession of an easy chair beside the open fire. "To tell you a secret," she went on laughingly, "I like my cousins Ned and Zoe Travilla immensely, and am always glad for an excuse to pay them a visit. But that Miss Deane — oh, she's just too sweet for anything!" making a grimace expressive of her disgust and aversion, "and a consummate, incorrigible flirt. Any one of the male sex can be made to serve her purpose, from a boy of sixteen to a man of seventy-five."

"I think you are correct about that,' said Zoe. "And, do you know, she is forever making covert sneers at my youth, and it's perfectly exasperating to me."

"Sour grapes," laughed Ella. "I wouldn't let it vex me in the least. It's all to hide her envy of you because you are really young and married too. I know very well she's dreadfully afraid of being called an old maid."

"I suspected as much," Zoe remarked. "But don't you think gentlemen are more apt to be pleased with her than ladies?"

"Yes, they don't see through her as her own sex do. And

she is beautiful and certainly a brilliant talker. I'd give a good deal for conversational powers equal to hers."

"So would I," Zoe said with an involuntary sigh.

Ella gave her a keen, inquiring look, and Zoe flushed hotly under it.

"Shall we go down now?" she asked. "It is nearly dinner time, and we shall have to dine alone unless someone drops in unexpectedly," she added as they left the room together and passed down the stairs arm in arm.

"If Arthur should, wouldn't it be a trial to Miss Deane to have to dine in her own room?" exclaimed Ella with a gleeful laugh.

"Why, what do you mean?" asked Zoe, opening her eyes wide with surprise.

"That she would not have the slightest objection to becoming Mrs. Dr. Conly."

"But you don't think there's any danger?" queried Zoe, by no means pleased with the idea of having the lady in question made a member of the family connection.

"No, I certainly hope not. It wouldn't be I that would want to call her sister," returned Ella emphatically.

"I should think Art had sufficient insight to see through her," said Zoe. "But no — on second thought, I'm not so sure. Ned will have it that it's more than half my imagination when I say she sneers at me."

"That's too bad," said Ella. "But Art is older than Ned by some years, and has probably had more opportunity to study character."

"Yes," replied Zoe, speaking with some hesitation, not liking to admit that anyone was wiser than her husband, little as she was inclined to own herself in the wrong when he differed from her.

CHAPTER FIFTH

Is there no constancy in earthly things?
No happiness in us, but what must alter?

ZOE DROVE over to the village in good season to meet the last train for that day, coming from the direction in which Edward had gone, ardently hoping he might be on board.

The carriage was brought to a standstill near the depot, and she eagerly watched the arrival of the train. She scanned the little crowd of passengers who alighted from it.

But Edward was not among them, and now it was quite certain that she should not see him before another day.

Just as she reached that conclusion, a telegram was handed her.

> Can't be home before tomorrow or
> next day. Will return as soon as
> possible. E. TRAVILLA.

To the girl-wife the message seemed but cold and formal. "So different from the way he talks to me when he is not vexed or displeased, as he hardly ever is," she whispered to herself with starting tears during the solitary drive back to Ion. "I know it's silly — telegrams can't be loving and kind. It wouldn't do, of course — but I can't help feeling as if he is angry with me, because there's not a bit of love in what he says. And, oh, dear, to think he may be away two nights, and I'm longing to tell him how sorry I am for being so cross this morning, and before that, too, and to have him take me in his arms and kiss me, and say all is right between us, that I don't know how to wait a single minute!"

She reached home in a sad and tearful mood. Ella, however, proved so entertaining and mirth-provoking a companion, that the evening passed quickly and by no means unpleasantly.

But when the two had retired to their respective apartments, Zoe felt very lonely, and said to herself that she would rather have Edward there, even silent and displeased, as he had been for several days past, than to be without him.

Her last thought before falling asleep and her first on awaking next morning were of him.

"Oh, dear!" she sighed half aloud, as she opened her eyes and glanced round the room, "what shall I do if he doesn't come today? I'll have to stand it, of course, but what does a woman do who has no husband?" And for the first time she began to feel sympathy for Miss Deane as a lonely maiden lady.

She thought a good deal about her unwelcome guest while attending to the duties of getting dressed, and determined to treat her with all possible kindness during the remainder of her enforced stay at Ion. So, meeting, on her way to the breakfast room, the old Negress who had been given charge of Miss Deane through the night, she stopped her and asked how her patient was.

"Jes' pow'ful cross dis hyar mawnin', Miss Zoe," was the reply in a tone of disgust. "Dar isn't one ob de fambly dat would be makin' half de fuss ef dey'd sprained bofe dey's ankles. Doan ye go nigh her, honey, fear she bite yo' head off.'

"Indeed, I sha'n't, Aunt Phillis, if there's any danger of that," laughed Zoe. "But as she can't jump up and run after me, I think I shall be quite safe if I don't go within arm's length of her sofa."

"She's pow'ful cross," repeated Aunt Phillis. "She done call dis chile up time an' again fru de night, and when I ax her, 'Whar yo' misery at?' she say, 'In my ankle, ob c'ose, yo' ole fool you! Cayn't yo' hab nuff sense to change de dressin'?' "

"Who is that has been so polite and complimentary to you, Aunt Phillis?" cried a merry voice in their rear.

Ella was descending the stairway at whose foot they stood, as they perceived, on turning at the sound of her voice.

"Good morning, cousin. How bright and well you are looking!" said Zoe.

"Just as I feel. And how are you, Mrs. Travilla? I trust you did not spend the night in crying over Ned's absence?" was the happy rejoinder.

"No, not nearly all of it," returned Zoe, catching her spirit of fun.

"Mawnin', Miss Ella," said the old nurse, dropping a curtsey. " 'Twas de lady what sprain her foot yisteday I was talkin' 'bout to Miss Zoe."

"Ah! How is she?"

"I doan' t'ink she gwine die dis day, Miss Ella," laughed the nurse, "she so pow'ful cross, and dey do say folks is dat way when dey's gittin' bettah."

"Yes, I have always heard it was a hopeful sign, if not an agreeable one," Ella remarked. "Was that the breakfast bell I heard just now?"

"Yes," said Zoe. "I hope you feel ready to do justice to your meal?"

As they seated themselves at the table, Zoe, glancing toward Edward's vacant chair, remarked with a sigh that it seemed very lonely to sit down without him.

"Well, now," said Ella, "I think it's quite nice to take a meal occasionally without the presence of anybody of the masculine gender."

"Perhaps that is because you have never been married," said Zoe.

"Perhaps so," returned her cousin, laughing, "yet I don't think that can be all that ails me, for I have heard married women express the same opinion quite frequently. What shall we do with ourselves today, Zoe? I've no notion of devoting myself exclusively to Miss Deane's entertainment, especially if she is really as cross as reported."

"No, indeed! I couldn't bear to let you, even if you were willing,' replied Zoe with decision. "I consented to your taking my place in that only because I supposed you found her agreeable — while to me she is anything else."

"Suppose we call on her together, after a little, and let the length of our stay depend upon the enjoyment our presence seems to afford her," suggested Ella.

"Agreed," said Zoe. "Then I will supply her with plenty of reading matter, which, as she professes to be so very intellectual, ought to entertain her far better than we can. Shall we ride after that?"

"Yes, and take a promenade on the verandas. We'll have to take our exercise in those ways, as the roads are not yet fit for walking.

"Yes," said Zoe, "but I hope that by afternoon they will be good enough for driving, as I mean to drive over to the depot to meet the late train, hoping to find Ned on it."

"Don't expect him till tomorrow," said Ella.

"Why not?" queried Zoe, looking as if she could hardly endure the thought.

"Because in that case, your disappointment, if you have one, will be agreeable."

"Yes, but on the other hand, I should lose all the enjoyment of looking forward through the whole day, to seeing him this evening. Following your plan, I shouldn't have half so happy a day as if I keep to my own."

"Ah! That's an entirely new view of the case," Ella said in her merry, laughing tones.

Miss Deane did not seem to enjoy their society, and they soon withdrew from her room, Zoe having done all in her power to provide her with every comfort and amusement available in her case.

"I'm glad that's over," sighed Zoe, when they were alone again. "And now for our ride, if you are ready, Ella. I ordered my pony for myself and mamma's for you; and I see that they are at the door."

"Then let us don our riding habits and be off at once," said Ella.

"Where are we going?" she asked as they cantered down the avenue.

"To the village, if you like. I want to call at the post office."

"In hopes of finding a note from Ned, I suppose. I don't believe there can be one that would bring you later news than yesterday's telegram. But I have no objection to making sure, and would as soon ride in that direction as any other."

Nothing from Edward was found at the office, and the young wife seemed much disappointed, till Ella suggested that that looked as if he expected to be at home before night.

It was a cheering idea to Zoe. She brightened up at once, and in the afternoon drove over the same road, feeling almost certain Edward would be on the incoming train, due about the time she would reach the village, or rather at the time she had planned to be there. Ella, who had asked to accompany her, was slow with her dressing, taxing Zoe's patience pretty severely by thus causing ten minutes' detention.

"Come, now, don't be worried. It won't kill Ned to have to wait ten or fifteen minutes,' she said laughingly, as she stepped into the carriage and seated herself by Zoe's side.

"No, I dare say not,' returned the latter, trying to speak with perfect pleasantness of tone and manner. "And he isn't one of the impatient ones who can never bear to be kept waiting a minute, like myself," she added with a smile. "Now, Uncle Ben, drive pretty fast, so that we won't be so very far behind time."

"Fas' as I kin widout damagin' de hosses, Miss Zoe," answered the coachman. "Marse Ed'ard allus tole me be keerful ob dem and de roads am putty bad sence de big storm."

Zoe glanced at her watch as they entered the village. "Drive directly to the depot, Uncle Ben," she said. "It's fully fifteen minutes past the time for the train to be in."

"I ain't heard de whistle, Miss Zoe," he remarked as he turned his horses' heads in the desired direction.

"No, nor have I," said Ella, "and we ought to have heard it fully five minutes before it got in. There may have been a delay. That is nothing unusual," she hastened to add, as she saw that Zoe had suddenly grown very pale.

The carriage drew up before the door of the depot, and the girls leaned from its windows, sending eager, searching glances from side to side and up and down the track.

No train was in sight and the depot seemed strangely silent and deserted.

"Oh!" cried Zoe, "what can be the matter?"

"I suppose the train must have got in some time ago — perhaps before we left Ion," replied Ella in a reassuring tone, "and all the passengers have dispersed to their homes or wherever they were going."

"No, there could not have been time for all that," Zoe responded in accents full of anxiety and alarm.

"Our watches may be much too slow," suggested Ella, trying to reassure both herself and her cousin, yet trembling with apprehension as she spoke.

"No, it isn't possible that they and all the timepieces in the house could be so far from correct," said Zoe despairingly.

"Dar doan' 'pear to be nobody 'bout dis hyar depot," remarked Uncle Ben reflectively, "but I reckon dar's somebody comin' to 'splain de mattah. Wha's de 'casion ob dis mos' onusual state ob t'ings?" he added as a woman, who had been watching the carriage and its occupants from the open door of a neighboring house, came running in their directions.

"What de mattah, Aunt Rhoda?" he queried, as she reached the side of the vehicle, almost breathless with excitement and exertion.

"Why, Uncle Ben, dar — dar's been a accident to de kyars, dey say, an' dey's all broke up, and de folks roun' here is all — "

"Where? Where?" exclaimed Ella, while Zoe sank back against the cushions, quite unable to speak for the moment.

"Dunno, miss," was the reply, "but," pointing up the road, "it's out dat way, 'bout a mile, I reckon. Yo see, de kyars was a comin' fas' dis way, and 'nudderole injine whiskin' 'long dat way, and dey bofe comes togedder wid a big crash, breakin' de kyars and de injines bofe of 'em till dey's good for nuffin' but kin'lin' wood. And de folks what's ridin' in de kyars is all broke up too, dey says, and de doctahs and eberybody — "

"Edward!" gasped Zoe. "Drive us there, Uncle Ben,

drive with all your might! Oh, Edward, my husband, my husband!" and she burst into hysterical weeping.

Ella threw her arms about her. "Don't, dear Zoe, oh, don't cry so! He may not be hurt. He may not have been on that train at all."

Ben had already turned and whipped up his horses and now they dashed along the road at a furious rate.

Zoe dropped her head on Ella's shoulder, answering only with tears and sobs and moans till the carriage came to a sudden standstill.

"We's got dar, Miss Zoe," said Uncle Ben in a subdued tone full of grief and sympathy.

She lifted her head, and her eyes instantly fell upon a little group, scarcely a yard distant, consisting of several men, among whom she recognized Dr. Conly, gathered about an apparently insensible form lying on the ground.

Ella and Ben saw it too. She suddenly caught the reins from his hands. He sprang from the carriage and, lifting Zoe in his strong arms as if she had been but a child, set her on her feet and supported her to the side of the prostrate man. The little crowd respectfully made way for her, at the words spoken by Ben in a voice half choked with emotion, "Hit's Marse Ed'ard's wife, gen'lemen."

It was Edward lying there motionless and with a face like that of a corpse.

With an agonized cry, Zoe dropped on her knees at his side and pressed her lips passionately to his.

There was no response, no movement, not the quiver of an eyelid; and she lifted her grief stricken face to that of the doctor, with a look of anguished inquiry in the beautiful eyes fit to move a heart of stone.

"I do not despair of him, yet, dear Cousin Zoe," Arthur said in a low, moved tone. "I have found no external injury, and it may be that he is only stunned."

The words had scarcely left his lips when Edward drew a sighing breath and opened his eyes, glancing up into Zoe's face bending over him in deepest, tenderest solicitude.

"Ah, love! Is it you?" he murmured faintly and with a smile. "Where am I? What has happened?"

"Oh, Ned, dear, dear Ned! I thought you were killed!" she sobbed, covering his face with kisses and tears.

"There has been an accident and you got a blow that stunned you," answered the doctor. "But I think you are all right now, or will be very soon."

"An accident!" Edward repeated with a bewildered look, and putting his hand to his head. "What was it?"

"A collision on the railroad," Arthur said. "There is an ambulance here. I think I will put you in it and have you taken home at once. 'Tis only a few miles and not a rough road."

"Yes, yes, home is much the best place," he sighed, again putting his hand to his head.

"Are you in pain?" asked Arthur.

"Not much, but I feel strangely confused. I should like to be taken home as soon as possible. But not to the neglect of anyone who may have been more seriously hurt than I," he added, feebly raising his head t look about him.

"There are none such," Arthur answered. "You perhaps remember that the cars were nearly empty of passengers. No lives were lost, and no one, I think, worse hurt than yourself."

"And I?" returned Edward in a tone of inquiry.

"Have escaped without any broken bones, and I trust will be all right in a few days."

"Oh, Ned! How glad I am it is no worse!" sobbed Zoe, clinging to his hand while the tears rolled fast down her cheeks.

"Yes, little wife," he said, gazing lovingly into her eyes.

"There, I positively forbid any more talking," said Arthur with a mixture of authority and playfulness. "Here is the ambulance. Help me to lift him, men," to the bystanders. "And you, Cousin Zoe, get into your carriage and drive on behind it, or ahead if you choose."

"Can't I ride in the ambulance beside him?" she asked almost imploringly.

"No, no, you will both be more comfortable in doing as I have directed."

"Then, please go with him yourself," she entreated.

"I shall do so, certainly," he answered, motioning her away, then stooping to assist the others in lifting the injured man.

Zoe would not stir till she had seen Edward put into the ambulance and made as comfortable for his ride home as circumstances would permit. Then, as the vehicle moved slowly off, she hurried to her carriage.

Ben helped her in, sprang into his own seat, and, as he took the reins from Ella, Zoe gave the order, "Home now, Uncle Ben, keeping as close behind the ambulance as you can."

"Oh, don't, Zoe! You oughtn't to!" expostulated Ella. Perceiving that her cousin was crying violently behind her veil. "I don't think Ned is very badly hurt. Didn't you hear Arthur say so?"

"He only expressed such a hope. He didn't say certainly," sobbed Zoe. "And when people are in danger, doctors always try to hide it from their friends.

"Arthur is perfectly truthful," asserted Ella, with some warmth. "He may keep his opinions to himself at times, but he never builds people up with false hopes. So cheer up, coz," she added, squeezing Zoe's hand affectionately.

"I know that what you say of Cousin Arthur is all true," sobbed Zoe, "but I could see he had fears as well as hopes. And — and — Ned doesn't seem a bit like himself. He has such a dazed look, as if not quite in his right mind."

"But he knew you and Art, and it is to be expected that a man would feel dazed after such a shock as he must have had."

"Yes, of course. Oh, I'm afraid he's dreadfully, dreadfully hurt, and will never get over it!"

"Still," returned Ella, "try to hope for the best. Don't you think that is the wiser plan always?"

"I suppose so," said Zoe, laughing and crying hysterically, "but I can't be wise tonight. Indeed, I never can."

CHAPTER SIXTH

And, if division come, it soon is past,
Too sharp, too strange and agony to last.

—MRS. NORTON

CHRISTINE AND Aunt Phillis, who had been left in charge of Miss Deane, had had a sore trial of patience in waiting upon her, humoring her whims, listening to her fretting and complaints, and trying to soothe and entertain her.

"Where is your mistress?" she asked at length. "Pretty manners she has to leave a suffering guest to the sole care of servants."

"Yes, miss, I'se alluz t'ought Miss Zoe hab pretty manners and a pretty face," replied Aunt Phillis, "but dere is ladies what habn't none, an doan' git pleased wid nuffin' nor nobody, an' cayn't stan' no misery nowhars 'bout deirselves, but jes' keep frettin' and concessantly displainin' 'dis t'ing and dat, like dey hasn't got nuffin' to be thankful for.'"

"Impudence!" muttered Miss Deane, her eyes flashing angrily. Then bidding her attendants to be quiet, she settled herself for a nap.

She was waked by a slight bustle in the house, accompanied by sounds as if a number of men were carrying a heavy burden through the entrance hall and up the wide stairway leading to the second story.

"What's the matter? What's going on? Has anything happened?" she asked, starting up to a sitting posture.

Christine had risen to her feet, pale and trembling, and stood listening intently.

"I must go and see," she said and hurried from the room, Aunt Phillis shambling after her in haste and trepidation.

"Stay!" cried Miss Deane. "Don't leave me alone. What are you thinking of?"

But they were already out of hearing. "I was never so shamefully treated anywhere as I am here," muttered the angry lady, sinking back upon her pillows. "I'll leave this house tomorrow, if it is a possible thing, and never darken its doors again."

Listening again, she thought she heard sounds of grief — sobbing and wailing, groans and sighs.

She was by no means deficient in curiosity, and it was exceedingly trying to be compelled to lie there in doubt and suspense.

The time seemed very much longer than it really was before Aunt Phillis came back, sobbing, wiping her eyes on her apron.

"What is the matter?" asked Miss Deane impatiently.

"Dere's — dere's been a awful commission on de railroad,' sobbed Aunt Phillis, "and Marse Ed'ard's 'most killed."

"Oh, dreadful," said Miss Deane. "Have they sent for his mother?"

Aunt Phillis only shook her head doubtfully and burst into fresh and louder sobs.

" 'Most killed! Dear me!" sighed the lady. "And he was so young and handsome! It will quite break his mother's heart, I suppose. But she'll get over it. It takes a vast deal of grief to kill."

"P'raps Marse Ed'ard ain't gwine ter die," said the old nurse, checking her sobs. "Dey does say Doctah Arthur kin 'most raise de dead."

"Well, I'm sure I hope Mr. Travilla won't die," responded Miss Deane, "or prove to be permanently injured in any way. — Ah, Christine!" as the latter reentered the room, "what is the story about a railroad accident? Is Mr. Travilla killed?"

"No, no, he not killed," replied Christine in her broken English. "How bad hurt, I not know to say, but not killed."

Meantime, Edward had been taken to his room, and

put comfortably to bed, while Zoe, seated in her boudoir, waited anxiously for the doctor's report of his condition.

Ella was with her, and now and then tried to speak a comforting word, which Zoe scarcely seemed to hear. She sat with her hands clasped in her lap, listening intently to catch every sound from the room where her injured husband lay. She looked pale and anxious, and occasionally a tear would roll quickly down her cheek.

At last the door opened and Arthur stepped softly across the room to her side.

"Cheer up, little cousin," he said kindly. "Edward seems to be doing very well, and if you will be a good, quiet little woman, you may go and sit by his side."

"Oh, thank you! I'll try," she said, starting up at once. "But mayn't I talk to him at all?"

"Not much tonight," was the reply, "not more than seems absolutely necessary. And you must be particularly careful not to say anything that would have the least tendency to excite him."

"Oh, then he must be very, very ill — terribly injured!" she cried, with a burst of tears and sobs.

"That does not necessarily follow," Arthur said, taking her hand and holding it in a kindly pressure. "But you must be more composed or," playfully, "I shall be compelled to exert my authority so far as to forbid you to go to him."

"Oh, no, no! Don't do that!" she cried pleadingly. "I'll be calm and quiet, indeed, indeed I will."

"That's right," he said. "I think I may venture to try you."

"But won't you please tell me just how much you think he is hurt?" she pleaded, clinging to his hand and looking beseechingly into his face.

"My dear little cousin," he said in a tenderly sympathizing tone, "I wish to do all in my power to relieve your anxiety, but am as yet in some doubt myself as to the extent of his injuries. He is a good deal shaken and bruised, but, as I have said before, there are no broken bones. And, unless there should be some internal injury which I have not yet discovered, he is likely to recover entirely in a few days or weeks."

"But you are not sure? Oh, how could I ever bear it if he should —" She broke off with a burst of violent weeping.

He led her to a seat, for she seemed hardly able to stand. Her whole frame was shaking with emotion.

"Try not to meet trouble half way, little cousin," he said gently. " 'Sufficient unto the day is the evil thereof,' and 'As thy days so shall they strength be.' It is God's promise to all who put their trust in Him, and cannot fail. All His promises are yea and amen in Christ Jesus."

"Yes, I know," she said, making a strong effort to control herself. "And you do hope Ned will soon be well?"

"I certainly do," he responded in cheerful accents. "And now, if you will wipe away your tears, and promise to be very good and quiet, I will take you to him. He was asking for you when I left the room."

She gave the desired promise and he led her to the bedside.

"I have brought you your wife, Ned," he said in a quiet tone, "and mean to leave her with you for a while, but you are to be a good boy, and not indulge in much chatter with her."

"We'll be good. I'll answer for her and myself too," Edward returned with a tenderly affectionate smile up into Zoe's face, as she bent over him and touched her lips to his forehead.

She dared not trust herself to speak, but silently put her hand in his, dropped on her knees by the bedside, and laid her pretty head on the pillow which his rested.

"My own darling!" he murmured softly pressing the hand he held. "My own precious little wife!"

Once more Arthur enjoined quiet, then went out and left them alone together.

He paid a professional visit to Miss Deane, satisfied her curiosity in regard to Edward's injuries and learned with pleasure that she was quite resolved to go home the next morning.

"Of course, Mrs. Travilla should give all her attention to her husband now," she remarked, "and I shall be only in the way. One disabled person is quite enough to have in a house at one time. So if you, doctor, will be so kind as to have the ambulance sent out for me directly after breakfast, I'll be much obliged."

"I will do so," he said. "The journey will do you no harm, and you will probably be better cared for and happier in your own home than here, under the circumstances."

Zoe's poor heart was longing to pour itself out into her husband's ear in words of contrition, penitence, and love; and only the fear of injuring him enabled her to restrain her feelings, and remain calm and quiet, kneeling there close by his side with her hand in his. She couldn't rest till she told him how very, very sorry she was for the petulance of the past few days, and especially for the cold rejection of his invitation to accompany him on his drive to Roselands, how firmly resolved never again to give him like cause to be displeased with her, and how dearly she loved him.

But she must refrain, from fear of exciting him. She must wait till all danger from that was past.

It was hard, yet there was strong consolation in the certainty that his dear love was still hers. She read it in his eyes as they gazed fondly into hers; felt it in the tender pressure of his hand; heard it in the tones of his voice as he called her his "darling, his precious little wife."

Yet she was tormented with the fear that his accident had affected his mind and memory for the time, so that he had forgotten the unkindness of the morning; and that, when returning health and vigor should recall the facts to his remembrance, he would again treat her with the coldness and displeasure merited by her behavior.

"But," she comforted herself, "if he does, it will not last long. He is sure to forgive and love me as soon as I tell him how sorry I am."

She did not want to leave him to take either food or rest, but Arthur insisted that she should go down to tea, and later to bed, leaving Edward in his care. She finally yielded to his persuasions, and exertion of medical authority.

She objected that it was quite useless to go to bed. She was positively sure she could not sleep a wink. But her head had scarcely touched the pillow before she fell into a profound slumber, for she was quite worn out with anxiety and grief.

It was broad daylight when she woke. The events of yesterday flashed instantly upon her mind, and she sprang from her bed and began dressing in haste.

She must learn as speedily as possible how Edward was — not worse surely, for Arthur had promised faithfully to call her at once if there should be any unfavorable change during the night. Still, a light tap at the door made her start and turn pale, and she opened it with trembling hand.

Ella stood there with a bright, smiling countenance. "Good morning, coz," she said merrily, "I bring good news — two pieces of it. Ned is almost himself again. Arthur is entirely satisfied that there is no serious injury — internal or otherwise. And Miss Deane has already set out for her home, leaving me to give you her adieus. Now, are you not happy?"

"Indeed, indeed I am!" cried Zoe, dancing about the room in ecstasy, her eyes shining and her cheeks flushing with joy.

"May I go to him at once?" she asked, stopping short, with an eager, questioning look.

"Yes, Art says you may, and Ned is asking for you. How fond he is of you, Zoe, though, I think, no fonder than you are of him."

"I don't deserve it," responded Zoe, with unwonted humility, answering the first part of the remark.

"I don't see but you do," said Ella. "Can I help you with your dressing? I know you are in a hurry to get to him."

"Thank you. I don't think you can, but I'll be done in five minutes."

Edward lay watching for her coming, listening for the sound of her light footsteps, and, as she opened the door, looked up and greeted her with a tenderly affectionate smile.

"Oh, Ned! Dear, dear Ned!" she cried, hastening to the bedside. "How like yourself you look again!"

"And feel, too, love," he said, drawing her down till their lips met in a long kiss.

Arthur had stepped out on her entrance and they were quite alone together.

"God has been very good to us, darling, in sparing us to each other," Edward said in low, moved tones.

"Oh, yes, yes!" she sobbed. "And I didn't deserve it, for I was so cross to you day before yesterday when you asked me to go with you, and I'd been cross for days before that. Can you, will you, forgive me, dear Ned?"

"I have not been blameless and we will exchange forgiveness," he said, drawing her closer till her head rested against his shoulder.

"It is so good of you to say that," she sobbed. "Oh, if you had been killed as I thought for one minute you were, I could never have had an hour of peace or comfort in this world! Those unkind words would have been the last I ever spoke to you, and I should never have been able to forget them, or the sad look that your face must have worn as you turned away. I didn't see it, for I had rudely turned my back to you, but I could imagine it, for I knew you must have been hurt, and grieved, too."

"So I was, little wife," he said tenderly, and passing his hand caressingly over her hair and cheek, "but a few moments' honest retrospect showed me that I was not blameless, had not been as forbearing and affectionate in my treatment of my darling little wife, for the past few days, as I ought to have been, and I resolved to tell her so on the first opportunity."

"Oh, Ned! I don't deserve such a kind, loving husband!" she sighed, "and you ought to have a great deal better wife."

"I am entirely satisfied with the one I have," lifting her hand to his lips. "There isn't a woman in the world I would exchange her for."

"But I often do and say things you don't approve," she murmured with a regretful sigh.

"Yes, but have I not told you more than once, that I do not want a piece of perfection for my wife, lest there should be far too strong a contrast between her and myself?"

"But there wouldn't be," she asserted. "I don't believe there's another man in all the world quite so dear and good as my husband."

"Sweet flattery from your lips," he returned laughingly. "Now, dearest, go and eat your breakfast. I have had mine."

"Ned, do you know our tormentor is gone?" she asked, lifting her head and looking into his eyes with a glad light in her own.

"Yes, and am much relieved to know it," he replied. "And dearest, she shall never come again, if I can prevent it."

CHAPTER SEVENTH

Tell me the old, old story

"MY DEAR ZOE, what a happy face!" was Ella's pleased exclamation as the two met in the breakfast room.

"Very bright, indeed!" said Arthur, who had come in with Zoe, smiling kindly upon her as he spoke.

"Because it reflects the light and joy in my heart," she returned. "Wouldn't it be strange if I were not happy in knowing that my husband is not seriously hurt? Oh, we have been so happy together that I have often feared it could not last!"

"There seems every reasonable prospect that it will,' Arthur said as they seated themselves at the table. "You are both young and healthy, your tastes are congenial, and you have enough of this world's goods to enable you to live free from troublesome cares and exhausting labors."

Zoe was in so great haste to return to Edward, that she could scarce refrain from eating her breakfast more rapidly than was consistent with either politeness toward her guests or a due regard for her own health, but she tried to restrain her impatience. Arthur, who perceived and sympathized with it, exerted himself for her entertainment, telling amusing anecdotes, and making mirth-provoking remarks.

Ella, perceiving his designs, joined in, in the same strain. Zoe presently entered into their mood and they seemed, as in fact they were, a light-hearted and happy little breakfast party — both Arthur and Ella feeling greatly relieved by the favorable change in their cousin, not for Zoe's sake alone, but also because of their own affection for him.

Edward no longer needed Arthur as nurse. Zoe claimed the right to a monopoly of the, to her, sweet task of waiting upon him, and attending to his wants. So Arthur resigned in that capacity, but was to continue his visits as physician.

He and Ella returned to Roselands shortly after leaving the breakfast table, and Zoe, in joyous, tender mood, took her place by her husband's bedside.

He welcomed her with a loving smile, taking her hand in his, and carrying it to his lips.

"Arthur has condemned me to lie here for a full week," he said. "It would seem a weary while in the prospect, but for the thought of having, through it all, the sweet companionship of my darling little wife."

"Dear Ned, how good of you to say so!" she murmured, kneeling beside the bed and laying her cheek to his. "I don't believe there's another creature in the world that thinks my society of much account."

"If you are right in that, which I very much doubt," he said with a smile of incredulity, "it only shows their want of taste and makes no difference to us, does it, love, since we are all the world to each other?"

"I am sure it makes no difference to me," she responded, "if you love and are pleased with me. It's very little I care what anybody else may think or say about me. But, oh, isn't it nice to be alone together again?"

"Very nice."

"And remember, you are to make all possible use of me — as nurse, reader — when you feel that you would like to listen to a book or newspaper — as secretary, everything."

"Yes, dearest, I expect to employ you in all those capacities by and by. But at present, I want nothing but to have you sit by my side and talk to me while I hold your hand, and feast my eyes on the face that is to me the dearest in all the world."

At that, the pretty face was suffused with blushes and smiles. "I'm so happy, so very happy!" she murmured, stealing an arm round his neck. "It is such a change from yesterday, when for a little while, I — I thought you —

were gone, and — and without my having had a chance to ask your forgiveness."

The sobs came thick and fast as she went on. "Oh, Ned, dear, dear Ned! I — I don't mean ever to be cross to you again, especially when we are going to part even for an hour."

"No," he said with emotion, and drawing her closer to him, "we should not have parted so. We had promised each other we would not, and I should have gone to you and made it up with you before leaving the house."

"It was all my fault," she sobbed, "and if — if you had been taken from me, I could never have had another happy moment."

"Thank God that we are spared to each other!" he said with fervent gratitude. "And now, dear wife, let us try to forget that there has been ever any coldness or clashing between us. Let us enjoy the present, and be as happy in each other as if no cloud, even the slightest, had ever come over our union as husband and wife."

"Yes," she said. Then, lifting her face, and gazing earnestly into his, "How pale and exhausted you look!" she cried in alarm. "I have talked and let you talk too much and too excitingly. I'm afraid Cousin Arthur will say I am a poor sort of nurse. Now," withdrawing herself from his embrace and gently rearranging his pillows and smoothing the bedclothes, "shut your eyes and try to sleep. I'll stay close beside you and be as quiet as a mouse."

With a faint smile, he did as he was bidden, and she fulfilled her promise to the letter, watching beside him with love and solicitude for two hours, till his eyes again opened and met hers, gazing so tenderly upon him with an answering look of ardent affection.

"You have had a good nap and look quite refreshed dear,' she said, bending over him and softly stroking his hair with her little white hand.

"Yes, I feel much better," he said. "And you, love — have been sitting there all the time?"

"Of course I have," she answered happily. "Did you think

I would break my word, or feel any desire to go away and leave you?"

"I know you to be the most devoted of nurses when it is I who require your services," he returned with a tenderly appreciative smile. "You are the best of little wives. But you must be very weary, and I want you now to go and take some exercise in the open air."

"Is that an order?" she asked playfully.

"Not yet," he returned in the same tone, "but, if not obeyed as a request, it may become — something stronger."

"Well," she said laughing, "it won't hurt me if it does. You can't hurt me in that way anymore, for do you know, Ned," and she bent lovingly over him, pressing a kiss upon his forehead, "I have become such a silly thing, that I actually enjoy obeying you — when you don't order me as if you thought I wouldn't do as you wish and you mean to force me to do it."

"Forgive me, love, that I have ever done it in that spirit," he said remorsefully and coloring deeply.

"Ned, I haven't anything to forgive," she said with sudden energy and warmth of affection.

"Then you will obey about the air and exercise?" he asked, returning to his playful tone.

"Presently, sir, when I have seen you eat something. It's time for that now, according to the doctor's directions."

She rang for refreshments, saw him take it, then left him for a short time in the care of old Aunt Phillis while she donned her riding hat and habit, mounted her pony, and flew over several miles of road and back again.

She seemed to bring a breath of fresh air with her when she returned to his side.

"My darling," he said, smiling up at her, "how the roses glow on your cheeks and how bright your eyes are! Give me a kiss, and then sit down close by my side."

"I obey both orders most willingly," she said merrily, as she bent down and kissed him on lips and forehead and cheek, then took possession of the chair she had vacated on leaving the room.

"Now, sir, what next?"

"Move your chair round a trifle, so that I can have a better view of your face."

She smilingly obeyed. "There! Does that satisfy your lordship?"

"Quite. Now talk to me."

"About what?"

"Anything you please. The principal thing is to hear the music of your voice."

"Suppose I sing, then."

"Yes, yes!" eagerly, "that's just what I should enjoy. Let it be 'I Love to Tell the Story.' "

Zoe had a beautiful voice. Soft and sweet and clear it rose —

> 'I love to tell the story
> Of unseen things above,
> Of Jesus and His glory,
> Of Jesus and His love.
> I love to tell the story,
> Because I know it's true:
> It satisfies my longings
> As nothing else can do.
>
> I love to tell the story:
> 'Twill be my theme in glory,
> To tell the old, old story,
> Of Jesus and His love.
>
> I love to tell the story:
> More wonderful it seems,
> Than all the golden fancies
> Of all our golden dreams.
> I love to tell the story,
> It did so much for me;
> And that is just the reason
> I tell it now to thee.
>
> I love to tell the story;
> 'Tis pleasant to repeat

~ 57 ~

What seems, each time I tell it,
More wonderfully sweet.
I love to tell the story,
For some have never heard
The message of salvation
From God's own Holy Word.

I love to tell the story;
For those who know it best,
Seem hungering and thirsting
To hear it like the rest.
And when in scenes of glory,
I sing the new, new song,
'Twill be the old, old story,
That I have loved so long.' "

The last note died away and for a moment there was silence in the room. Edward lay gazing into his wife's eyes with a look of sad, yearning tenderness.

"Oh, Ned! Why, why do you look so at me?" she asked, with a sudden burst of tears and dropping her face on the pillow beside his.

He had been holding her hand while she sang. He kept it still, and, laying his other one gently on her head, "Zoe, my darling," he said in tone tremulous with emotion, "it is the one longing desire of my heart that you may learn the full sweetness of that old, old story. Oh, love! Sometimes the thought, 'What if my precious wife should miss heaven and our union be only for time and not for eternity,' sends so keen a pang to my heart, that I know not how to endure it."

"Oh, Ned! Surely I shall not miss it," she said with a sob. "My father and mother were such good Christians, and you, my own husband, are so good too."

"Ah, my darling!" he sighed, "that hope is but a spider's web. Do you not remember that passage in Ezekiel, 'Though these three men, Noah, Daniel, and Job, were in it, they should deliver but their own souls by their righteousness, saith the Lord God'? And it is repeated again and again, 'Though Noah, Daniel and Job were in it, as I live, saith the Lord God, they shall deliver neither son nor daughter; they shall but deliver their own souls by their righteousness.' Zoe, dear, no righteousness but the imputed righteousness of Christ can save the soul from death. He offers it to you, love; and will you continue to reject it?"

"Ned," she sobbed, "I wish I had it. I often think I would be a Christian if I only knew how, but I don't."

"Do you not?" he asked in some surprise. "I will try to make it plain. Jesus offers you a full and free salvation, purchased by what He has done and suffered in your stead, that 'God might be just, and yet the justifier of him who believeth in Jesus.'

" 'Believe on the Lord Jesus Christ, and thou shalt be saved.'

"He bids you come to Him, and says, 'Him that cometh to me, I will in no wise cast out.' "

"But how shall I come?" she asked. "Tell me just how."

"How do you come to me, love, when you feel that you have displeased me, and want to be reconciled?"

"Oh! You know I just come and acknowledge that I've been hateful and cross, and say how sorry I am, and that I don't mean to behave so any more, and ask you to forgive and love me. And, dear Ned, you are always so willing and ready to do that, you hardly wait till I've said my say before you put your arms round me and hug and kiss me and it's all right between us."

"Yes, dearest, and God, our heavenly Father, is far more ready to receive and forgive us when we turn to him with sorrow for our sins, confessing them and pleading for pardon in the name and for the sake of His dear Son, our Saviour."

"I'm afraid I don't feel half so sorry as I ought."

"Who of us does? But we are not to wait for that. We must come to Him to be shown the evil of our natures, the sinfulness of our lives.

" 'Him hath God exalted with His right hand to be a Prince and a Saviour, for to give repentance to Israel, and forgiveness of sins.' "

"But how am I to make myself believe?" she asked.

" 'By grace are ye saved through faith, and that not of yourselves; it is the gift of God.' So you see, we have to go to Jesus in faith, for salvation from the guilt and love of sin, and from eternal death.

"The plan of salvation is very simple — its very simplicity seems to cause many to stumble. They don't know how to believe that it is offered them as a free gift. They think they must do something to merit it, but it cannot be bought. It is 'without money and without price.' 'Whosoever will, let him take the water of life freely.' Come to Jesus, dear one. Come now, for only the present moment is yours. Delay is most dangerous, for the invitation may be withdrawn at any time."

"If I could only see Him! If I could hear His voice!" she sighed.

"That you cannot, yet you know I am not nearer to you, or more willing to hear a petition from you than He is."

At that moment a well-known step was heard in the hall without, and as Zoe rose hastily, wiping her eyes, Arthur tapped at the door.

CHAPTER EIGHTH

I bless thee for kind looks and words
Showered on my path like dew,
For all the love in those deep eyes,
A gladness ever new.

— MRS. HEMANS

A WEEK HAD PASSED since Edward's accident, and he now exchanged his bed, during the day, for an easy chair.

He and Zoe had just finished taking their breakfast together in her boudoir when a servant came in with the mail.

There were letters from Viamede — one for Edward from his mother, one for Zoe from Betty Johnson.

Both brought the unwelcome tidings that little Grace, Raymond and Violet's baby were very ill with scarlet fever.

Edward read aloud his mother's announcement of the fact. "Yes," said Zoe, "Betty tells me the same thing. Oh, Ned! How sorry I am for poor Vi! It would be hard enough for her if she had the captain with her, to help bear the burden and responsibility, and to share in her grief if they should die."

"Yes, it is hard for her, and I am glad she has mamma and grandpa and grandma with her. Mamma says Dick Percival is attending the children, and there is talk of telegraphing Arthur.

"Ah," glancing from the window, "here he comes! He will perhaps bring us later news."

Arthur did so. The children were worse than at the date of the letters. He had just received his summons, and would obey it immediately, taking the next train, had called to tell them and see how Edward was.

"Almost entirely recovered, tell my mother," Edward said in reply to the query, "and you needn't feel any anxiety in regard to this one of your patients," he added playfully.

"I leave him in your care, Zoe," said Arthur; "and if he does not do well, I shall hold you responsible."

"Then you must lay your commands upon him to obey my orders," she said with a merry glance from one to the other.

"Would that be anything new in his experience?" asked the doctor with mock gravity.

"It won't do to question us too closely," returned Zoe, coloring and laughing.

"She is a good little wife and tolerably obedient," laughed Edward. "Really, would you believe it? She told me once she actually enjoyed obeying — under certain circumstances, and so, I suppose, should I. Zoe, you mustn't be too hard on me."

"Oh! I intend to be very strict in seeing the doctor's orders carried out," she said. "And I expect to enjoy my brief authority immensely."

Dr. Conly took leave almost immediately, for he had no time to spare, and the reading of the letter was resumed.

Betty's was a long one, giving a full account, from her point of view, of the contest between Mr. Dinsmore and Lulu Raymond in regard to her refusal to take music lessons of Signor Foresti after he had struck her. None of the family had mentioned the affair in their letters, even Rosie feeling that she had no warrant to do so, and the story was both new and interesting to Zoe.

Lulu had not yet submitted when Betty wrote, so the story as told in her letter left the little girl still in banishment at Oakdale Academy.

Zoe read the letter aloud to Edward.

"Lulu is certainly the most ungovernable child I have ever seen or heard of," he remarked at its conclusion. "I often wonder at the patience and forbearance grandpa and mamma have shown toward her. In their place, I should have had her banished to boarding school long ago — one at a distance, too, so that she could not trouble me, even during holidays."

"So should I," said Zoe. "She hasn't the least shadow of a claim upon them."

"No, the captain feels that and is duly grateful. It is evident, too, that Lulu's lack of gratitude, and her bad behavior, are extremely mortifying to him."

"But don't you think, Ned, it was rather hard to insist on her going back to that ill-tempered, abusive old music teacher?"

"Yes," he acknowledged with some hesitation. "I rather wonder at grandpa.'

"I wonder how it is going to end," said Zoe. "They are both so very determined, I should not like to stand in Lulu's shoes, nor yet in his."

A second letter from Betty, received a fortnight later, told how it ended — though Betty, not being in Lulu's confidence as Evelyn was, knew nothing of Captain Raymond's letter to his daughter, or of Lulu's confession in reply to it, so her story ended with the statement that Lulu had at last submitted, been restored to favor, and was at Magnolia Hall with Evelyn as a companion — all the children who were in health having been banished from Viamede to save them from the danger of catching the dreaded fever.

But to go back to the morning when the first installment of her story was received — "It must be a very anxious time for them — the family at Viamede, I mean," remarked Edward musingly. "And poor, dear Vi is so young to have such burdens to bear. What a blessing that she has mamma with her!"

"Yes," said Zoe. "And, oh, I hope the children will get well! They are such darlings, both Gracie and the baby. I feel very sorry they are so ill and yet I can't help rejoicing that my dear husband is able to sit up again.

"Is that quite heartless in me?" she asked, laying her hand on one of his, which rested on the arm of his easy chair, for she was seated in a low rocker, close at his side.

"I think not," he answered, smiling down into her eyes. "It will do them no good for us to make ourselves unhappy. We will sympathize with and pray for them, but at the same time be thankful and joyful because of all God's goodness to us and them. 'Rejoice in the Lord always: and again I say rejoice.' 'Rejoicing in hope, patience in tribulation.' "

"You have certainly obeyed that last injunction," remarked Zoe, looking at him with affectionate admiration, "so patient and cheerful as you have been since your injury! Many a man would have grumbled and growled from morning to night, while you have been so pleasant, it was a privilege to wait on you.'

"Thank you," he said laughingly. "It is uncommonly good of you to say that, but I'm afraid you are rather uncharitable in your judgment of 'many men.'

"Mamma has not yet heard of my accident," he remarked presently, "and wonders over my long silence. I'll write to her now, if you will be so kind as to bring me my writing desk."

"I'm doubtful about allowing such exertion," she said. "You are left under my orders, you remember, and I'm to be held responsible for your continued improvement."

"Nonsense! That wouldn't hurt me," he returned with an amused smile, "and if you won't get the desk, I'll go after it myself."

"No, you mustn't. I sha'n't allow it," she said, knitting her brows and trying to look stern.

"Then get it for me."

"Well," she said reflectively, "I suppose there'll have to be a compromise. I'll get the desk if you'll let me act as your secretary.'

"We'll consider that arrangement after you have brought it."

"No, you must agree to my proposition first."

"Why, what a little tyrant you are!" he laughed. "Well, I consent. Now will you please bring the desk?"

"Yes," she said, jumping up and crossing the room to where it stood, "and if you are very good, you may write a postscript with your own hand."

"I'll do it all with my own hand," he said as she returned to his side.

"Why, Ned!" she exclaimed in surprise, "I thought you were a man of your word!"

"And so I am, I trust,' he said, smiling at her astonished look, then catching her right hand in his. "Is not this mine?" he asked. "Did not you give it to me? — Let me see — nearly two years ago?"

"Yes, I did," she answered, laughing and blushing with pleasure and happiness. "You are right; it is yours. So you have every right to use it, and must do so."

"Ah!" he said, " 'a willful woman will have her way,' I see. There never was a truer saying. No, that won't do," as she seated herself with the desk in her lap. Put it on the table. I can't have you bending over to write on your lap and so growing round shouldered, especially in my service."

"Anything to please you," she returned merrily, doing as he directed. "I suppose my right hand is not all of me that you lay claim to?"

"No, indeed! I claim you altogether as my better and dearer half," he said, his tone changing from jest to earnest and the light of love shining in his eyes.

She ran to him at that, put her arms round his neck, and laid her cheek to his. "No, Ned, I can't have you say that," she murmured. "You who are so good and wise, while I am such a silly and faulty thing, not at all worthy to be your wife. Whatever made you marry me?"

"Love," he answered, drawing her closer and fondly caressing her hair and cheek — "love that grows stronger and deeper with every day we live together, dearest."

"Dear Ned, my own dear husband!" she said, hugging him tighter. "Words could never tell how much I love you, or how I rejoice in your love for me. You are truly my other, my best half, and I don't know how I could live without you."

"Our mutual love is a cause for great gratitude to God," he said reverently. "There are so many miserably unhappy couples, I feel that I can never be thankful enough for the little wife who suits me so entirely."

"You are my very greatest earthly blessing," she replied, lifting her head and gazing into his face with eyes shining with joy and love, "and your words make me very, very happy. Now," releasing herself from his embrace, "it's time to attend to business, isn't it? I am ready to write if you will dictate.' And she seated herself before the desk and took up her pen.

It was not a lengthy epistle. He began with an acknowledgment of the receipt of his mother's letter, expressed his sympathy in the sorrow and suffering at Viamede, gave a brief account of his accident, consequent illness, and partial recovery, highly eulogizing Zoe as the best of wives and nurses.

When he began that, her pen ceased its movement, and was held suspended over the paper, while, blushing deeply, she turned to him with a remonstrance.

"Don't ask me to write that. I am ashamed to have mamma see it in my handwriting.

"Go on," he said. "She will know they are my words and not yours."

"Well, I obey orders," she replied with a smile, "but I don't half like to do it."

"Then let me," he said. "If you hold the desk on the arm of my chair for five minutes and give me the pen, I can finish up the thing easily, and without the least danger of hurting my precious self."

She did as directed. "There, now lie back in your chair and rest," she said when he had finished his note, and signed his name. "You do look a little tired," she added with an anxious glance at him as she returned the desk to the table.

"Nonsense! Tired with that slight exertion!" he responded merrily. "You may read that over, and see if it wants for any corrections."

She did so, then, turning toward him with an arch smile, asked, "May I criticize?"

"I should be happy to have the benefit of your criticism," he said, laughing, "but don't make it too severe, please."

"Oh, no! I was only thinking that mamma, judging of her by myself, would not be half satisfied with such a bare statement of facts, and that I had better write a supplement, giving her more of the particulars."

"I highly approve the suggestion," he answered, "only

stipulating that you shall not spend too much time over it, and shall read it to me when finished."

"I'm afraid it won't be worth your hearing."

"Let me judge of that. If not worth my hearing, can it be worth mamma's reading?"

"Perhaps so," she said with a blush, "because what I tell will be news to her, but not to you."

"Ah! I hadn't thought of that. But I shall want to hear it all the same, and take my turn at criticism."

"If you are not more severe than I was, I can stand it," she said. "And now please keep quiet till I am done."

He complied, lying back at his ease and amusing himself with watching her, admiring the graceful pose of her figure, the pretty face bending over the paper, and the small, white, shapely hand that was gliding swiftly back and forth.

"Come," he said at last, "you are making quite a long story of it."

"Mamma won't think so," she retorted without looking up. "And you know you are not obliged to hear it."

"Ah! But that is not the objection. I want to hear every word of it, but I cannot spare my companion and nurse so long."

She turned to him with a bright smile. "What can I do for you, dear? Just tell me. The letter can be finished afterward, you know."

"I want nothing but you," was the smiling rejoinder. "Finish your letter, and then come and sit close by my side.

"But no, you must take your accustomed exercise in the open air."

Considering a moment, "I think," he said, "I'll have you order the carriage for about the time you are likely to be done there, and we'll have a drive together."

She shook her head gravely. "You are not fit for any such exertion."

"Uncle Ben and Solon shall help me down the stairs and into the carriage, so there need be no exertion about it."

"I won't consent," she said. "The doctor left you in my

charge, and his orders were that you should keep quiet for the next few days."

"You prefer to go alone, do you?"

"Yes, rather than have you injured by going with me."

"Come here," he said, and laying down her pen, she obeyed.

He took both her hands in his, and gazed with mock gravity up into her face as she stood over him. "What a little tyrant you are developing into!" he remarked, knitting his brows. "Will you order the carriage, and take a drive in my company?"

"No."

"Then what will you do?"

"Go by myself, or stay at home with you, just as you bid me."

"What a remarkable mixture of tyranny and submission," he exclaimed, laughing as he pulled her down to put his arm round her and kiss her first on one cheek, then on the other. "I'll tell you what we'll do — you finish that letter, read it to me, and take the benefit of my able criticisms; then I'll try to get a nap while you take your drive or walk, whichever you prefer."

"That will do nicely," she said, returning his caresses. "If you will be pleased to let me go, I'll order the carriage, finish the letter in five minutes, hear the able criticisms, put my patient to bed, and be off for my drive."

"Do so," he said, releasing her.

From this time forward, till the children were out of danger, and Edward was able to go about and attend to his affairs as usual, there were daily letters and telegrams passing between Viamede and Ion. Then Dr. Conly came home and almost immediately on his arrival drove over to Ion to see for himself if his patient there had entirely recovered, and to carry some messages and tokens of affection from the absent members of the family.

It was late in the afternoon that he reached Ion, and he found Edward and Zoe sitting together in the parlor — she with a bit of embroidery in her hands, he reading aloud to her.

Arthur was very warmly welcomed by both.

"Cousin Arthur, I'm delighted to see you!" cried Zoe, giving him her hand.

"And I no less so," added Edward, offering his. "How did you leave them all at Viamede?"

"All in health, except, of course, the two little ones who have been so ill," he said, taking the chair Edward drew forward for him. "And we consider them out of danger, with the careful attention they are sure to have."

"How have mamma and Vi stood the anxiety and nursing?" asked Edward.

"Quite as well as could have been expected. They have lost a little in flesh and color, but will, I think, soon regain both, now that their anxiety is relieved.

"And you, Ned, are quite yourself again, I should say, from appearances?"

"Yes, and I desire to give all credit to the nurse in whose charge you left me," returned Edward with a smiling glance at Zoe.

"As is but fair," said Arthur. "I discovered her capabilities before I left."

"She made the most of her delegated authority," remarked Edward gravely. "I was allowed no will of my own. It was not till I had entirely recovered from my injuries that she had no longer the shadow of an excuse for depriving me of my liberty."

"I thought it was a good lesson for him," retorted Zoe. "I've read somewhere that nobody is fit to rule who hasn't first learned to obey."

"Ah! But that I learned before I was a year old," said Edward, laughing.

"Nobody would have thought it, seeing the trouble I had to make you obey," said Zoe.

"Now, Cousin Arthur, tell us all about Viamede, and what you did and saw there."

"It is a lovely place," he said. "I expected to be disappointed after the glowing accounts I had heard, but I feel like saying, 'The half has not been told me.' " With that he plunged into an enthusiastic description of the mansion, its grounds, and the surrounding country.

"I was loath to leave it," he said in conclusion.

"And you make me more desirous to see it than ever," said Zoe.

"Oh, do tell us. Had Captain Raymond been heard from before you left? We have seen by the papers that the report of the loss of his vessel was untrue, and, of course, we were greatly relieved."

"Yes, letters came from him the day before I started home. Fortunately, they had been able to keep the report from Vi and little Gracie, but Max and Lulu had heard it and were terribly distressed, I was told."

"They are very fond of their father," remarked Zoe.

"Yes, as they have good reason to be," said Arthur. "He is a noble fellow and one of the best husbands and fathers."

"Did you hear anything in particular about Lulu?" Zoe asked.

"No, I think not," he said reflectively, "nothing but that she, Max and Evelyn Leland were staying, by invitation, at Magnolia Hall.

"Ah, yes! I remember now that Betty told me there had been some trouble between Uncle Horace and Lulu in regard to her taking lessons of a music teacher whom she greatly disliked, and that because of her obstinate refusal he had banished her from Viamede, entering her as a boarder at the academy the children were attending, and that her distress of mind over the illness of her little sisters, and the sad report about her father had led her to submit."

"Much to Vi's relief, no doubt," remarked Edward. "Poor Vi! She is devotedly attached to her husband, but Lulu is a sore thorn in her side."

"I don't believe she has ever acknowledged as much, or could be induced to," said Zoe.

"No," assented Edward, "but it is evident to those who know her well, nevertheless. She tries hard to conceal the fact, and has wonderful patience with the willful, passionate child, really loving her for her father's sake."

"And for her own, too, if I mistake not," Arthur said. "There is something quite lovable about Lulu in spite of her very serious faults."

"There is," said Edward. "I have felt it strongly myself at times. She is warmhearted, energetic, very generous, and remarkably straightforward, truthful and honest."

Dr. Conly had risen, as if to take leave.

"Now, Cousin Arthur," said Zoe, "please sit down again, for we cannot let you leave us till after tea."

Edward seconded the invitation.

"Thank you both," Arthur said, "but — "

"But — no buts," interrupted Zoe merrily. "I know you were about to plead haste, but there is the tea bell now. So you will not be delayed, for you have to take time for your meals."

"Then I accept," he said, "rejoicing in the opportunity to spend a little longer time in your very pleasant society."

CHAPTER NINTH

*Here are a few of the unpleasantest words
that ever blotted paper.*

EDWARD AND ZOE now began to look forward to the return
of the family as a desirable event not very far in the future.
They had been extremely happy in each other during almost
the whole time of separation from the rest, but now they
were hungering for a sight of "mamma's sweet face," and
would by no means object to a glimpse of those
grandparents, sisters, and children.

At length a letter was received, fixing the date of the
intended departure from Viamede, and stating by which
train the party would probably reach the neighboring
village of Union, where carriages must be in readiness to
receive and convey them to Ion.

And now Edward and Zoe began counting the days. The
little matron put on more housewifely airs than was her
wont, and was in great glee over her preparations for a
grand reception and welcoming feast to the loved travelers.

She insisted on much cleaning and renovating, and on
the day of the arrival robbed the greenhouses and
conservatories for the adornment of the house, the table,
and her own person.

Edward laughingly asserted that he was almost, if not
quite, as much under her orders at that time as when left
in her charge by the doctor, and could have no peace but
in showing himself entirely submissive, and ready to
carry out all her schemes and wishes.

Fairview also was getting ready to receive its master and
mistress, but the indoor preparations there were overseen
by Mrs. Lacey of the Laurels — Edward's Aunt Rose.

It was the last of April — lovely spring weather had

come, and the head gardeners and their subordinates of both places found much to do in making all trim and neat against the expected arrival of the respective owners. Of these matters Edward took a general oversight.

He and Zoe were up earlier than their wont on the morning of the long-looked-for day, wandering about the gardens before breakfast.

"How lovely everything looks!" exclaimed Zoe in delight. "I am sure mamma will be greatly pleased and praise you to your heart's content, Cuff," she added, turning to the gardener at work near by.

"Ya'as, Miss Zoe," he answered with a broad grim of satisfaction. "Dat's what I'se been workin' for, an' spects to hab sho', kase Miss Elsie, she doan' nebber grudge nuffin' in de way ob praise nor ob wages, when yo's done yo' bes', ob co'se; an' dis chile done do dat, sho's yo' bawn."

"Yes, I'm sure you have, Cuff," said Edward kindly. "The flowers look very flourishing. There's not a dead leaf or a weed to be seen anywhere. The walks are clean and smooth as a floor — nothing amiss anywhere, so far as I can perceive."

They moved on, walking slowly and inspecting carefully as they went, yet finding nothing to mar their satisfaction.

They had reached the front of the house and were about to go in when a boy on horseback came cantering up the avenue, and handed a telegram to Edward.

Tearing it hastily open, "From grandpa," he said. "Ah! They will be here by the next train!"

"Half a day sooner than they or we expected," cried Zoe, half joyfully, half in dismay, struck with a momentary fear that her preparations could not be quite complete in time.

EDWARD HASTENED to reassure her. "Altogether, good news, isn't it?" he said. "We can be quite ready, I am sure, and will escape some hours of waiting, while they gain time for rest and refreshment before the arrival of the family party who are to gather here from the Oaks, Roselands, the Laurels, and the Pines."

"Oh, yes, yes! It is ever so nice! And I'm as glad as can

be," she cried rapturously. "Now let us make haste to get to our breakfast and then to attend to the finishing touches needed by the house and our own persons."

"Stay," said Edward, detaining her as she was starting up the steps into the veranda. "We should sent word to Fairview, but it will be time enough after breakfast. Suppose we ride over there immediately upon leaving the table and carry the news ourselves? The air and exercise will do you good."

"It would be very nice," she returned meditatively, "but I am afraid I shall hardly have time."

"Yes, you will," he said. "You can give your orders and let Christine and Aunt Dicey see them carried out."

"But I want my taste consulted in the arrangement of the flowers," she objected.

"Plenty of time for that after we get back," he said. "And I want your help in deciding whether everything is exactly as it should be in the grounds at Fairview. Shall I order the horses?"

"Yes, I'll go, of course, if you wish it, and enjoy it greatly, I know."

They were very merry over their breakfast and during their ride, for they were young, healthy, happy in each other. The morning air was delicious, and not a cloud was to be perceived in either the natural sky above their heads or in their future. All was bright and joyous, and they seemed to have naught to do with sorrow or care, or any of the evils that oppressed the hearts and darkened the lives of many of their fellow creatures.

Their tidings were received with joy by the retainers at Fairview, nearly everything being in readiness for the reception of its master and mistress.

Edward and Zoe had agreed that it was not at all necessary to inform the expected guests of the evening of the change in the hour for the arrival of the homecoming party they intended to welcome.

"The meeting will be quite as early as anticipated," remarked Edward, "and it will do no harm for mamma and the others to have a chance to rest a little before seeing so many."

"They will enjoy themselves all the better, I'm sure," said Zoe.

They were cantering homeward as they talked. Arrived there, Zoe set to work at the pleasant task of adorning the house — mamma's boudoir in particular — with beautiful and sweet scented flowers, and contrived to be delightfully busy in their arrangement till some little time after Edward had gone with the carriages to meet and bring home the travelers.

All came directly to Ion, except the Fairview family, who sought their own home first, but promised to be present for the evening festivities.

The journey had been taken leisurely, and no one seemed fatigued but the little convalescents, who were glad to be put immediately to bed.

"Mamma, dear, dearest mamma!" cried Zoe, as the two clasped each other in a close embrace. "I am so, so glad to see you!"

"Tired of housekeeping, little woman?" Elsie asked, with an arch look and smile.

"No, mamma, not that, though willing enough to resign my position to you," was the happy rejoinder. "But my delight is altogether because you are so dear and sweet, that everybody must be the happier for your presence."

"Dear child, I prize and fully return your affection," Elsie said in reply.

For each one, Zoe had a joyous and affectionate greeting, till it came to Lulu's turn.

At her she glanced doubtfully for an instant, then gave her a hearty kiss, saying to herself, "Though she did behave so badly, I'm sure she had a good deal of provocation."

Lulu had noted the momentary hesitation, and flushed hotly under it, but the kiss set all right and she returned it as warmly as it was given.

"It seems nice to see you and Uncle Edward again, Aunt Zoe!" she said, "and nice to get back to Ion, though Viamede is so lovely."

"Yes," chimed in Rosie. "Viamede is almost an earthly paradise, but Ion is the homiest home of the two."

Lulu had been on her very best behavior ever since the termination of the controversy between Mr. Dinsmore and herself in regard to her tutelage by Signor Foresti. She had returned to Ion full of good resolutions, promising herself that, if permitted to continue to live at Ion, she would henceforward be submissive, obedient, and very determined in her efforts to control her unruly temper.

But was she to be allowed to stay there? No objection had been raised by any of the family. But remembering her father's repeated warning that if she proved to be troublesome to these kind friends, he would feel compelled to take her away from Ion and send her to a boarding school, she awaited his decision with much secret apprehension.

It was quite too soon to look for a response to her confession, written from Magnolia Hall, or a letter from him to her mamma, grandma Elsie, or grandpa Dinsmore, giving his verdict in regard to her. And, at times, she found the suspense very hard to bear.

Thus far, Evelyn Leland had been the sole confidant of her doubts, fears, and anxieties on the subject. Not even Max had been made acquainted with the contents of either her father's letter to her or her reply to it.

She had managed to conceal her uneasiness from him and also from Grandma Elsie and Violet, the time and attention of both ladies being much occupied with the care of the little invalids.

But, on the evening of this day, Grace and baby Elsie were fast asleep, the one in bed, the other in her dainty crib, at an early hour. Violet bethought her of Lulu in connection with the expected assembling of a large family party.

"I must see that the child is suitably attired," she said to herself, and, deferring her own dressing, went at once to the little girl's room.

She found her already dressed — suitably and tastefully, too — and sitting by a window in an attitude of dejection, her elbow on the sill, her head in her hand. She was not looking out — her eyes were downcast and her countenance was sad.

"What is the matter, Lulu, dear?" Violet asked in gentle tones, as she drew near and laid her soft white hand caressingly on the bowed head. "Are you sorry we are at home again?"

"Oh, no, no, Mamma Vi! It's not that. I should be very glad to get back, if I were only sure of being allowed to stay," Lulu answered, lifting her head and hastily wiping a tear out of the corner of her eye. "But I — I'm dreadfully afraid papa will say I can't, that I must be sent away somewhere, because of having been so disobedient and obstinate."

"I hope not, dear," Violet said. "You have been so good ever since you gave up and consented to do as grandpa wished."

"Thank you for saying that, Mamma Vi. I have been trying with all my might — asking God to help me, too," she added low and reverentially, "but papa doesn't know that, and he has been very near banishing me two or three times before. Oh, I don't know how to wait to hear from him! I wish a letter would come!"

"It is almost too soon to hope for it yet, dear child. But I trust we may hear before very long," said Violet.

At that moment there came a little tap at the door and the sweetest of voices asked, "Shall I come in?"

"Oh, yes, mamma!"

"Yes, Grandma Elsie!" answered the two addressed.

"I thought our little girl might like some help with her dressing for the evening," Elsie said, advancing into the room. "But — is anything wrong? I think you are looking troubled and unhappy, Lulu."

Violet explained the cause, and Elsie said, very kindly, "I don't want you sent away, Lulu, dear. No one could desire a better-behaved child than you have been of late. And I have written to your father to tell him so, and ask that you may stay with us still. So cheer up and hope for the best, little girl," she added with a smile and an affectionate kiss.

Lulu had risen and was standing by Elsie's side. As the latter bent down to bestow the caress, her arms were thrown impulsively about her neck with a glad, grateful exclamation, "Oh, Grandma Elsie, how good you are to me! I don't know how you could want to keep me here when I've been so bad and troublesome so many times."

"I trust you have been so for the very last time, dear child," Elsie responded. "Think how it will rejoice your father's heart if he learns that you have at length conquered in the fight with your naturally quick, willful temper, which has been the cause of so much distress to both him and yourself."

"I do think of it very often, Grandma Elsie," Lulu returned with a sigh that seemed to come from the depths of her heart. "And I do want to please papa and make him happy, but — oh, dear! When something happens to make me angry, I forget all about it and my good resolutions till it's too late. The first thing I know, I've been acting like a fury, and disgracing myself and him."

"Yet don't be discouraged, or ever give up the fight," Elsie said. "Persevere, using all your own strength and asking help from on high, and you will come off conqueror at last."

About the same time that this little scene was enacting at Ion, Elsie Leland, passing the door of Evelyn's room, thought she heard a low sob coming from within.

She paused and listened. The sound was repeated, and she tapped lightly on the door. There was no answer, and opening it, she stole softly in.

Evelyn sat in an easy chair at the farther side of the room, her face hidden in her hands, an open letter lying in her lap.

"My poor child! Is it bad news?" Elsie asked, going up to the little girl and touching her hair caressingly.

"It is heartbreaking to me, Aunt Elsie, but read and judge for yourself," Evelyn replied in a voice choking with sobs. And taking up the letter, she placed it in her aunt's hand.

Elsie gave it a hasty perusal, then, tossing it indignantly aside, took the young weeper in her arms, bestowing upon her tender caresses and soothing words.

"It is hard, very hard for you, dear, I know. It would be

for me in your place; but we must just try to make the best of it."

"Yes," sobbed Evelyn, "but I could hardly feel more fully orphaned if my mother were dead. And papa has not been gone a year. Oh, how could she? How could she! You see, Aunt Elsie, she talks of my joining her as soon as I am my own mistress, but how can I ever think of it now?"

"We — your uncle and I — would be very loath to give you up, darling; and, if you can only be content, I think you may always have a happy home here with us," Elsie said with another tender caress.

"Dear auntie, you and uncle have made it a very happy home to me," returned Evelyn gratefully, wiping away her tears as she spoke, and forcing a rather sad sort of smile. "I should be as sorry to leave it as you could possibly be to have me do so."

Evelyn was of a very quiet temperament, rarely indulging in bursts of emotion of any kind, and Elsie soon succeeded in restoring her to calmness, thought her eyes still showed traces of tears. Her expressive features again wore the look of gentle sadness that was their wont in the first weeks of her sojourn at Fairview, but which had gradually changed to one of cheerfulness and content.

"Now, Eva, dear, it is time we were getting ready for our drive to Ion," Elsie said. "Shall I help you change your dress?"

"I — I think, if you will excuse me, auntie," Evelyn returned with hesitation, "I should prefer to stay at home. I'm scarcely in the mood for merry-making."

"Of course, you shall do as you like, dear child," was the kindly response. "But it is only to be a family party, and you need not be mixed up with any fun or frolic — I don't suppose there will be anything of the kind going on — and you will probably enjoy a private chat with your bosom friend, Lulu. You know, there are plenty of corners where you can get together by yourself. I think you would find it lonely staying here, and Lulu would not half enjoy her evening without you."

"You are right, auntie. I will go," Evelyn answered more cheerfully than she had spoken since reading her letter. "I will dress at once, but shall not need any help except advice about what I shall wear."

Elsie gave it, and, saying the carriage would be at the door in half an hour, went back to her own apartments to attend to the proper adornment of her own pretty person.

Soon after her little talk with Grandma Elsie and Mamma Vi, Lulu, still unable to banish the anxiety which made her restless and uneasy, wandered out into the shrubbery, where she presently met Max.

"I've been all round the place," he said, "and I tell you, Lu, it's in prime order. Everything's as neat as a pin. Don't the grounds look lovely, even after Viamede?"

"Yes," she sighed, glancing round from side to side with a melancholy expression of countenance quite unusual for her.

"What's the matter, Sis?" he asked with some surprise. "I hope you're not sick."

"No, I'm perfectly well," she answered. "But the prettier the place looks, the sorrier I feel to think I may have to go away and leave it."

"Who says you are to go away?" he demanded, " — not Grandma Elsie or Mamma Vi either, I am sure, for they are both too kind; and, in fact, I don't believe anybody here wants to send you off."

"Maybe not," she said, "but I'll have to go if papa says so; and, oh, Max, I'm so afraid he will, because of — all that — all the trouble between Grandpa Dinsmore and me about the music lessons."

"I didn't suppose papa had been told about it," he remarked half inquiringly.

"Yes," she said, "I confessed every bit of it to him in that letter I wrote at Magnolia Hall."

"Bully for you!" cried Max heartily. "I knew you'd own up at last, like a brick, as you are."

"Oh, Max! You forget that Mamma Vi does not approve of slang," she said. "But I don't deserve a bit of praise for confessing, because I had to. Papa wrote to me that he was sure I'd been misbehaving — though nobody had told him a single word about it — and that I must write at once and tell him everything."

"Well, I'm glad you did, and I hope he won't be hard on you, Lu. Still, I wouldn't fret, though," he added in a consolatory tone, "because there's no use trying to cross the bridge before you come to it, 'specially when you mayn't come at all."

"That's quite true, but it's a great deal easier to preach than to practice," she said. "Maxie, would you be sorry to have me sent away?" she asked, her voice taking on a beseeching tone.

"Why, of course I should," he said. "We've gone through a good deal together, and you know we've always been rather fond of each other, considering that we're brother and sister," he added laughingly. "Ah, here comes Eva," and he lifted his hat with a profound bow as a turn in the walk brought them face to face with her.

"Oh, Eva! I'm so glad you've come early!" exclaimed Lulu.

"I, too," said Max, "but if you have any secrets for each other's private ear, I'll be off."

"Your company is always agreeable, Max," Evelyn said with a faint smile, "and I should be sorry to drive you away."

"Thanks," he said, "but I'll have to go, for I hear Grandpa Dinsmore calling me."

He hastened to obey the call, and the two girls, each putting an arm about the other's waist, paced to and fro along the gravel walk.

"How is Fairview looking?" asked Lulu.

"Lovely — it couldn't be in better order, and there are a great many flowers in bloom. One might say just the same of Ion."

"Yes, it is even prettier than Fairview, I have always thought. But that's a sweet place to be and Aunt Elsie and Uncle Lester are delightful to live with. I only wish I was as sure as you are of such a sweet home."

"Don't worry, Lu. I hope your father will let you stay on

here," Evelyn said in an affectionate tone, "but, indeed, I don't think you have any reason to envy me."

She ended with so profound a sigh that Lulu turned a surprised, inquiring look upon her, asking, "have you had any bad news, Eva? I know you have been looking anxiously for a letter from your mother."

"Yes, it has come. I found it waiting for me at Fairview, and — " She paused for a moment, her heart too full for speech.

"And it was bad news? Oh, I am so sorry!" said Lulu. "I hope it wasn't that she wants you to go away from here — unless I have to go too, and we can be together somewhere"

"No, it was that — not now. Mamma knows that, because of the way papa made his will, I must stay with Uncle Lester till I come of age. She talks of my going to her then, but I cannot — oh, I never can, for — Lulu, she's married again, to an Italian count. And it is not a year since my dear, dear father was taken from us."

Evelyn's voice was tremulous with pain, and she ended with a burst of bitter weeping.

"Oh, how could she!" exclaimed Lulu. "I don't wonder you feel so about it, Eva. A horrid Italian, too!" she added, thinking of Signor Foresti. "I'd never call him father!"

"Indeed, I've no idea of doing that," Eva said indignantly. "I only hope he may never cross my path. And so I — feel as if my mother is lost to me. You are far better off than I, Lulu. You have your own dear father still living, and Aunt Vi is so lovely and sweet."

"Yes, I am better off than you," Lulu acknowledged emphatically, "and if I hadn't such a bad temper, always getting me into trouble, I'd be a girl to be envied."

CHAPTER TENTH
Lulu's Sentence

PENDING CAPTAIN RAYMOND'S verdict in regard to Lulu, life at Ion fell into the old grooves, for her as well as the other members of the family.

Studies were taken up again by all the children, including Evelyn Leland, where they had been dropped — Mr. Dinsmore and his daughter giving instruction and hearing recitations as formerly.

This interval of waiting lasted over two months, a longer period of silence on the part of husband and father than usual; but, as they learned afterward, letters had been delayed in both going and coming.

Captain Raymond, in his good ship, far out on the ocean, was wearying for news from home, when his pressing want was most opportunely supplied by a passing vessel.

She had a heavy mail for the man-of-war, and a generous share of it fell to her commander.

He was soon seated in the privacy of his own cabin with Violet's letter open in his hand. It was sure to receive his attention before that of any other correspondent.

With a swelling heart he read of the sore trial she had been passing through, in the severe illness of Gracie and the babe. Deeply he regretted not having been there to lighten her burdens with his sympathy and help in the nursing. And though, at the time of writing, she was able to report that the little sufferers were considered out of danger, he could not repress a fear, amid his thankfulness, that there might be a relapse, or the dread disease might leave behind it, as it so often does, some lasting ill effect.

He lingered over the letter, re-reading passages here and

there, but at length laid it aside, and gave his attention to others bearing the same postmark.

There was a short one from Max, which stirred his heart with fatherly love and pride in his boy. That came next after Violet's; then, he opened Lulu's bulky packet.

He sighed deeply as he laid it down after a careful perusal, during which his face had grown stern and troubled, and, rising, paced the cabin to and fro, his hands in his pockets, his head bowed on his chest, which again and again heaved with a deep-drawn sigh.

"What I am to do with that child, I do not know," he groaned within himself. "If I could make a home for her, and have her constantly with me, I might perhaps be able to train her up aright and help her to learn the hard lesson of how to rule her own spirit.

"I could not do that, however, without resigning from the service. That would be giving up my only means of earning a livelihood for her as well as the others and myself. That is not to be thought of. Nor could I forsake the service without heartfelt regret, were I a millionaire."

The captain was a man of prayer. Some moments were spent on his knees, asking guidance and help for himself, and a change of heart for his wayward daughter. Then, again seating himself at his writing table, he opened yet another letter, one whose superscription he recognized as that of a business agent in one of the far Western States.

His face lighted up as he read and a verse flashed across his mind: "And it shall come to pass, that before they call, I will answer; and while they are yet speaking, I will hear."

That sheet of paper was the bearer of most strange, unlooked-for tidings — a tract of wild land, bought by him for a trifle years before, and long considered of little or no value, had suddenly become — by the discovery that it contained rich mineral deposits, and the consequent opening of mines, and laying out of a town upon it — worth many thousands, perhaps millions of money.

And he — Captain Raymond — was the undisputed owner of it all — of wealth beyond his wildest dreams. He could scarce believe it. It seemed impossible. Yet it was undoubtedly true — and a bright vision of a lovely home with his wife and children about him rose up before his mind's eye, and filled him with joy and gratitude to the Giver of all good.

He would send in his resignation and realize the vision at the earliest possible moment.

But stay! Could he now, in the prime of life, forsake the service for which he had been educated, and to which he had already given many of his best years? Could he be content to bid farewell to the glorious old ocean so long his home, so beautiful and lovable in its varied moods, and settle down upon the unchanging land, quite reconciled to its sameness? Would he not find in himself an insatiable longing to be again upon the ever-restless sea, treading once more the deck of his gallant ship, monarch of her little world, director of all her movements?

It was not a question to be decided in a moment. It requires time for thought — a careful consideration of seemingly conflicting duties, a careful balance of inclinations and interests, and for seeking counsel of his best, his almighty and all-wise Friend.

At Ion, as the summer heats approached, the question was mooted, "Where shall we spend the next two or three months?" After some discussion, it was decided that all should go north to Cape May for a time — afterward they would break up into smaller parties and scatter to different points of interest, as they might fancy.

Lester and Elsie Leland would spend a portion of the season at Cliff Cottage — Evelyn's old home — taking her and Lulu with them.

Edward and Zoe, too, and probably some of the others, would visit there.

All necessary arrangements had been made, and they were to start the next day, when at last letters were received from Captain Raymond.

Lulu's heart beat very fast at sight of them. She had been full of delight at the prospect of her northern trip, especially the visit to be paid with Evelyn to her former home, the latter having in their private talks dwelt upon its many attractions, and the life she had led there in the sweet companionship of her beloved father.

"Would there be anything in papa's letter to prevent the carrying out of the cherished plan?" Lulu asked herself, as, in fear and trembling, she watched Violet opening with eager fingers the packet handed her at the breakfast table.

Max and Gracie, too, looked on with interest equal to Lulu's, but in their case there was only joyous expectancy unmingled with dread.

"There is something for each of us, as usual," Violet said presently, with a smiling glance from one to another — "Max, Lulu, Gracie, and myself."

Lulu received hers — only a folded slip of paper — and, asking to be excused, stole away to the privacy of her own room to read it.

> *My Dear Little Daughter,*
> *The story of your misconduct has*
> *given a very sad heart to the father*
> *who loves you so dearly. I forgive you,*
> *my child, but can no longer let you*
> *remain at Ion to be a trouble and*
> *torment to our kind friends there. I*
> *shall remove you elsewhere as soon as*
> *I can settle upon a suitable place. In*
> *the meantime, if you are truly sorry for*
> *the past, you will, I am sure, earnestly*
> *strive to be patient, submissive and*
> *obedient to those who have you in*
> *charge.*
>
> *Your loving father,*
> *L. Raymond.*

The paper fell from Lulu's hand and fluttered to the floor, as she folded her arms upon the sill of the window beside which she had seated herself, and rested her head upon them.

"And that's all — just that I am to go away, nobody knows where, to be separated from Max and Gracie and everyone else that I care for. And when papa comes home, maybe he won't visit me at all, of if he does, it will be for only a little bit, because, of course, he will want to spend most of his leave where the others are. Oh dear! Oh dear! I wish I'd been good! I wish I'd been born sweet-tempered and patient, like Gracie. I wonder if papa will ever, ever let me come back!

"But perhaps Grandpa Dinsmore and Grandma Elsie will never invite me again. I wouldn't in their place, I'm sure."

The captains' letter to his wife made the same announcement of his intentions in regard to Lulu, adding, that, for the present he would have her disposed of as should seem best to them — Mr. Dinsmore, his daughter, and Violet herself — upon consultation together. He had entire confidence, he said, in their wisdom and their kind feeling toward his wayward, troublesome, yet still beloved child, so that he could trust her to their tender mercies without hesitation.

He went on to say (and, ah, with what a smile of exultation and delight those words were penned!) that "there was a possibility that he might be with them again in the fall, long enough to find a suitable home for Lulu; and, in the meantime, would they kindly seize any opportunity that presented itself, to make inquiries in regard to such a place?"

Violet read that portion of his letter aloud to her mother and grandfather, then asked if they saw in it anything necessitating a change in their plans for the summer.

They did not, and were glad for Lulu's sake that it was so.

Lulu, in the solitude of her room, was anxiously considering the same question, and presently went with it to her mamma, taking her father's note in her hand.

Finding Violet alone in her dressing room, giving the captain's missive another perusal, "Mamma Vi," she said, "what — what does papa tell you about me?" She spoke hesitatingly, her head drooping, her cheeks hot with blushes. "I mean, what does he say is to be done with me?"

Violet pitied the child from the bottom of her heart. "I wish, dear," she said, "that I could tell you he consented to mamma's request to let us try you here a little longer, but — doesn't he say something about it in his note to you?"

"Yes, Mamma Vi," Lulu answered chokingly, "he says he can't let me stay here any longer, to be such a trouble and torment to you all, and will put me somewhere else as soon as he can find a suitable place. But he doesn't say what is to be done with me just now."

"No, dear, he leaves that to us — grandpa, mamma, and me — and we have decided that no change in the arrangements for the summer need be made."

Oh, Mamma Vi! How good and kind you all are!" cried Lulu in a burst of unrestrained gratitude, and her tears began to fall.

Violet was quite moved by the child's emotion. "You have been a dear good girl of late, and we feel glad to take you with us," she said, drawing her to her side and giving her an affectionate kiss. "Your father says there is a possibility that he may be at home with us again for a while in the fall. He expects to settle you somewhere then. But if you continue to be so good, perhaps he may relent and allow you still to have a home with us. I am quite sure that such a child as you have been for the last two or three months would be heartily welcome to us all."

"It's ever so good of you to say that, Mamma Vi," returned the little girl, furtively wiping her eyes, "and I'm determined to try with all my might. I'd want to do it to please papa, even if I knew there wasn't one bit of hope of his letting me stay. I don't think there is much, because, if he decides a thing positively, he's very apt to stick to it."

"Yes, I know, but he will doubtless take into account that circumstances alter cases," Violet answered lightly, and with a pleasant smile. "And at all events, you may be quite sure that whatever small influence I may possess will be exerted on your behalf."

"I am sure you have a great deal, Mamma Vi, and I thank you very much for that promise," Lulu said, turning to go.

But at that instant a quick, boyish step sounded in the hall without, and Max's voice at the door asked, "Mamma Vi, may I come in?"

"Yes," she said, and in he rushed with a face full of excitement. "Lu, I've been looking everywhere for you!" he cried. "What do you think? Just see that!" and he held up a bit of paper, waving it triumphantly in the air while he capered round the room in an ecstasy of delight.

"What is it?" asked Lulu. "Nothing but a strip of paper, as far as I can see."

"That's because you haven't had a chance to examine it," he said, laughing with pleasure. "It's a check with papa's name to it, and it's good for fifty dollars. Now do you wonder I'm delighted?"

"No, not if it's yours. Did he give it to you?"

"Half of it — the other half's to be divided between you and Gracie, and it's just for pocket money for this summer."

"Oh, that is nice!" exclaimed Violet. "I am very glad for you all."

Lulu looked astounded for an instant; then the tears welled up into her eyes as she said falteringly, "I — don't deserve it, and — I thought papa was vexed with me. I should never have expected he'd give me a single cent."

"He's just a splendid father, that's what he is!" cried Max, with another bound of exultant delight. "He says that if we go to the mountains and grandpa thinks I can be trusted with a gun, I'm to have the best that can be bought. And, if I'm a splendid boy all the time, when he comes home I shall have a fine pony of my own."

Then sobering down, "I'm afraid, though, that he can't afford all that, and I shall tell him so, and that I don't want him to spend too much of his hard-earned pay on his only son."

"Good Boy!" Violet said with an approving smile, "but I know it gives your father far more pleasure to lay out money for his children than to spend it on himself."

Still, she wondered within herself, for a moment, if her husband had in some way become a little richer than he was when last he described his circumstances to her. Had he had a legacy from some lately deceased relative or friend? (Surely no one could be more deserving of such remembrance.) Or had he an increase of pay? But no, he would surely have told her if either of those things had happened, and with that thought, the subject was dismissed from her mind.

He had not told her of his good fortune — the sudden, unexpected change in his circumstances. He wanted to keep it secret till he could see the shining of her eyes, the lighting up of her face, as she learned that their long separations were a thing of the past — that in the future they would have a home of their own, and be as constantly together as Lester and Elsie, Edward and Zoe.

But his mind was full of plans for making her and his children happy by means of his newly acquired wealth, and he had not been able to refrain from some attempt to do so at once.

"I don't want papa to waste his money on me, either," Lulu said. "I'd rather never have any pocket money than have him do without a single thing to give it to me."

"Dear child, I know you would," Violet said. "But take what he has sent and be happy with it. That is what he desires you to do. And I think you need have no fear that he will want for anything because of having sent it to you."

"Let me see that, won't you Maxie?" Lulu asked, following her brother from the room.

He handed her the check, and she examined it curiously.

"It has your name on it," she remarked.

"Yes, it is drawn payable to me," returned Max, assuming an air of importance.

"But," said Lulu, still examining it critically, "how can you turn it into money?"

"Oh, I know all about that," laughed Max. "Papa explained it to me the last time he was at home. I just write my name on the back of that and take it to a bank, and they'll give me the fifty dollars."

"And then you'll keep half and divide the other half between Gracie and me. That will be twelve dollars and fifty cents for each of us, won't it?"

"No, it isn't divided equally. Papa says you are to have fifteen dollars and Gracie ten — because you are older than she is, you know."

"But she's better, and deserves more than I," said Lulu. "Anyway, she shall have half, if she wants it."

"No, she doesn't," said Max. "I told her about it, and she thinks ten dollars to do just what she pleases with is a great fortune."

"When will we get it, Max?"

"What — the money? Not till after we go North. Grandpa Dinsmore says it will be best to wait till then, as we won't care to spend any of it here. Oh, Lu! — you are going along, I suppose? — what does papa say about — about what you told him in your last letter?"

"You may read for yourself, Max," replied Lulu, putting the note into his hand.

She watched his face while he read, and knew by his expression that he was sorry for her, even before he said so, as he handed it back.

"But perhaps papa may change his mind, if you keep on being as good as you have been ever since you left that school," he added. "But you haven't told me yet whether you are still to go North with us, or not."

"Yes, Mamma Vi says I am. She says papa says in his letter to her that they may do what they think best with me for the present — and they will take me along. It's good of them, isn't it?"

To that Max gave a hearty assent. "They are the kindest people in the world," he said.

CHAPTER ELEVENTH

How terrible is passion!

THE SUMMER PASSED quickly and pleasantly to our friends of Ion and Fairview. The plans they had made for themselves before leaving home were carried out, with, perhaps, some slight variations.

Lulu had her greatly desired visit to Cliff Cottage, and enjoyed it nearly as much as she had hoped to, a good deal less than she would if she could have quite forgotten her past misconduct and its impending consequences.

As matters stood, she could seldom entirely banish the thought that the time was daily drawing nearer when her father's sentence would be carried out, to her sad exclusion from the pleasant family circle of which she had now been so long a member.

She had experienced the truth of the saying that blessings brighten as they take flight, and would have given much to undo the past, so that she might prove herself worthy of a continuance of those she had rated so far below their real value, that, in spite of her father's repeated warnings, she had wantonly thrown them away.

She kept her promise to Violet and strove earnestly to deserve a repeal of her sentence, though her hope of gaining it was very faint. All summer long she had exercised sufficient control over her temper to avoid any outbursts of passion and generally had behaved quite amiably.

By the first of October the two families were again at home at Ion and Fairview, pursuing the even tenor of their way, Lulu with them, as of old, no new home having yet been found for her. No one cared to make much effort in that direction. It was just as well, Mr. Dinsmore, Elsie his daughter, and Violet thought, simply to let things take their course till her father should return, and take matters into his own hands.

There was no certainty when that would be — his letters still alluded to his coming that fall as merely a possibility.

But Lulu had been so amiable and docile for months past, that no one was in haste to be rid of her presence. Even Rosie was quite friendly with her, had ceased to tease and vex her, and mutual forbearance had given each a better opinion of the other than she had formerly entertained.

But Lulu grew self-confident and began to relax her vigilance. It was so long since her temper had got decidedly the better of her that she thought it conquered, or so nearly so that she need not be continually on the watch against it.

Rosie brought home with her a new pet — a beautiful puppy as mischievous as he was handsome.

Unfortunately it happened again and again that something belonging to Lulu attracted his attention and was seriously damaged or totally destroyed by his teeth and claws. He chewed up a pair of kid gloves belonging to her. It did not mend matters that Rosie laughed as though it was a good joke, and then told her it was her own fault for not putting them in their proper place when she took them off. He tore her garden hat into shreds; he upset her inkstand; tumbled over her workbasket, tangling the spools of sewing silk and cotton; jumped upon her with muddy paws, soiling a new dress and handsome sash; and, at last, capped the climax by defacing a book of engravings belonging to Mr. Dinsmore which she had carelessly left in his way.

Then her anger burst forth and she kicked the dog till his howls brought Rosie running to the rescue.

"How dare you, Lulu Raymond!" she exclaimed with flashing eyes as she gathered Trip in her arms, and soothed him with caresses. "I'll not allow my pet to be so ill used in my own mother's house!"

"He deserves a great deal more than I gave him," retorted

Lulu, quivering with passion, "and if you don't want him hurt, you'll have to keep him out of mischief. Just look what he has done to this book!"

"One of grandpa's handsome volumes of engravings!" cried Rosie, aghast. "But who left it lying there?"

"I did."

"Then you are the one to blame and not my poor little Trip, who, of course, knew no better. How is he to tell that books are not meant for gnawing quite as much as bones?"

"What is the matter, children?" asked Mr. Dinsmore, stepping out upon the veranda where the little scene was enacting. It surprises me to hear such loud and angry tones."

For a moment each girlish head drooped in silence, hot blushes dying their cheeks; then Lulu, lifting hers said, "I'm very sorry, Grandpa Dinsmore. I oughtn't to have brought this book out here, but it wouldn't have come to any harm if it hadn't been for that troublesome dog that's as full of mischief as he can be. I don't believe it was more than five minutes that I left the book lying there on the settee. And when I ran back to get it, and put it in its place, he had torn out a leaf and nibbled and soiled the cover, as you see.

"But, if you'll please not be angry, I'll save up all my pocket money till I can buy you another copy."

"That would take a good while, child," Mr. Dinsmore answered. "It is a great pity you were so careless. But I'll not scold you, since you are penitent, and so ready to make all the amends in your power. Rosie, you really must try to restrain the mischievous propensities of your pet."

"I do, grandpa," she said, flashing an angry glance at Lulu, "but I can't keep him in sight every minute. If people will leave things in his way, I think they are more to blame than he is if he spoils them."

"Tut, tut! Don't speak to me in that manner," said her grandfather. "If your dog continues to damage valuable property, he shall be sent away."

Rosie made no reply, but colored deeply as she turned and walked with her pet in her arms.

"Now, Lulu," said Mr. Dinsmore, not unkindly, "remember in the future you are not to bring a valuable book such as this out here. If you want to look at them, do so in the library."

"Yes, sir, I will. I'm very sorry about that; but if you'll tell me, please, how much it would cost to buy another just like it, I'll write to papa. I know he will pay for it."

"I thought you proposed to pay for it yourself," remarked Mr. Dinsmore grimly.

"Yes, sir, but I don't wish to keep you waiting. Papa wouldn't wish it. He sends his children pocket money every once in a while, and I'd ask him to keep back what he considered my share till it would count up to as much as the price of the book."

"Well, child, that is honorable and right," Mr. Dinsmore said in a pleasanter tone, "but I think we will let the matter rest now till your father comes, which I trust will be before a very great while."

Rosie, knowing that her grandfather was quite capable of carrying out his threat, lacking neither the ability nor the will to do so, curtailed the liberty of her pet and exerted herself to keep him out of mischief.

Still, he occasionally came in Lulu's way, and when he did was very apt to receive a blow or kick.

He had a fashion of catching at her skirts with his teeth and giving them a jerk, which was very exasperating to her — all the more so, that Rosie evidently enjoyed seeing him do it.

A stop would have been put to the "fun" if the older people of the family had happened to be aware of what was going on, but the dog always seemed to seize the opportunity when none of them were by, and Lulu scorned to tell tales.

One morning, about a week after the accident to the book, Lulu, coming down a little before the ringing of the breakfast bell, found Max on the veranda.

"Don't you want to take a ride with me after breakfast, Lu?" he asked. "Mamma Vi says I can have her pony, and as Rosie doesn't care to go, of course you can ride hers."

"How do you know Rosie doesn't want to ride?" asked Lulu.

"Because I heard her tell her mother she didn't, that she meant to drive over to Roselands with Grandpa Dinsmore instead, that he had told her he expected to go there to see Cal about some business matter, and would take her with him. So you see, her pony won't be wanted, and Grandma Elsie has often said we could have it whenever it wasn't in use or tired, and of course it must be quite fresh this morning."

"Then I'll go," said Lulu with satisfaction, for she was extremely fond of riding, especially when her steed was Rosie's pretty, easy-going pony, Gyp.

So Max ordered the two ponies to be in readiness, and as soon as breakfast was over, Lulu hastened to her room to prepare for her ride.

But in the meantime Mr. Dinsmore had told Rosie he had, for some reason, changed his plans and should wait till afternoon to make his call at Roselands.

Then Rosie, glancing from the window and seeing her pony at the door, ready saddled and bridled, suddenly decided to take a ride, ran to her room, donned riding hat and habit, and was down again a little in advance of lulu.

Max, who was on the veranda waiting for his sister, felt rather dismayed at sight of Rosie, as she came tripping out in riding attire.

"Oh, Rosie, excuse me," he said. "I heard you say you were going to drive to Roselands with your grandpa, and so, as I was sure you wouldn't be wanting your pony, I ordered him saddled for Lu.'

"That happened very well, because he is here now all ready for me," returned Rosie laughing as she vaulted into the saddle, hardly giving Max a chance to help her. "Lu can have him another time. Come, will you go with me?"

For an instant Max hesitated. He did not like to refuse Rosie's request, as she was not allowed to go alone outside the grounds, yet was equally averse to seem to desert Lu.

"But," he thought, "she's sure to be in a passion when she finds this out, and I can't bear to see it."

So he sprang upon his waiting steed, and as Lulu, ready dressed for her ride and eager to take it, stepped out upon the veranda, she just caught a glimpse of the two horses and their riders disappearing down the avenue.

She turned white with anger at the sight, and stamped her

foot in a fury, exclaiming between her clenched teeth, "It's the meanest trick I ever saw!"

There were several servants standing near, one of them little Elsie's nurse, an old Negress, Aunt Dinah, who, having lived in the family for more than twenty years, felt herself privileged to speak her mind upon occasion, particularly to its youngest members.

"Now, Miss Lu," she said, "dat's not de propah way fo' you to talk 'bout dis t'ing, kase dat pony b'longs to Miss Rosie, an' co'se she hab de right to ride him befo' anybody else."

"You've no call to put in your word and I'm not going to be lectured and reproved by a servant!" retorted Lulu passionately, and turning quickly away, she strode to the head of the short flight of steps leading down into the avenue and stood there leaning against a pillar with her back toward the occupants of the veranda. Her left arm was round the pillar and in her right hand was held her little riding whip.

She was angry at Dinah, furiously angry at Rosie, and when the next minute something — Rosie's dog she supposed — tugged at her skirts, she gave a vicious backward kick without turning her head.

Instantly a sound of something falling, accompanied by a faint, frightened little cry and a chorus of shrieks of dismay from the older voices flashed upon her the terrible knowledge that she had sent her baby sister rolling down the steps to the hard gravel walk below.

She clutched at her pillar, almost losing consciousness for one brief moment in her dreadful fright.

Violet's agonized cry as she came rushing from the open doorway, "My baby, oh, my baby! She's killed!" roused her and she saw Dinah pick up the little creature from the ground and place it in her mother's arms, where she lay limp and white like a dead thing, without sense or motion. The whole household, young and old, black and white, gathered round in wild excitement and grief.

No one so much as glanced at her or seemed to think of

her at all — their attention was wholly occupied with the injured little one.

She shuddered as she caught a glimpse of her deathlike face, then put her hand over her eyes to shut out the fearful sight. She felt as if she were turning to stone with a sense of the awful thing she had done in her mad passion. Then, suddenly seized with an overwhelming desire to hide herself from all these eyes that would presently be gazing accusingly and threateningly at her, she hurried away to her own room and shut and locked herself in.

Her riding whip was still in her hand. She tossed it on to the window sill, tore off her gloves, hat and habit, and threw them aside, then, dropping on her knees beside the bed, buried her face in the clothes, sobbing wildly, "Oh, I've killed my little sister, my own dear little baby sister! What shall I do? What shall I do?"

Moments passed that seemed like hours — faint sounds came up from below. She heard steps and voices, and — was that Mamma Vi crying — crying as if her heart would break — saying over and over again, "My baby's dead! My baby's dead! Killed by her sister, her cruel, passionate sister!" Would they come and take her (Lulu) to jail? Would they try her for murder and hang her? Oh, then papa's heart would break, losing two of his children is such dreadful ways.

"Oh, wouldn't it break anyhow when he heard what she had done — when he knew the baby was dead and that she had killed her, even if she should not be sent to prison and tried for murder?"

At length someone tried the door, and a little sobbing voice said, "Lulu, please let me in."

She rose, staggered to the door, and unlocked it. "Is it only you, Gracie?" she asked in a terrified whisper, opening it just far enough to admit the little slender figure.

"Yes, there's nobody else here," said the child. "I came to tell you the baby isn't dead, but the doctor has come and, I believe, he doesn't feel sure she won't die. Oh, Lu! How could you?" she asked with a burst of sobs.

"Oh, Gracie, I didn't do it on purpose! How could you

think so? I mean, I didn't know it was the baby—I thought it was that hateful dog."

"Oh, I'm glad! I couldn't b'lieve it, though some of them do!" exclaimed Gracie in a tone of relief.

Then, with a fresh burst of tears and sobs, "But she's dreadfully hurt, the dear little thing! I heard the doctor tell Grandpa Dinsmore he was afraid she'd never get over it, but he mustn't let mamma know yet, 'cause maybe she might."

Lulu paced the room, wringing her hands and sobbing like one distracted.

"Oh, Gracie!" she cried, "I'd like to beat myself black and blue! I just hope papa will come home and do it, because I ought to be made to suffer ever so much for hurting the baby so."

"Oh, Lu, no!" cried Gracie, aghast at the very idea. "It wouldn't do the baby any good. Oh, I hope papa won't whip you!"

"But he will! I know he will, and he ought to," returned Lulu vehemently. "Oh, hark!"

She stood listening intently, Grace doing the same. They had seemed to hear a familiar step that they had not heard for many a long month. Yes, there it was again, and with a low cry of joy, Grace bounded to the door, threw it open, but closed it quickly behind her, and sprang into her father's arms.

"My darling, my precious little daughter!" he said, clasping her close, and showering kisses on her face. "Where is everyone? You are the first I have seen, and — why, how you have been crying! What is wrong?"

"Oh, papa! The baby — the baby's 'most killed," she sobbed. "Come, I'll take you to her and mamma!"

Fairly stunned by the sudden dreadful announcement, he silently submitted himself to her guidance, and suffered her to lead him into the nursery, where Violet sat in a low chair with the apparently dying babe on her lap, her mother, grandfather and his wife, and the doctor, grouped about her.

No one noticed his entrance, so intent were they upon

the little sufferer, but just as he gained her side, Violet looked up and recognized him with a low cry of mingled joy and grief.

He bent down and kissed the sweet, tremulous lips, his features working with emotion. "My wife, my dear love, what — what is this? What ails our little one?" he asked in anguished accents, turning his eyes upon the waxen baby face; and bending still lower, he softly touched his lips to her forehead.

No one replied to his question, and gazing with close scrutiny at the child, "She has been hurt?" he said, half in assertion, half inquiringly.

"Yes, captain," said Dr. Conly, "she has had a fall — a very severe one for so young and tender a creature."

"How did it happen?" he asked in tones of mingled grief and sternness.

No one answered, and after waiting a moment, he repeated the question, addressing it directly to his wife.

"Oh, do not ask me, love!" she said entreatingly, and he reluctantly yielded to her request. But light began to dawn upon him, sending an added pang to his heart. Suddenly he remembered Lulu's former jealousy of the baby, her displeasure at her birth; and with a thrill of horror, he asked himself if this could be her work.

He glanced about the room in search of her and Max. Neither was there.

He passed noiselessly into the next room, then into the one beyond—his wife's boudoir—and there found his son.

Max sat gazing abstractly from a window, his eyes showing traces of tears.

Turning his head as the captain entered, he started up with a joyful but subdued cry, "Papa!" then threw himself with bitter sobbing into the arms outstretched to receive him.

"My boy, my dear boy!" the captain said, in moved tones. "What is this dreadful thing that has happened? Can you tell me how your baby sister came to get so sad a fall?"

"I didn't see it, papa. I was out riding at the time."

"But you have heard about it from those who did see it?"

"Yes, sir," the lad answered reluctantly, "but — please, papa, don't ask me what they said."

"Was Lulu at home at the time?"

"Yes, sir."

"Would she be able to tell me all about it, do you think?"

"I haven't seen her, papa, since I came in," Max answered evasively.

The captain sighed. His suspicions had deepened to almost certainty.

"Where is she?" he asked, releasing Max from his embrace and turning to leave the room.

"I do not know, papa," answered Max.

"Where was the baby when she fell? Can you tell me that?" asked his father.

"On the veranda, sir — so the servants told me."

"Which of them saw it?"

"Aunt Dinah, Agnes, Aunt Dicey — nearly all the women, I believe, sir,"

The captain mused a moment.

"Was Lulu there?" he asked.

"Yes, sir, and papa — if you must know just how it happened — I think she could tell you all about it as well as anybody else, or maybe better. And you know she always speaks the truth."

"Yes," the captain said, as if considering the suggestion, "however, I prefer to hear the story first from someone else."

He passed on through the upper hall and down the stairs, then on out to the veranda, where he found a group of servants — of whom Aunt Dicey was one — excitedly discussing the very occurrence he wished to inquire about.

They did not share the reluctance of Violet and Max, but answered his questions promptly, with a very full and detailed account of the affair.

They gave a graphic description of the rage Lulu was thrown into at the sight of Rosie galloping away on the pony she had expected to ride. They repeated her angry retort in reply to Aunt Dinah's reproof, and told, without any extenuation of the hard facts, how the baby girl, escaping from the nurse's watchful care for a moment, had toddled along to her sister, caught at her skirts for support, and received a savage kick that sent her down the steps to the gravel walk below.

The captain heard the story with ever increasing, burning indignation. Lulu's act seemed the very wantonness of cruelty — a most cowardly attack of a big, strong girl upon a tiny, helpless creature, who had an indisputable claim upon her tenderest protecting care.

By the time the story had come to an end, he was exceedingly angry with Lulu. He felt that in this instance it would be no painful task to him to chastise her with extreme severity — in fact, he dared not go to her at once, lest he should do her some injury. He had never yet punished a child in anger. He had often resolved that he never would, but would always wait till the feeling of love for the delinquent was uppermost in his heart, so that he could be entirely sure his motive was a desire for the reformation of the offender and not the gratification of his own passion.

Feeling that he had a battle to fight with himself ere he dared venture to discipline the child and that he must have solitude for it, he strode away down the avenue, turned into a part of the grounds little frequented, and there paced back and forth, his arms folded on his chest, his head bent, his heart going up in silent prayer for strength to rule his own spirit, for patience and wisdom according to his need.

Then he strove to recall all that was lovable about his wayward daughter, and to think of every possible excuse for the dreadful deed she had done, yet without being able to find any that deserved the name.

At length, feeling that the victory was at least partially won, and filled with anxiety about the baby, he began to retrace his steps toward the house.

In the avenue he met Edward and Zoe, who greeted

him with joyful surprise, not having before known of his arrival.

The expression of his countenance told them that he was already informed of the sad occurrence of the morning, and Edward said with heartfelt sympathy, "It is but a sad homecoming for you, captain, but let us try to hope for the best. It is possible the little darling has not received any lasting injury."

A silent pressure of the hand was the captain's only reply for the moment. He seemed too much overcome for speech.

"Such a darling as she is!" said Zoe. "The pet of the whole house, and just the loveliest little creature I ever saw."

"Did you — either of you — see her fall?" asked the captain huskily.

"Yes," said Zoe, "I did. Violet and I happened to be at the window of the little reception room over looking the veranda and were watching the little creature as she toddled along, and — " But Zoe paused, suddenly remembering that her listener was the father of Lulu as well as of her poor little victim.

"Please go on," he said with emotion. "What was it that sent her down the steps?"

"Lulu was standing there," Zoe went on, hesitating, and coloring with embarrassment, "and I saw the baby's hands clutch at her skirts — "

Again she paused.

"And Lulu, giving the tender, toddling child a savage kick, caused the dreadful catastrophe?" he groaned, turning away his face. "You need not have feared to tell me. I had already heard it from the servants who were eyewitnesses, and I only wanted further and undoubtedly reliable testimony."

"I think" said Edward, "that Lulu really had no idea what it was she was kicking at. I happened to be sout in the grounds, and coming round the corner of the house just in time to catch her look of horror and despair as she half turned her head and saw the baby fall."

"Thank you," the captain said feelingly. "It is some relief to her unhappy father to learn of the least extenuating circumstance."

CHAPTER TWELFTH

Anger resteth in the bosom of fools.

— ECCLESIASTES 7:9

Foolishness is bound in the heart of a child; but the rod of correction shall drive it far from him.

— PROVERBS 22:15

"HE SEEMS TO FEEL terribly about it, poor man!" remarked Zoe with a backward glance at the retreating form of Captain Raymond as he left them and pursued his way to the house.

"Yes, and no wonder," said Edward. "Not for worlds would I be the father of such a child as Lulu!"

"Nor I her mother," said Zoe. "So I'm glad it was you I got for a husband instead of Captain Raymond."

"Only for that reason?" he queried, facing round upon her in mock astonishment and wrath.

"Oh, of course!" she returned laughing, then sobering down with a sudden recollection of the sorrow in the house. "But, oh, Ned! How heartless we are to be joking and laughing when poor Vi and the captain are in such distress!"

"I'm afraid you are right," he assented with a sigh. "Yet I am quite sure we both feel deeply for them and are personally grieved for the injury to our darling little niece."

"Yes, indeed! The pretty pet that she is!" returned Zoe, wiping her eyes.

Gracie was on the veranda looking for her father, and, catching sight of him in the avenue, ran to meet him.

"How is baby, now? Can you tell me?" he asked, taking her hand and stooping to give her a kiss.

"Just the same, I suppose, papa," she said. "Oh, it's very hard to see her suffer so! Isn't it, papa?"

He nodded a silent assent.

"Papa," she asked, lifting her tearful eyes to his face with a pleading look, "have you seen Lulu yet?"

"No."

"Oh, papa, do go now! It must be so hard for her to wait so long to see you, when you've just come home."

"I doubt if she wants to see me," he said with some sternness of look and tone.

"Oh, dear papa, don't punish her very hard. She didn't hurt the baby on purpose."

"I shall try to do what is best for her, my little girl, though I very much doubt if that is exemption from punishment," he said with an involuntary sigh. "But if she is in haste to see me," he added, "there is nothing, so far as I am aware, to prevent her from coming to me."

"But she is afraid, papa because she has been so very, very naughty."

"In that case, is it not kinder for me to keep away from her?"

"Oh, papa! You know she always wants things — bad things — over."

"The bad thing she has brought upon the poor baby will not be over very soon," he said sternly. "I must go now to the babe and your mamma."

He did so, and sharing Violet's deep grief and anxiety, and perceiving that his very presence was a comfort and support to her, he remained at her side for hours.

Hours, that to Lulu seemed like weeks or months. Alone in her room, in an agony of remorse and fear, she waited and watched and listened for her father's coming, longing for, and yet dreading it, more than words could express.

"What would his anger be like?" she asked herself.

"What terrible punishment would he inflict? Would he ever love her again, especially if the baby should die?

"Perhaps he would sent her away to some very far off place, and never, never come near her any more."

Naturally of a very impatient temperament, suspense and passive waiting were well nigh intolerable to her. By turns she walked the floor, fell on her knees by the bedside, and buried her face in a pillow, or threw herself into a chair by table or window, and hid it on her folded arms.

"Oh! Would this long day, this dreadful, dreadful waiting for -what? ever come to an end?" she asked herself over and over again.

Yet, when at last the expected step drew near, she shuddered, trembled and turned pale with affright, and, starting to her feet, looked this way and that with a wild impulse to flee. Then, as the door opened, she dropped into her chair again and covered her face with her shaking hands.

She heard the door close, the step drew nearer, nearer, and stopped close at her side. She dared not look up, but felt her father's eyes gazing sternly upon her.

"Miserable child!" he said at length, "do you know what your terrible temper has wrought? Do you know that in your mad passion you have nearly or quite killed your little sister? That even should she live, she may be a life-long sufferer in consequence of your fiendish act?"

"Oh, papa, don't!" she pleaded in broken accents, cowering and shrinking as if he had struck her a deadly blow.

"You deserve it," he said. "Indeed, I could not possibly inflict a worse punishment than your conduct merits. But what is the use of punishing you? Nothing reforms you! I am in despair of you! You seem determined to make yourself a curse to me instead of the blessing I once esteemed you. What am I to do with you? Will you compel me to cage or chain you up like a wild beast, lest you do someone a fatal injury?"

A cry of pain was her only answer and he turned and left the room.

"Oh!" she moaned, "it's worse than if he had beaten me half to death! He thinks I'm too bad even to be punished, because nothing will make me good. He says I'm a curse to him, so he must hate me, though he used to love me dearly, and I loved him so, too! I suppose everybody hates me now, and always will. I wish I was dead and out of their way. But, oh, no, I don't, for I'm not fit to die. Oh! What shall I do? I wish it was I that was hurt instead of the baby. I'd like to go away and hide from everybody that knows me. Then I shouldn't be a curse and trouble to papa or any of them."

She lifted her head and looked about her. It was growing dusk. Quick as a flash came the thought that now was her time — now, while almost everybody was so taken up with the critical condition of the injured little one — now, before the servants had lighted the lamps in rooms and halls.

She would slip down a back stairway, out into the grounds, and away, she cared not whither.

Always impulsive, and now full of mental distress, she did not pause a moment to consider, but, snatching up a hat and coat lying conveniently at hand, stole noiselessly from the room, putting them on as she went.

She gained a side door without meeting anyone, and the grounds seemed deserted as she passed round the house and entered the avenue, down which she ran with swift footsteps, after one hasty glance around to make sure that she was not seen.

She reached the great gates, pushed them open, stepped out, letting them swing to after her, and started on a run down the road.

But the next instant someone had caught her — a hand was on her shoulder, and a stern, astonished voice cried, "Lulu, is it possible this can be you? What are you doing out here in the public road alone, and in the darkness of evening? Where were you going?"

"I — I — don't want — to tell you, papa," she faltered.

"Where were you going?" he repeated, in a tone that said an answer he would have and that at once.

"Nowhere — anywhere to get away from this place,

where everybody hates me!" she replied sullenly, trying to wrench herself free. "Please, let me go, and I'll never come back to trouble you any more."

He made no reply to that, but simply took her hand in a firm grasp, and led her back to the house, back to her own room, where he shut himself in with her, locking the door on the inside.

Then he dropped her hand, and began pacing the floor to and fro, seemingly in deep and troubled thought, his arms folded, his head bowed upon his chest.

A servant had brought in a light during Lulu's absence, and now, looking timidly up at her father, she saw his face for the first time since they had bidden each other farewell a year before. It struck her as not only very pale, stern, and grief-stricken, but very much older and more deeply lined than she remembered it. She did not know that the change had been wrought almost entirely in the last few hours, yet recognized it with a pang nevertheless.

"Papa is growing old," she thought. "Are there gray hairs in his head, I wonder?" Then there came dimly to her recollection some Bible words about bringing a father's gray hairs down with sorrow to the grave. "Was her misconduct killing her father?" She burst into an agony of sobs and tears at the thought.

He lifted his head, and looked at her gravely, and with mingled sternness and compassion.

"Take off that hat and coat, get your nightdress, and make yourself ready for bed," he commanded, then, stepping to the table, sat down, drew the lamp nearer, opened her Bible lying there, and slowly turned over the pages as if in search of some particular passage, while she moved slowly about the room, trembling and tearfull;y obeying his order.

"Shall I get into bed, papa?" she asked tremulously, when she had finished.

"No, not yet. Come here."

She went and stood at his side, with drooping head and fast-beating heart, her eyes on the carpet, for she dared not look in his face.

He seemed to have found the passage he sought; and, keeping the book open with his left hand, he turned to her as she stood at his right.

"Lucilla," he said, and his accents were not stern, though very grave and sad, "you cannot have forgotten that I have repeatedly and positively forbidden you to go wandering alone about unfrequented streets and roads, even in broad daylight; yet you attempted to do that very thing tonight in the darkness, which of course, makes it much worse."

"Yes, papa, but I — I didn't ever mean to come back."

"You were running away?"

"Yes, sir, I — I thought you would be glad to get rid of me," she sobbed.

He did not speak again for a moment, and when he did, it was in moved tones.

"Supposing I did desire to be rid of you — which is very far from being the case — I should have no right to let you go, for you are my own child, whom God has given to me to take care of, provide for, and train up for His service. You and I belong to each other as parent and child. You have no right to run away from my care and authority, and I have none to let you do so. In fact, I feel compelled to punish the attempt quite severely, lest there should be a repetition of it."

"Oh, don't, papa!" she sobbed. "I'll never do it again."

"It was an act of daring, willful disobedience," he said, "and I must punish you for it. Also, for the fury of passion indulged in this morning. Read this, and this, aloud," he added, pointing to the open page. She obeyed, reading faltering, sobbingly — .

" 'Foolishness is bound in the heart of a child; but the rod of correction shall drive it far from him.' … 'Withhold not correction from the child: for if thou beatest him with the rod, he shall not die. Thou shalt beat him with the road, and shalt deliver his soul from hell.' "

"You see, my child, that my orders are too plain to be misunderstood," he said, when she had finished. "And they must be obeyed, however unwelcome to me or to you."

"Yes, papa, and — and I — I — 'most want you to whip

me for hurting the baby so. I suppose nobody believes I'm sorry, but I am. I could beat myself for it, though I didn't know it was the baby pulling at my skirt. I thought it was Rosie's dog."

"It is not exactly for hurting the baby," he said. "If you had done that by accident, I should never think of punishing you for it, but for the fury of passion that betrayed you into doing it, I must punish you very severely.

"I shudder to think what you may come to, if I let you go on indulging your fiery, ungovernable temper. Yes, and to think what it has already brought you to," he added with a heavy sigh.

"You can never enter heaven unless you gain the victory over that, as well as every other sin. And, my daughter, there are but two places to choose from as our eternal home — heaven and hell. And I must use every effort to deliver your soul from going to that last — dreadful place!"

He rose, stepped to the window where her little riding whip lay, came back to her, and for the next few minutes she forgot mental distress in sharp, physical pain, as the stinging, though not heavy, blows fell thick and fast on her thinly covered back and shoulders.

She writhed and sobbed under them, but neither screamed nor pleaded for mercy.

When he had finished, he sat down again, and drew the weeping child in between his knees, put his arm about her in tender, fatherly fashion, and made her lay her head on his shoulder; but he said not a word. Perhaps his heart was too full for speech.

Presently Lulu's arm crept round his neck. "Papa," she sobbed, "I — I do love you, and I — I'm glad you wouldn't let me run away — and that you try to save me from losing my soul. But, oh, I can't be good! I wish, I wish I could!" she ended, with a bitter, despairing cry.

He was much moved.

"We will kneel down and ask God to help you, my poor, dear child," he said.

He did so, making her kneel beside him, while, with his

arm still about her, he poured out a prayer so earnest and tender, so exactly describing her feelings and her needs, that she could join in it with all her heart. He prayed like one talking to his Father and Friend, whom he knew was both able and willing to do great things for him and his.

When they had risen from their knees, she lifted her eyes to his face with a timid, pleading look.

He understood the mute petition, and, sitting down again, drew her to his knee, and kissed her several times with grave tenderness.

"I wanted a kiss so badly, papa," she said. "You know, it is a whole year since I had one, and you never came home before without giving me one just as soon as we met."

"No, but I never before had so little reason to bestow a caress on you," he said. "When I heard of your deed of this morning, I felt that I ought not to show you any mark of favor, at least not until I had given you the punishment you so richly deserved. Do you not think I was right?"

"Yes, sir," she answered, hanging her head, and blushing deeply.

"I will put you in your bed now, and leave you for tonight," he said. "I must go back to my little suffering baby and her almost heartbroken mother."

He led her to the bed and lifted her into it as he spoke.

"Papa, can't I have a piece of bread?" she asked humbly. "I'm so hungry!"

"Hungry!" he exclaimed in surprise. "Had you no supper?"

"No, sir, nor dinner either. I haven't had a bite to eat since breakfast."

"Strange!" he said, "but I suppose you were forgotten in the excitement and anxiety everyone in the house had felt ever since the baby's sad fall. And they may have felt it unnecessary to bring anything to you, as you were quite able to go to the dining room for it."

"I couldn't bear to, papa," she said with tears of shame and grief, "and, indeed, I wasn't hungry till a little while ago. But now I feel faint and sick for something to eat."

"You shall have it," he replied, and went hastily from the

room, to return in a few minutes, bringing a bowl of milk and a plentiful supply of bread and butter.

He set them on the table and bade her come and eat.

"Papa, you are very kind to me, ever so much kinder than I deserve," she said tremulously, as she made haste to obey the order. "I think some fathers would say I must go hungry for tonight."

"I have already punished you in what I consider a better way, because it could not injure your health," he said, "while going a long time without food would be almost sure to do so. It is not my intention ever to punish my children in a way to do them injury. Present pain is all I am willing to inflict, and that only for their good."

"Yes, papa, I know that," she said with a sob, setting down her bowl of milk to wipe her eyes. "So, when you punish me, it doesn't make me quit loving you."

"If I did not love you, if you were not my own dear child," he said, laying his hand on her head as he stood by her side, "I don't think I could be at the trouble and pain of disciplining you as I have tonight. But eat your supper. I can't stay with you much longer, and I want to see you in bed before I go."

As she laid her head on her pillow again, there was a flash of lightning, followed instantly by a crash of thunder and a heavy downpour of rain.

"Do you hear that?" he asked. "Now, suppose I had let you go when I caught you trying to run away? How would you feel, alone out of doors, in the darkness and storm, no shelter, no home, no friends, no father to take care of you, and provide for your wants?"

"Oh, papa! It would be very, very dreadful!" she sobbed, putting her arm round his neck as he bent over her. "I'm very glad you brought me back, even to punish me so severely, and I don't think I'll ever want to run away again."

"I trust not," he said, kissing her goodnight. "And you must not leave this room till I give you permission. I intend that you shall spend some days in solitude — except when I see fit to come to you — that you may have plenty of time and opportunity to think over your sinful conduct and its dire consequences."

CHAPTER THIRTEENTH

*I'm on the rack;
For sure, the greatest evil man can know
Bears no proportion to the dread suspense.*

"Is there any change, doctor?" asked Captain Raymond, meeting Arthur Conly in the hall.

"Hardly," was the reply, "certainly none for the worse."

"Will she get over it, do you think?" The father's tones were unsteady as he asked the question.

"My dear captain, it is impossible to tell yet," Arthur said feelingly, "but we must try to hope for the best."

Their hands met in a warm clasp.

"I shall certainly do so," the captain said. "But you are not going to leave us — especially not in this storm?"

"No, I expect to pass the night in the house, ready to be summoned at a moment's notice, should any change take place."

"Thank you. It will be a great satisfaction to us to know we have you close at hand." And the captain turned and entered the nursery, which Arthur had just left.

Violet, seated by the side of the crib where her baby lay, looked up on her husband's entrance, greeting him with a smile of mingled love and sadness.

"Your dear presence is such a comfort and support!" she murmured as he drew near. "I don't like to lose sight of you for a single moment."

"Nor I of you, dearest," he answered, bending down to kiss her pale cheek, then taking a seat close beside her, "but I had to seek solitude for a time while fighting a battle with myself. Since that I have been with Lulu."

He concluded with a heavy sigh, and for a moment both

were silent; then he said with grave tenderness, "I fear you will find it hard to forgive her. It has been no easy thing for me to do so."

"I cannot yet," returned Violet, a hard look that he had never seen there before stealing over her face. "And that is an added distress, for 'if ye forgive not men their trespasses, neither will your Father forgive your trespasses.' I think I can if my baby recovers, but should she — be taken away — or — or, worse by far, live to be a constant sufferer — oh, how can I ever forgive the author of that suffering? Pray for me, my dear husband," she sobbed, laying her head on his shoulder.

"I will, I do, my darling," he whispered, passing his arm about her, and drawing her closer, "and I know the help you need will be given."

" 'Ask, and it shall be given you.' "

"Perhaps it may aid the effort, if I tell you Lulu did not intentionally harm her little sister, and is greatly distressed at her state. She thought it was Rosie's dog pulling at her skirts. And, I own, that that explanation makes the sad affair a little less heart-rending to me, though I could not accept it as any excuse for an act done in a fury of passion, and have punished her very severely for it — that is, for her passion. I think it is right under the circumstances, that you should know that I have, and that it is my fixed purpose to keep her in solitary confinement, at least so long as the baby continues in a critical condition."

"Oh! I am glad to know it was not done purposely," Violet exclaimed — though in a tone hardly raised above a whisper — lifting her tearful eyes to his face with a look of something like relief. "Knowing that, I begin to feel that it may be possible to forgive and forget, especially if the consequences do not prove lasting," she added with a sob, turning her eyes to the little face on the pillow. "But I certainly take no delight in the severity of her punishment. In fact, I fear it may destroy any little affection she has had for her baby sister."

"No," he said, "I am not at all apprehensive of that.

When she found I was about to punish her, she said she almost wanted me to, that she felt like beating herself for hurting the baby, then went on to explain her mistake — thinking it was the dog tugging at her dress — and I then gave her fully to understand that the chastisement was not for hurting the baby, but for indulging in such a fury of passion, a fault that I have punished her for on more than one former occasion — telling her, too, that I intended to chastise her every time I knew of her being guilty of it."

The sound of a low sob caused the captain to turn his head, to find his little Grace standing at the back of his chair, crying bitterly, though without much noise.

He took her hand, and drew her to his side. "What is the matter, daughter?" he asked tenderly.

"Oh, papa! I'm so sorry for Lulu," she sobbed. "Please, mayn't I go to her for a little while?"

"No, Gracie. I cannot allow her the pleasure of seeing you, either tonight or for some days."

"But, papa, you said — you told mamma just now — that you had already punished her very severely, and must you keep on?"

"Yes, my child, so far as to keep her in solitude, that she may have plenty of time to think about what she has brought upon herself and others by the indulgence of an ungovernable temper. She needs to have the lesson impressed upon her as deeply as possible."

"I'm so sorry for her, papa!" repeated the gentle little pleader.

"So am I, daughter," he said, "but I think that to see that she has the full benefit of this sad lesson will be the greatest kindness I can do her. And my little Grace must try to believe that papa knows best.

"Now, give me a goodnight kiss and go to your bed, for it is quite time you were there."

As he spoke, he took her in his arms, and held her for a moment in a close embrace. "Papa's dear little girl!" he said softly. "You have never given me a pang, except for your feeble health."

"I don't want to, papa. I hope I never, never shall!" she returned, hugging him tight.

Leaving him, she went to Violet, put her arms about her neck, and said in her sweet, childish treble, "Dear mamma, don't feel so dreadfully about baby. I've been asking God to make her quite, quite well, and I do believe He will."

When she had left the room, the captain found himself alone with his young wife and their little one. Again her head was on his shoulder, his arm about her waist.

"My husband, my dear, dear husband," she murmured, "I am so glad to have you here! I cannot tell you how I longed for you when the children were so ill. Oh, if we could only be together always, as Lester and Elsie, Edward and Zoe are!"

"My love, my life," he said in low tones, tremulous with feeling, "what if I should tell you that your wish is already accomplished?"

She gave him a glance of astonishment and incredulity.

"It is even so. I mean all I have said," he answered to the look. "I have sent in my resignation. It has been accepted, and I have come home — no, I have come here to make a home for you and my children, hoping to live in it with you and them for the rest of my days."

Her face was radiant. "Oh, can it be true?" she cried, half under her breath — for even in her glad surprise, the thought of her suffering babe and her critical condition was present with her. "Are we not to be forced apart again in a few days or weeks — not to go spending more than half our lives at a distance from each other?"

"It is quite true, my darling," he answered, then went on to tell, in a few brief sentences, how it had come about.

"It cost me a struggle to give up the service," he said in conclusion. "Perhaps I might not have decided as I did, but for the thought that if I should be needed by my country at some future day, I could offer her my services. The thought was that at the present, wife and children needed me more, probably, than she. I felt that Lulu, in particular, needed my oversight and training. The task of bringing her up was too difficult, too trying, to be left to other hands than those of her father, and I felt that still more sensibly since hearing of this day's doings," he added in a tone of heartfelt sorrow.

"I think you are right," Violet said. "She is more willing to submit to your authority than to that of anybody else, as, indeed, she ought to be. In a home that she will feel is really her own, her father's house, and with him constantly at hand, to watch over and help her to correct her faults, there is hope, I think, that she may grow to be all you desire."

"Thank you, love, for saying it," he responded with emotion. "I could not blame you if now you thought her utterly irreclaimable."

"No, oh, no!" she answered earnestly. "I have great hopes of her with her father at hand to help her in her struggle with her temper. For I am sure she does struggle against it, and I must acknowledge that for months past she has been as good and lovable a child as one could desire. I don't know a more lovable one than she is when her temper does not get the better of her. And, as Gracie says, whenever it does, 'she gets sorry very soon.' "

"My darling," he said, pressing the hand he held, "you are most kind to be so ready to see what is commendable in my wayward child. I cannot reasonably expect even you to look at her with her father's partial eyes. And dearly as I certainly do love her, I have been exceedingly angry with her today; so angry that, for a time, I dared not trust myself to go near her — I who ought to have unlimited patience with her, knowing, as I do, that she inherits her temper from me."

"I don't know how to believe that, my dear, good husband," Violet said, gazing up into his face with fond, admiring eyes, "for I have never seen any evidence of it. If you have such a temper, you have certainly gained complete mastery of it. And that may well give us hope for Lulu."

"I do not despair of her," he said, "though I was near doing so today—for a time — after hearing a full account of her passionate behavior — her savage assault, as it seemed to be, upon her baby sister."

"Oh!" moaned Violet, bending over the little one with fast falling tears — for she was moaning as if in pain, "my baby, my poor, precious baby! How gladly mamma would bear all your suffering for you, if she could!" Oh, Levis, what shall we do if she is taken from us?"

"Dear wife, I hope we may not be called to endure that trial," he said, "but, in any case, we have the gracious promise, 'As thy days, so shall thy strength be.' And that blessed assurance, for our consolation, in regard to her, 'He shall gather the lambs with His arms, and carry them in His bosom.'"

" 'Tis a very sweet promise, but, oh, I don't know how to resign her, even to Him," she said, weeping bitterly.

"Nor I, but we will try to leave it all with Him. We will rejoice if she is spared to us, and, if not, we will be glad to know that she is so safe, so happy with Him — gathered with His arm, carried in His bosom."

"Yes, yes," she sobbed, "it would be only for ourselves we would need to grieve, not for her, sweet pet."

Elsie, Violet's mother, came into the room at that moment.

"My dear Vi," she said tenderly, "you are looking sadly worn and weary. I want you and the captain to take your rest tonight, while Arthur and I will care for the baby.

"Thank you, dearest mamma," Violet replied, "but rest and sleep are quite as necessary to you as to me, and, besides, I could not bear to leave her."

"I took a nap on purpose to be able to sit up tonight," Elsie said. "Also, I am less exhausted by mental distress than her mother is, dearly as I love her. Can you not trust her to me with the doctor sharing the vigil?"

"I could trust your nursing sooner than my own, mother," Violet answered. "It is not that, but I cannot tear myself away from my darling while she is in so critical a state."

"And I," said the captain, "while warmly thanking you and the doctor, cannot consent to leave either wife or baby tonight."

So, finding they were not to be persuaded to rest, the others left them to watch over the little one through the night.

The morning brought a slight change for the better, yet no certainty of recovery; but even that barely perceptible improvement, joined to the delightful prospect of always having her husband at home, cheered Violet greatly.

They had talked much of that through the night, beguiling the long hours of their tedium with many a bright plan for the future, always hoping that "baby" would be a sharer in their realization.

The captain hoped to buy or build in the near neighborhood of Ion, that Violet need not be separated from her mother — a separation he most desirous to avoid on his own account, also, for he entertained a very high regard and warm affection for his mother-in-law, averring that it would be scarcely possible for him to love her better were he her own son.

He had resigned to Violet the pleasure of telling the joyful news to her mother and the whole family, except the children; reserving to himself the right to communicate the glad tidings to them when, and in what way, he should deem best.

Lulu, he said, was to be kept in ignorance of it till the time of her imprisonment expired.

At a very early hour in the morning, Elsie and the doctor came to the relief of the watchers. Arthur noted and announced improvement, thus reviving hope in the anxious hearts of the parents. Before retiring for a few hours' rest and sleep, Violet whispered to them the news that had gladdened her heart in spite of its heavy load of grief and fear.

They both rejoiced with her, and bade her hope for the best in regard to her babe.

Pain, mental and physical, kept Lulu awake a good while after her father left her, but at length she fell into a deep sleep which lasted far beyond her customary hour for rising — the house being very still because of the baby's illness and the blinds being down in her room so that their was neither light nor noise to rouse her.

Her first thoughts on awakening were a little confused. Then, as with a flash, all the events of yesterday came to her remembrance, bringing with them bitter upbraidings of conscience and torturing anxieties and fears.

Would the baby die? Oh! Perhaps she was already dead and she a murderess — the murderess of her own little sister — her father's child!

If that were so, how could she ever look him or anybody else in the face again? And what would be done to her? Was there any danger that she would be put in prison? Oh! That would be far worse than being sent to a boarding school, even where the people were as strict and as disagreeable as possible!

And she would be sorry, oh, so sorry to lose the baby sister, or to have her a sufferer from what she had done, for life, or for years, even could she herself escape all evil consequences.

All the time she was attending to the duties of getting dressed, these thoughts and feelings were in her mind and heart, and her fingers trembled so that it was with difficulty she could manage buttons and hooks and eyes, or stick in a pin.

She started at every sound, longing, yet dreading — as she had done the previous day — to see her father, for who could tell what news he might bring her from the nursery?

Glancing at the little clock on the mantel, when at last she was quite dressed and ready for her breakfast, she saw that it was more than an hour past the usual time for that meal. Yet, no one had been near her, and she was very hungry; but, even if her father had not forbidden her to leave the room, she would have preferred the pangs of hunger to showing her face in the dining room.

Presently, however, footsteps — not those of her father — approached her door.

"Miss Lu," said a voice she recognized as that of her mamma's maid, "please open de doah. Hyar's yo' breakfus."

The request was promptly complied with and Agnes entered, carrying a waiter laden with a bountiful supply of savory and toothsome viands.

"Dar it am," she remarked when she had set it on the

table. "I s'pose mos' likely yo' kin eat ef de precious little darlin' is mos' killed by means ob yo' bein' in a passion an' kickin' ob her — de sweet honey — down de steps."

And turning swiftly about, her head in the air, the girl swept from the room, leaving Lulu standing in the middle of the floor, fairly struck dumb with indignation, astonishment, and dismay.

"How dared Agnes — a mulatto servant girl — talk so to her! But was the baby really dying? Would papa never come to tell her the truth about her? She wouldn't believe anything so dreadful till she heard it from him. Very likely Agnes was only trying to torment her, and make her as miserable as possible."

She had sunk, trembling into a chair, feeling as if she should never want to eat again, but with that last thought, her hopes revived, hunger once more asserted its sway, and she ate breakfast with a good deal of appetite and relish.

But, when hunger was appeased, fears and anxieties renewed their assault. She grew half distracted with them as hour after hour passed on and no one came near her except another maid, to take away the breakfast dishes and tidy the room.

On her, Lulu turned her back, holding an open book in her hand and pretending to be deeply absorbed in its contents, though not a word of the sense was she taking in, for, intense as was her desire to learn the baby's condition, she would not risk any more such stabs to her sensitiveness and pride as had been given by Agnes.

This one came, did her work, and went away again in silence, but all the time she was in the room Lulu felt that she was casting glances of disgust and disfavor at her. She could not breathe freely till the girl had left the room.

She thought surely the dinner hour would bring her father, but it did not. Her wants were again supplied by a servant.

CHAPTER FOURTEENTH

The dread of evil is the worst of ill.

ON LEAVING THE breakfast room, Violet hastened back to the nursery; but the captain, calling Max and Grace into her boudoir, said, as he took the little girl on his knee and motioned Max to a seat by his side, —

"I have some news for you, my children. Can you guess what it is?"

"Something good, I hope, papa," said Max. "You look as if it was."

"I am very much pleased with my share of it," the captain said, smiling, "and I shall know presently, I presume, what you two think of yours. What would you like it to be, Gracie?"

"That my papa was never, never going away anymore," she answered promptly, lifting loving eyes to his face.

"There couldn't be better news than that," remarked Max, "but," with a profound sigh, "of course, it can't be that."

"Ah! Don't be quite so sure, young man," laughed his father.

"Papa, you don't mean to say that that is it?" queried Max breathlessly.

"I do. I have resigned from the navy, and hope soon to have a home ready for my wife and children, and to live in it with them as long as it shall please God to spare our lives."

Tears of joy actually came into the boy's eyes, while Gracie threw her arms round their father's neck, and half smothered him with kisses.

"Oh, papa, papa!" she cried, "I'm so glad, I don't know what to do! I'm the happiest girl in the world! — Or should be, if only the dear baby was well," she added, with springing tears.

"Yes," he sighed, "we cannot feel other than sad while she is suffering and in danger. But she is a trifle better this morning and we will hope the improvement may continue till she is entirely restored."

"She's such a darling!" said Max, "just the brightest, cutest baby that ever was seen! Mamma Vi has taught her to know your photograph, and whenever she sees it, she says, 'Papa,' as plainly as I can. She calls me too, and Lu. Oh! I don't know how Lulu could — " He broke off without finishing his sentence.

"Lu didn't do it on purpose," sobbed Gracie, pulling out her handkerchief to wipe her eyes.

"No," sighed the captain. "I am quite sure she had no intention of harming her little sister, yet she is responsible for it as the consequence of indulging in a fit of rage. She feels that, and I hope the distress of mind she is now suffering because of the dreadful deed she has done in her passion will be such a lesson to her that she will learn to rule her own spirit in the future."

"Oh, I do hope so!" said Grace. "Papa, does Lulu know your good news?"

"No, I have not told her yet, and I intend to keep her in ignorance of it for some days, as part of her deserved punishment. I do not want her to have anything to divert her mind from the consideration of the great sin and danger of such indulgence of temper."

"You haven't quit loving her, papa? You won't?" Grace said, half entreatingly, half inquiringly.

"No, daughter, oh no!" he replied with emotion. "I don't know what would ever make me quit loving any one of my dear children."

He drew her closer, and kissed her fondly as he spoke.

"I am glad of that, papa," said Max feelingly, "for though I do mean to be always a good son to you, if I ever should do anything very, very bad, I'd not be afraid to confess it to you. I could stand punishment, you know; but I don't think I could bear to have you give up being fond of me."

A warm pressure of the lad's hand was the captain's only reply at first, but presently he said, "I trust you will always be perfectly open with me, my dear boy. You don't think, do you, that you could have a better — more concerned — earthly friend than your father?"

"No, sir! Oh, no, indeed!"

"Then make me your confidant," his father said with a smile and look that spoke volumes of fatherly pride and affection. "Let me into all your secrets. Now that I am to be with you constantly, I shall take a deeper interest than ever in all that concerns you — if that is possible — in your studies, your sports, your thoughts and feelings. You may always be sure of my sympathy and such help as I can give in any right and wise undertaking."

"I'll do that, papa!" Max exclaimed with a sudden, glad lighting up of his face. "Why, it'll be as good as having the brother I've often wished for!" he added with a pleased laugh, "better in some ways, anyhow, for you'll be so much wiser than any boy and keep me out of scrapes with your good advice."

"Papa," queried Grace, with a little bashful hesitation, "mayn't I have you for my friend, too?"

"Yes, indeed, my darling little girl!" he answered with a hug and kiss. "I should like to be quite as intimate with you as I hope to be with Max."

"With Lulu, too?" she asked.

"Yes, with every one of my children."

Max had averted his face to hide his amusement at his little sister's question in regard to her father's friendship for herself, for the timid, sensitive girl could hardly bear to be laughed at. But now he turned to his father again with the query, "Papa, where are we going to live?"

"I don't know yet, Max," the captain answered, "but I hope to be able to buy or build somewhere in this neighborhood, as I should be loath to take your mamma far away from her mother — myself either, for that matter. And I presume you would all prefer to live near these kind friends?"

"I am sure I should," said Max. "But, papa — " he paused, coloring and casting down his eyes.

"Well, my boy, what is it? Don't be afraid to talk freely to your intimate friend," his father said in a kindly tone, and laying a hand affectionately on the lad's shoulder.

"Please don't think me impertinent, papa," Max said, coloring still more, "but I was just going to ask how you could live without your pay, as I heard you say it was nearly all you had."

"I am not at all offended at the inquiry," was the kindly reply. "The intimacy and confidences are not to be all on one side, my boy. I am quite willing you should know that I am able to do without the pay. Some land belonging to me in the Far West has so risen in value as to afford me sufficient means for the proper support of my family, and education of my children."

"Oh, that is good!" cried Max, clapping his hands in delight. "And if it is used up by the time I'm grown and educated, I hope I'll be able to take care of you and provide for you as you do now for me."

"Thank you, my dear boy," the captain said with feeling. The day may come when you will be the stay and staff of my old age, but, however that may be, you may be sure that nothing can add more to your father's happiness than seeing you growing up to honorable and Christian manhood."

"Yes, sir. It's what I want to do." Then, a little anxiously, after a moment's thought, "Am I to be sent away to school, sir?"

"I have not quite decided that question, and your wishes will have great weight with me in making the decision. I shall keep Lulu at home and educate her myself — act as her tutor, I mean — and if my boy would like to become my pupil also — ."

Oh, papa! Indeed, indeed I should!" exclaimed Max joyfully, as his father paused, looking smilingly at him, "and I'll try hard to do you credit as my teacher as well as my father."

"Then we will make the trial," said the captain. "If it

should not prove a success, there will be time enough after that to try a school."

"What about me, papa?" asked Grace wistfully, feeling as if she were being overlooked in the arrangements.

"You, too, shall say lessons to papa," he answered with tender look and tone. "Shall you like that?"

"Ever so much!" she exclaimed, lifting glad, shining eyes to his face.

"Now you may go back to your play," he said, gently putting her off his knee. "I must go to your mamma and our poor, suffering baby."

He went, but the children lingered a while where they were, talking over this wonderfully good news.

"Now," said Max, "if Lu had only controlled her temper yesterday, what a happy family we'd be!"

"Yes," sighed Grace, "how I do wish she had! Oh, I'm so sorry for her that she doesn't know this about papa going to stay with us all the time! 'Sides, she's 'specting to be sent away somewhere, and how dreadfully she must feel! Papa's punishing her very hard and very long, but of course he knows best, and he loves her."

"Yes, I'm sure he does," assented Max, "so he won't give her any more punishment than he thinks she needs. It'll be a fine thing for her, and all the rest of us, too, if this hard lesson teaches her never to get into a passion again."

Captain Raymond had intended to go to Lulu early in the day, but anxiety about the babe and sympathy for Violet kept him with them till late in the afternoon.

When at last he did go to his prisoner, he found her feverish with anxiety and fear for the consequences of her mad act of the day before.

She had been longing for his coming, moving restlessly about the room, feeling that she could not endure the suspense another moment. She had at length thrown herself into a chair beside the window, as was her wont in times of overwrought feeling, and buried her face on her folded arms, laid on the windowsill.

She started up wildly at the sound of his step and the opening of the door.

"Papa," she cried breathlessly, "oh, papa, what — what have you come to tell me? Is — is the baby — "

"She is living, but far from out of danger," he said, regarding her with a very grave, stern expression, but it softened as he marked the anguish in her face.

He sat down and drew her to his knee, putting his arm about her waist, and with the other hand clasping one of hers.

He was startled to feel how hot and dry it was.

"My child!" he exclaimed, "you are not well."

She dropped her head on his shoulder and burst into a passion of tears and sobs. "Papa, papa! What shall I do if baby dies? Oh, I would do or bear anything in the world to make her well!"

"I don't doubt it, daughter," he said, "but a bitter lesson we all have to learn is that we cannot undo the evil deeds we have done. Oh, let this dreadful occurrence be a warning to you to keep a tight rein upon your quick temper."

"Oh, I do mean to, indeed, I do!" she sobbed, "but that won't cure the dear baby's hurt. Papa, all day long I have been asking God to forgive me. Do you think He will?"

"I am sure that He has already done so, if you have asked with your heart and for Jesus' sake. But we will ask Him again for that, and to give you strength to fight against your evil nature as you never have fought, and to conquer."

"And to make the baby well, papa," she added sobbingly as he knelt with her.

"Yes," he said.

When they had risen from their knees, he bade her get her hat and coat saying, "You need fresh air and exercise. I will take you for a walk."

"I'd like to go, papa," she said, "but — "

"But what?"

"I — I'm afraid of — of meeting some of the family, and — and I don't want to see any of them."

"Perhaps we shall not meet them," he said, "and, if we do, you need not look toward them, and they will not speak to you. Put on your hat and coat at once. We have no time to lose."

She obeyed and presently they were walking down the avenue, not having met anyone on their way out of the house.

The captain moved on in silence, seemingly absorbed in sad thought and hardly conscious that Lulu was by his side.

She glanced wistfully up into his grave, stern face two or three times, then said humbly, pleadingly, "Papa, please may I put my hand in yours?"

"Certainly," he said, looking down at her very kindly as he took her hand and held it in a warm, affectionate clasp. "Child, you have not lost your father's love. You are very dear to me, in spite of all your naughtiness."

He slackened his pace, for he saw she was finding it difficult to keep up with him, and his attention was again attracted to the heat of her hand.

"You are not well, perhaps not able to walk?" he said inquiringly and in tender, solicitous accents.

"It is pleasant to be out in the air, papa," she answered, "but it tires me a good deal more than usual."

"We will not go far, then," he said, "and, if your strength gives out before we get back to the house, I will carry you."

They were in the road now, some distance beyond the avenue gates. At this moment a number of horsemen came in sight approaching from the direction opposite to that they were taking.

Perceiving them, Lulu uttered a sharp cry of terror and shrank behind her father, though still clinging to his hand.

"What is it, daughter?" he asked in surprise. "What do you fear?"

"Oh, papa, papa!" she sobbed, "are they coming to take me and put me in prison? Oh, don't let them have me!"

"Don't be frightened," he said soothingly. "Don't you see it is only some men who have been out hunting and are going home with their game?"

"Oh, is that all?" she gasped, the color coming back to her face, which had grown deadly pale. "I thought it was the sheriff coming to put me in jail for hurting the baby. Will they do it, papa? Oh, you won't let them, will you?"

"I could not protect you from the law," he said in a moved

~ 130 ~

tone, "but I think there is no danger that it will interfere. You did not hurt your sister intentionally, and she is still living. You are very young too, and, doubtless, everybody will think your punishment should be left to me, your father."

She was trembling like a leaf.

He turned aside to a fallen tree, sat down on it and took her in his arms. She dropped her head on his shoulder, panting like a hunted thing.

"These two days have been too much for you," he said pityingly. "And that fear has tormented you all the time?"

"Yes, papa. Oh, I thought I have to be hung if baby died, and — it was — so — dreadful — to think I'd killed her — even if they didn't do anything to me for it," she sobbed.

"Yes, very, very dreadful — perhaps more so to me — the father of you both — than to anyone else," he groaned.

"Papa, I'm heartbroken about it," she sobbed. "Oh, if I only could undo it."

He was silent for a moment, then he said, "I know you are suffering very much from remorse. This is a bitter lesson to you. Let it be a lasting one. I can relieve you of the fear of punishment from the law of the land. There is no danger of that now, but if you do not lay this lesson to your heart, there may come a time when that danger will be real for there is no knowing what awful deed such an ungovernable temper as yours may lead you to commit.

"But don't despair — you can conquer it by determination, constant watchfulness and the help from on high which will be given in answer to earnest prayer."

"Then it shall be conquered!" she cried vehemently. "I will fight it with all my might. And you will help me, papa, all you can, won't you, by watching me and warning me when you see I'm beginning to get angry, and punishing me for the least little bit of a passion? But oh, I forgot that you can't stay with me, or take me with you!" she cried with a fresh burst of sobs and tears. "Must you go back to your ship soon?"

"Not very soon," he said, "and I gladly promise to help you all I can in every way. I can do it with my prayers, even when not close beside you. But, my child, the struggle must be your own. All I can do will be of no avail unless you fight the battle yourself with all your strength.

"We will go home now," he added, rising and taking her hand in his.

But they had gone only a few steps when he stooped, and took her in his arms saying, "You are not able to walk. I shall carry you."

"But I am so heavy, papa," she objected.

"No, darling, I can carry you very easily," he said. "There, put your arm round my neck, and lay your head on my shoulder."

The pet name from his lips sent a thrill of joy to her heart, and it was very pleasant, very restful, to feel herself enfolded in his strong arms.

He carried her carefully, tenderly along, holding her close, as something precious that he began to fear might slip from his grasp. She had always been a strong, healthy child, and heretofore he had scarcely thought of sickness in connection with her, but now he was alarmed at her state.

"Are you in pain, daughter?" he asked.

"Only a headache, papa — I suppose because I've cried so much."

"I think I must have the doctor see you."

"Oh, no, no, papa! Please don't," she sobbed. "I don't want to see him or anybody."

"Then we will wait a little. Perhaps you will be all right again by tomorrow."

He did not set her down till they had almost reached the house, and he took her in his arms again at the foot of the stairway, and carried her to her room, where he sat down with her on his knee.

"Papa, aren't you very tired, carrying such a big, heavy girl?" she asked, looking regretfully into his face.

"No, very little," he answered, taking off her hat and laying his cool hand on her forehead. "Your head is very hot. I'll take off your coat and lay you on the bed, and I want you to stay there for the rest of the day. Go to sleep if you can."

"I will, papa," she answered submissively, then as he laid her down and turned to leave her, "Oh, I wish you could stay with me!" she cried, clinging to him.

"I cannot now, daughter," he said smoothing her hair caressingly. "I must go back to your mamma and the baby. But I will come in again to bid you goodnight, and see that you are as comfortable as I can make you. Can you eat some supper?"

"I don't know, papa," she answered doubtfully.

"Well, I will send you some, and you can eat it, or not, as you feel inclined."

CHAPTER FIFTEENTH

After the storm, a calm; after the rain, sunlight.

As CAPTAIN RAYMOND passed through the hall on which Lulu's room opened, a little girl, dressed in deep mourning, rose from the broad, low sill of the front window where she had been sitting waiting for the last few minutes, and came forward to meet him. She was a rather delicate-looking, sweet-faced child with large dark eyes full of intelligence.

"Captain Raymond?" she said inquiringly and with a timid look on her face.

"Yes," he said, holding out his hand to her with a fatherly smile, "and you, I suppose, are my Lulu's friend, Evelyn Leland?"

"Yes, sir. We — Uncle Lester, Aunt Elsie, little Ned and I — have been away visiting at some distance and did not hear of — of the baby's bad fall till we came home this afternoon. We are all so sorry, so very sorry! Aunt Elsie is with Aunt Vi now, and I-ooh, please, sir, may I go to Lulu?"

"My dear little girl, I should like to say yes, for your sake — and Lulu's, too — but for the present, I think it best not to allow her to see anyone," he said in a kindly tone and affectionately pressing the little hand she had put into his. "But," seeing the disappointment in her face, "I entirely approve of the intimacy and hope it will be kept up, for I think it has been of benefit to Lulu."

"Thank you, sir," she returned, coloring with pleasure. "But Lulu told me you had quite determined to send her away from here. I hope you will reconsider, and — let her stay," with a very coaxing look up into his face.

He smiled. "Can you keep a secret?" he asked. "One from only Lulu, and that for only a few days?"

"Try me, sir," she answered brightly.

"I will. I have left the navy and expect to settle down in this neighborhood. In that case, you and Lulu will not be separated, for my strongest reason for the change was that I might have her constantly with me and train her up as I think she should be trained — as perhaps no one but her father can train her."

Evelyn's face had grown very bright. "Oh, how delightful, how happy Lu will be when she hears it!" she exclaimed, "for, do you know, sir, she thinks there is nobody in the world to compare to her father?"

Those words brought a glad look into his face for the moment.

"Yes," he said, "she is a warm-hearted, affectionate child — a dear child, in spite of her quick temper."

A door had opened and closed. A step was coming down the hall, and a cheerful voice in his rear said, "Captain, I have good news for you. There has been a great, really wonderful change for the better in the last hour. The child will live, and I hope, I believe, entirely recover from the injuries caused by her fall."

Before the doctor's sentence was finished, the captain had turned and caught his hand in a vice-like grasp. His eyes filled, his chest heaved with emotions too big for utterance, he shook the hand warmly, dropped it, and, without a word, hurried into the nursery.

He found nearly the whole family gathered there, every face full of a great gladness.

The doctor, however, following him in, speedily cleared the room of all but two or three — only the two Elsies, besides himself and the parents were left.

Violet looked up at her husband as he entered with a face so bright and joyous that it recalled the days of their honeymoon.

"Oh, how happy I am! How good God has been to us!" she whispered, as he bent down to kiss her. "Our darling is spared to us! See how sweetly she is sleeping!"

"Yes," he returned in the same low tone, his features working with emotion. "And what double reason for joy and gratitude have I — the father of both the injurer and the injured!"

"Forgive me that I have felt a little hard to Lulu. I can and do forgive her now,' she said with sweet eyes looking penitently into his.

"Darling," he returned with emotion, "I have nothing to forgive, but shall be very glad if you can find any love in your heart, after this, for my wayward child, little as she merits it."

Then, without waiting for a reply, he turned to Mrs. Leland with a brotherly greeting, not having seen her before since his arrival at Ion.

"Vi has told me the glad tidings you brought her yesterday," she said as he held her hand in his, "and I can't tell you how delighted we all are to know that you have come to stay among us."

"And now I can rejoice in that to the full, my dear, dear husband," Violet said, dropping her head on his shoulder as he sat down by her side and put his arm about her.

For a little while they all sat silently watching the sleeping babe, then Arthur glanced at the clock and with a low tone promised to be back in an hour, rose and left the room.

"Excuse me for a little, dear," the captain said to Violet, and softly followed Arthur out to the hall.

"Can you spare a moment?" he asked.

"Yes, full five of them, if necessary," was the jovial reply.

Arthur's heart was so light in consequence of the improvement in his young patient that a jest came readily to his lips.

"Thank you," returned the captain warmly, then went on to describe Lulu's condition and ask what should be done for her.

"Relieve her mind as speedily as possible with the good news of the certainty of the baby's recovery, and, if you choose, the other glad tidings you brought us yesterday," Arthur answered. "The mental strain of the past two days has evidently been too much for her. She must have suffered greatly from grief, remorse, and terror. Relief from those will be the best medicine she could have, and probably will work a speedy cure. Good evening."

He hurried away and the captain went at once to Lulu.

She was on the bed where he had left her, but at the opening of the door, started up, and turned to him with a look of wild fright.

"Papa!" she cried breathlessly, "is — is the baby — ? Oh, no! How glad your face is!"

"Yes, baby is very much better, in fact, quite out of danger, the doctor thinks. And you? Have you not slept?" he asked, bending over her in tender solicitude, for she had fallen back on her pillow and was sobbing as if her heart would break, weeping for joy as she had before wept with sorrow, remorse, and penitence.

He lifted her from the bed, and sat down with her in his arms.

"Don't cry so, daughter dear," he said soothingly, softly caressing her hair and cheek. "It will make your head ache still more."

"I can't help it, papa. I'm so glad the dear baby will get well, and that I — I'm not a murderess. Papa, won't you thank God for me?"

"Yes," he said with emotion, " for you and myself and all of us."

When they had risen from their knees, "Now I hope you can sleep a while and afterward eat some supper," he said, lifting her and gently laying her on the bed again.

"Oh, papa! I wish you could stay with me a little longer," she cried, clinging to his hand.

"I cannot stay now, daughter," he said, "but I will come in again to bid you goodnight."

He leaned over her and kissed her several times. She threw her arm round his neck and drew him down closer.

"Dear, dear papa!" she sobbed, "you are the best father in the world! Oh, I wish I was a better girl! Do you think I — I'm a curse to you now?"

"I think — I believe you are going to be a very great blessing to me, my own darling," he answered in tones tremulous with emotion. "I fear I was hard and cruel in what I said when I came to you that first time last night."

"No, papa, I deserved it every bit, but it 'most broke my heart because I love you so. Oh, I do want to be a blessing to you, and I mean to try with all my might!"

"My dear little girl, my own little daughter, that is all I can ask," he said repeating his caresses.

Then he covered her up with tender care, and left her, weary, exhausted with the mental suffering of the last two days, but with a heart singing for joy over his restored affection and the assurance of the baby's final recovery.

She expected to stay awake till he came again, but in less than five minutes was fast asleep.

The captain found Max and Gracie hovering near as he passed out into the hall.

"Papa," they said, coming hastily forward, "may we go in to see Lulu now?" Max adding, "I was too angry with her at first to want to see her, but I've got over that now." Then Gracie said, "And mayn't she know now that we're going to keep you always at home?" taking his hand in both of hers and looking up coaxingly into his face.

"No, my dears, not tonight," he said. "She has cried herself sick — has a bad headache, and I want her to try to sleep it off."

"Poor Lu! She must have been feeling awfully all this time," Max said. "I wish I hadn't been so angry with her."

"You look very happy — you two," their father said smiling down on them.

"So do you, sir," returned Max, "and I'm so glad for you've been looking heartbroken ever since you came home."

"Pretty much as I have felt," he sighed, patting Gracie's cheek as he spoke.

"We are just as happy as we can be, papa," she said, "only I —"

"Well?" he said inquiringly as she paused, leaving her sentence unfinished.

"I'm just hungry to sit on your knee a little while, but" ruefully, "I s'pose you haven't time."

"Come into the nursery with me, and you shall sit there as long as you like and are willing to keep perfectly quiet so as not to disturb baby."

"Oh! Thank you, papa," she returned joyously, slipping her hand into his. "I'll be as quiet as a mouse."

"I hope my turn will come tomorrow," remarked Max. "I've a hundred questions I want to ask."

"As many as you like, my boy, when I have time to listen; though I don't promise to answer them all to your entire satisfaction," his father replied as he passed on into the nursery, taking Grace with him.

Max went downstairs where he found Evelyn Leland sitting alone in one of the parlors, waiting till her Aunt Elsie should be ready to go back to Fairview.

"Max," she said as he came in and took a seat at her side, "you have just the nicest kind of a father!"

"Yes, that's so!" he returned heartily. "There couldn't be a better one."

"I wish he would let me see Lu," Evelyn went on. "I was in hopes he would after the doctor told him the baby was sure to get well."

"I think he would, but that Lu has cried herself sick and he wants her to sleep off her headache. He refused to let Gracie and me in for that reason."

"Poor thing!" Evelyn exclaimed, tears springing to her eyes. "I should think it must have been almost enough to set her crazy. But how happy she will be when she hears that your father isn't going away again and means to keep her at home with him."

"Yes, indeed; she will go wild with joy. It's what all three of us have wanted to have happen more than anything else we could think of.

"I've often envied boys that could live at home with their fathers, though" he added with a happy laugh, "I've said to myself many a time that mine was enough nicer than theirs to make up for having to do without him so much of the time. At least, I'd never have been willing to swap fathers with one of 'em. No, indeed!"

"Of course not," said Evelyn. "And I'm so delighted that

Lu and I are not to be separated! I can hardly wait to talk with her about it and the good times we'll have together."

A nap and nice supper had refreshed Lulu a good deal, but she felt weak and languid and was lying on the bed when her father returned to her room.

She looked up at him wistfully as he came and stood beside her, then her eyes filled with tears.

"What is it?" he asked, lifting her from the bed, seating himself, and drawing her into his arms. "What is your petition? I read in your eyes that you have one to make."

"Papa, you won't send me away — very — soon, will you?" she pleaded in tremulous tones, her arms round his neck, her face hidden on his shoulder.

"Not till I go myself; then I shall take you with me."

"To a boarding school?" she faltered.

"No, I'm going to put you in a private family."

Her face was still hidden and she did not see the smile in his eyes.

"What kind of people are they, papa?" she asked with a deep-drawn sigh.

"Very nice people, I think. The wife and mother is a very lovely woman, and the four children — a boy and three girls — are, I presume, neither better nor worse than my own four. The gentleman, who will teach you himself, along with the others, and have the particular care and oversight of you, is perhaps rather stern and severe with anyone who ventures to disobey his orders, but I am quite certain that if you are good and obedient, he will be very kind and indulgent, possibly a trifle more indulgent than he ought to be."

Lulu began to cry again. "I don't like men teachers!" she sobbed. "I don't like a man to have anything to do with me. Please, please don't send me there, papa!"

"You want me to relent, and let you stay on here if they will have you?"

"No, no, papa! I don't want to stay here! I don't want to see anybody here again, except Max and Gracie because I'm so ashamed of — of what I've done. I couldn't look any of them in the face, for I know they must despise me."

"I am sure you are mistaken in that, my child," he said gravely. "But what is it you do desire?"

"To be with you, papa. Oh, if I could only go with you!"

"And leave Max and Gracie?"

"I'll have to leave them, anyhow, if you take me away from here, and though I love them very much, I love you a great deal better."

"I'm afraid you would have a doleful time on shipboard with no companions, nobody to see or speak to but your father and the other officers."

"I wouldn't care for that or anything, if I could only be with you. Papa, you don't know how I love you!"

"Then, I'll take you with me when I leave here, and you need never live away from me any more, unless you choose."

"Papa," she cried, lifting her head to look up into his face with glad, astonished eyes. "Do you really mean it? May I go with you?"

He held her close with a joyous laugh.

"Why, I understood you to say a moment since that you didn't want to be in the care of a man — any man."

"But you know I didn't mean you, papa."

"But I am the gentleman I spoke of a little while ago, as the one in whose care I intended to put you."

"Papa," she said with a bewildered look, "I don't understand."

Then he told her, and she was, as Max had foreseen, almost wild with delight.

"Oh!" she cried, "how nice, nice it will be to have a home of our very own, and our father with us all the time! Papa, I think I sha'n't sleep a wink tonight, I'm so glad."

"I trust it will not have that effect," he said. "I hesitated a little about telling you tonight, lest it might interfere with your rest. But you seemed so unhappy about your future prospects that I felt I must relieve you of the fear of being sent away among strangers."

"You are so very good and kind to me, papa," she returned gratefully. "Where is our dear home to be?"

"I don't know yet," he said. "I have not had time to look

about in search of house or land, but I hope to be able to buy or build a house somewhere in this region, as near Ion as a pleasant location can be found."

"I hope you'll find a house ready built, papa," she said. "I shouldn't know how to wait for one to be built."

"Not if, by waiting, we should, in the end, have a much nicer, pleasanter one?"

She considered a moment. "Couldn't we rent a house to live in while we get our own built?"

"I think that plan might answer quite well," he said with a smile. "I had no idea you were such a business woman. Probably that is what we will do, for I am as anxious to get to housekeeping as even you can be."

"But, papa," she exclaimed, with a look as if struck by a sudden and not very pleasant thought, "may I — will you be vexed if I ask you something?"

"Suppose you find out by asking?"

"I — I hope you won't think it's impertinence, papa, I don't mean it for that," she said with hesitation, hanging her head and blushing, "but — but — I hope it isn't Mamma Vi's money we're to live on?"

He put his hand under her chin and lifted her face so that he could look down into her eyes, and she drew a long breath of relief as she perceived that he was smiling at her.

"No," he said. "You come honestly by your pride of independence. I would no more live on Mamma Vi's money than you would."

"Oh, I'm so glad! But — then, how can you do without your pay, papa?"

"Because my heavenly Father has prospered me and given me money enough of my own (or, rather, lent it to me — for all that we have belongs to Him, and is only lent to us for a time) to provide all that is necessary for my family and to educate my children.

"Now, we had a long talk, which has, I trust, made my dear little girl much happier, and it is time for you to go to your bed for the night."

"I don't like to have you leave me," she said clinging to

~ 142 ~

his neck, "but you were very kind to stay so long. Won't you come soon in the morning?"

"You are not a prisoner any longer," he said caressing her. "You are free to leave this room and go where you choose about the house and grounds tomorrow."

"But I don't want to. Oh, papa! I can't face them! Mayn't I stay in my room till you are ready to take me to our own home?"

"You will have to face them sometime," he said, "but we will see what can be done about it. Would you like to see Max and Gracie tonight?"

"Gracie, ever so much, but Max — I — I don't know how he feels toward me, papa."

"Very kindly. He has been asking permission to come in to see you, and Gracie has pleaded quite hard for it, and to have you forgiven and told the good news."

"Gracie always is so dear and kind," she said tremulously, "and Maxie isn't often cross with me. Yes, papa, I should like to see them both."

"Your friend Evelyn was here this afternoon asking permission to come in to see you, but is gone now. You may see her tomorrow, if you want. Ah! I hear your brother and sister in the hall."

He opened the door and called to them. They came bounding in, so full of delight over the pleasant prospect opening before them, as hardly to remember that Lulu had been in such dreadful disgrace."

"Oh, Lu! Has papa told you the good news?" they cried.

"Yes."

"And aren't you glad?"

"Yes; glad as glad can be. But, oh, I wish the home was ready to go into tonight!"

Her father laughed. "I think you were born in a hurry, Lulu," he said. "You are never willing to wait a minute for anything.

"Well, I suppose you children would prefer to be left to yourselves for a while; so I will leave you. You may talk fifteen minutes together, but no longer, as it is your bedtime now — Gracie's at least."

"Oh, papa, don't go!" they all exclaimed in a breath.

"Please stay with us. We'd rather have you, a great deal rather!"

He could not resist their entreaties, so sat down and drew his two little girls into his arms while Max stationed himself close at his side.

"My dear children," he said, "you can hardly be happier in the prospect before us than your father is."

"Is Mamma Vi glad?" asked Lulu.

"Yes, quite as much rejoiced, I think, as any of the rest of us."

"But doesn't she want me sent away to school or somewhere?" asked Lulu with a wistful, anxious gaze into his face. "Is she willing to have me in the new home, papa?"

"Yes, daughter, more than willing. She wants you to be under your father's constant care and watchfulness, hoping that so he may succeed in teaching you to control your temper."

"She's very good and forgiving," was Lulu's comment in a low and not unmoved tone.

"Papa, when will you begin to look for the new home?" asked Grace, affectionately stroking his cheek and whiskers with her small white hand.

"I have been looking at advertisements," he said, "and now that baby is out of danger, I shall begin the search in earnest."

"Can we afford a big house and handsome furniture, papa?" queried Lulu.

"And to keep carriage and riding horses?" asked Max.

"I hope my children have not been so thoroughly spoiled by living in the midst of wealth and luxury, that they could not content themselves with a moderately large house and plain furniture?" he said gravely.

"I'd rather live that way with you, than have all the fine things and you not with us, dear papa," Lulu said, putting her arm round his neck and laying her cheek to his.

"I too."

"And I," said Max and Grace.

"And I," he responded, smiling affectionately upon

them, "would much prefer such a home with my children about me, to earth's grandest place without them. Millions of money could not buy one of my treasures!"

"Not me, papa?" whispered Lulu tremulously with her lips close to his ear.

"No, dear child, not even you," he answered, pressing her closer to his side. "You are no less dear than the others."

"I deserve to be," she said with tears in her voice. "It would be just and right, papa, if you did not love me half so well as any of your other children."

She spoke aloud this time, as her father had.

"We all have our faults, Lu," remarked Max, "but papa loves us in spite of them."

" 'God commendeth His love toward us, in that while we were yet sinners, Christ died for us,' " said his father. "The Bible bids us to 'be followers of God as dear children.' And oh, how we should hate sin when we remember that it crucified our Lord!"

There was a momentary silence. Then the children began talking joyfully again of the new home in prospect for them, and their hopes and wishes in regard to it.

Their father entered heartily into their pleasure and encouraged them to express themselves freely, until the clock, striking nine, reminded him that more than the allotted time for the interview had passed. Then he bade them say goodnight and go to their beds, promising that they should have other opportunities for saying all they wished on the subject.

CHAPTER SIXTEENTH

*'Tis easier for the generous to forgive
Than for offense to ask it.*

IN PASSING THROUGH the hall on his way from Lulu's room to the nursery, Captain Raymond met "Grandma" Elsie.

She stopped him and asked in a tone of kindly concern if Lulu was ill, adding that something she had accidentally overheard him saying to the doctor had made her fear the child was not well.

"Thank you, mother," he said. "You are very kind to take any interest in Lulu after what has occurred. No, she is not quite well. The mental distress of the last two days has been very great and has exhausted her physically. It could not, of course, be otherwise, unless she were quite heartless. She is full of remorse for her passion and its consequences, and my only consolation is the hope that this terrible lesson may prove a lasting one for her."

"I hope so, indeed," Elsie said with emotion. "Yes, she must have suffered greatly, for she is a warm-hearted, affectionate child, and would not, I am sure, have intentionally done her baby sister an injury."

"No, it was not intentional. Yet, as the result of allowing herself to get into a passion, she is responsible for it, as she feels and acknowledges.

"And so deeply ashamed is she, that she knows not how to face the family, or anyone of them, and therefore entreats me to allow her to seclude herself in her own room till I can take her to the home I hope to make for my wife and children ere long."

"Poor child!" sighed Elsie. "Tell her, Levis, that she

~ 146 ~

need not shrink from us as if we were not sinners as well as herself. Shall I go tomorrow morning, and have a talk with her before breakfast?"

"It will be a great kindness," he said flushing with pleasure, "and make it much easier for her to show herself afterwards at the table. But I ought to ask if you are willing to see her there in her accustomed seat?"

"I shall be glad to do so," Elsie answered with earnest kindliness of look and tone. "She was not banished by any edict of mine or papa's."

"No, I forbade her to leave her room while the baby was in a critical condition. Yet I think she had no disposition to leave it — shame and remorse causing a desire to hide herself from everybody."

"It strikes me as a hopeful sign," Elsie said, "and I do not despair of one day seeing Lulu a noble woman, the joy and pride of her father's heart."

She held out her hand as she spoke.

The captain grasped it warmly. "Thank you, mother, for those kind and hopeful words," he said with emotion. "For the last year or two, she has been alternately my joy and my despair, and I am resolved to leave no effort untried to rescue her from the dominion of her fierce temper.

"The task would doubtless have been far easier could I have undertaken it years ago in her early infancy. But I trust it is not yet too late to accomplish it, with the help and the wisdom I may have in answer to prayer."

"No, I am sure it is by no means a hopeless undertaking, looking where you do for needed strength and wisdom, and I rejoice almost for Lulu's sake as for Vi's that you have now come among us to stay. I will try to see her in the morning and do what I can to make it easy for her to join the family circle again.

"And now goodnight. I must not keep you longer from the wife who grudges every moment that you are absent from her side," she concluded, with a smile as sweet and beautiful as that of her girlhood days.

While the captain and his mother-in-law held this little

conversation in the upper hall, Zoe and Rosie were promenading the veranda, arm in arm. They had been talking of Violet and her baby, rejoicing together over its improved condition.

"How dreadful the last two days have been to poor Vi!" exclaimed Rosie, "even in spite of the homecoming of her husband, which has always before this made her so happy. In fact, it has been a dreadful time to all of us, and nobody to blame except that bad-tempered Lulu.

"At least, so I think," she added, conscience giving her a twinge, "though mamma says I ought to have let her have my pony, and taken my own ride later in the day if I wanted one."

"It would have been more polite and unselfish, wouldn't it?" queried Zoe, in a teasing tone. "I dare say it is what mamma herself would have done under the circumstances."

"I have no doubt of that," returned Rosie, "but mamma and I are two very different people. I can never hope to be as good and unselfish as she is and always has been so far as I can learn."

"Ah! But there's nothing like trying," laughed Zoe.

"Suppose you tell Lulu that, advising her to undertake the task of controlling her temper."

"She was quite a good while without an outbreak," said Zoe, "and really, Rosie, that dog of yours is extremely trying at times."

"It's quite trying to me that I've had to send him away, and can't have him about any more till Lulu's gone. I'll be sorry to have Vi leave Ion, but rejoiced to be rid of Lulu. I wonder if the captain still intends to send her away? I sincerely hope so, for Vi's sake. Poor little Elsie may be killed outright the next time Lulu has an opportunity to vent her spite upon her."

Oh, Rosie! How can you talk so?" exclaimed Zoe. "Haven't you heard that Lulu says she thought it was your dog she was kicking at? And she has been really sick with distress about the baby? As to sending her away to be trained and taught by strangers — her father has no idea of doing it. In fact — so Vi told Ned — the conviction that Lulu needed his constant oversight and control had a great deal to do in leading him to resign from the service and come home to live."

"Then, he's a very good father — a great deal better one than she deserves. But I'm sorry for Vi and her baby."

"You needn't be. Surely the captain should be able to protect them from Lulu," laughed Zoe.

Rosie laughed too, remarked that it must be getting late, and they went into the house.

"I DO WISH PAPA would come for me. I can't bear to go down alone to breakfast," Lulu was saying to herself the next morning, when a light step in the hall without caught her ear. Then there was a tap at the door, and, opening it, she found the lady of the house standing on the threshold.

"Good morning, my child," she said in pleasant, cheery tones and smiling sweetly as she spoke. Then, bending down, she gave the little girl a kiss.

"Good morning, Grandma Elsie," murmured Lulu, blushing deeply and casting down her eyes. "You are very kind to come to see me, and to kiss me, too, when I have been so bad. Please take a chair," she added, drawing one forward.

"Thank you, dear, but I would rather sit on the sofa yonder, with you by my side," Elsie said, taking Lulu's hand, and leading her to it. Then, when they had seated themselves, she put the other arm about the child's waist and drew her close to her side. "I feel that I have been neglecting you," she went on, "but my thoughts have been taken up with other things, and —"

"Oh, Grandma Elsie!" cried Lulu, bursting into tears. "I didn't deserve that you should show me the least kindness or think of me at all except as a very bad, disagreeable girl. I should think you'd want to turn me out of your house and say I should never come into it again."

"No, dear child, I have no such feeling toward you. If I

had, should I not be very much like that wicked servant to whom his lord had forgiven a debt of ten thousand talents, yet who refused to have compassion on his fellow servant who owed him a hundred pence? I should, indeed, for my sins against God have been far greater, and more heinous than yours against me or mine."

"But you were always such a good child when you were a little girl, and I am such a bad one."

"No, my dear, that is quite a mistake. I was not always good as a child, and I am very far from being perfect as a woman."

"You seem so to me, Grandma Elsie. I never know of your doing and saying anything the least bit wrong."

"But you, my child, see only the outward appearance, while God looks at the heart, and He knows that, though I am truly His servant, trying earnestly to do His will, I fall lamentably short of it."

"Grandma Elsie, I didn't know it was the baby. I didn't mean to hurt her."

"No, my dear, I know you didn't."

"But papa said he must punish me all the same, because it was being in a passion that made me do it. Grandma Elsie, if you had such a dreadful temper as mine, wouldn't you be discouraged about conquering it?"

"No, my child, not while I could find such words as these in the Bible. 'Oh, Israel, thou hast destroyed thyself: but in Me is thine help.' 'Thou shalt call His name Jesus, for He shall save His people from their sins.' 'He is able also to save them to the uttermost that come to God by Him.' 'God is faithful, who will not suffer you to be tempted above that ye are able, but will with the temptation make a way to escape, that ye may be able to bear it.' "

" 'His people,' " repeated Lulu. Then, with a sigh, "But I am not one of them, Grandma Elsie, so those promises are not for me."

"He invites you to become one of His people, and then they will be for you.

" 'Come unto Me, all ye that labor and are heavy laden,' Jesus says, 'and I will give you rest.'

"You feel yourself heavy laden with that unconquerable temper, do you not?"

"Yes, ma'am."

"Then, that invitation is for you, and it will not be unconquerable with the Lord to help you.

" 'The God of Israel is He that giveth strength and power unto His people.' 'And they that stumbled are girded with strength.' You cannot doubt that you are included in the invitation, for it is 'Whosoever will, let him take the water of life freely.' And the time to come is now. 'Now is the accepted time; behold, now is the day of salvation.' "

The breakfast bell rang at that moment, and Grandma Elsie, rising, took Lulu's hand saying, "Come, my dear, you need not shrink from joining us at the table. No one will be disposed to treat you unkindly."

As she spoke the door opened and Captain Raymond and Violet came in. They exchanged morning greetings with their mother, while Lulu, with eyes cast down and cheeks aflame, half shrank behind her, ashamed and afraid to meet Violet's gaze.

But Violet bent down and kissed her affectionately, saying in a kindly tone, "I hope you are feeling better than you did yesterday?"

"Oh, mamma Vi!" Lulu cried, throwing her arm round her young stepmother's neck and bursting into tears, "is baby getting better? And will you forgive me? I am, oh, so sorry!"

"Yes, dear, baby is improving fast, and it is all forgiven, so far as I am concerned," was the gentle reply.

Then the captain kissed his little girl good morning and they all went down to the breakfast room together.

The worst was over to Lulu in having seen Violet, yet it was quite an ordeal for her to face the rest of the large family. But each one spoke pleasantly to her. Rosie alone bestowed so much as an unkind look upon her, and that was wasted, for Lulu, expecting it from that quarter more than any other, constantly averted her gaze from Rosie, keeping her eyes down, or turned in another direction.

Dr. Conly had joined them as they sat down and presently addressed the captain. "I hear, Raymond that you would like to buy in this neighborhood."

"Yes, if I can find a suitable place — one that will satisfy my wife as well as myself," the captain answered with a smiling glance at Violet.

"Well, Vi, how would Woodburn answer, so far as you are concerned?" queried Arthur.

"Woodburn! Is it for sale?" she cried delightedly. "Oh, Levis!" turning to her husband, "it is a lovely old place! A visit there was always a great treat to me as a child."

"And it is really for sale?" exclaimed several voices in chorus, all eyes turning inquiringly upon Dr. Conly.

"Yes, so Miss Elliott told me yesterday," replied Arthur. "She was slightly indisposed and sent for me, and, while telling me her ailments, remarked that she was very lonely since her sister Margaret had married and gone, leaving her sole occupant — not taking servants into account — of that large house with its extensive grounds. So she had at last decided, she said, to comply with her sister's urgent request to sell the place and take up her abode with them.

"She had thought of advertising, and asked my advice about it. Of course, I thought at once of you and Vi, captain, told her I knew of a gentleman who might like to become a purchaser, and that I would promise her a call from him today to look at the place. Will you redeem my promise?"

"Gladly," responded the captain, "especially as Vi expressed so strong a liking for the place. Will you go with me, my dear?"

"I hardly like to leave my baby yet," she answered dubiously. "But if you should feel entirely satisfied with the house, the grounds, and the price asked for them, you could not please me better than by making the purchase."

"There! If Miss Elliott only knew it, she might consider the estate as good as sold," remarked Zoe.

"If she is willing to take a reasonable price, I presume

she might," said Arthur. "Captain, I will go there directly from here. Will you drive over with me and take a look at the place?"

"Yes, thank you, and have a talk with the lady, if you will give me an introduction."

Max and Lulu, sitting side by side at the table, exchanged glances — Lulu's full of delight, Max's only interested. He shook his head in response to hers.

"What do you mean? Wouldn't you like it?" she asked in an undertone.

"Yes, indeed! But I'm pretty sure papa couldn't afford such a place as that. It must be worth a good many thousands."

Lulu's look lost most of its brightness. Still, she did not quite give up hope, as the conversation went on among their elders — Woodburn and the Elliotts continuing to be the theme.

"Will it be near enough to Ion?" Captain Raymond asked, addressing Violet more particularly. "What is the distance?"

"Something over a mile, they call it," said Mr. Dinsmore.

"That is as near as we can expect to be, I suppose," said Violet.

"And with carriages and horses, bicycles, tricycles and telephones, we may feel ourselves very near neighbors indeed," remarked Edward. "When the weather is too inclement for mamma or Vi to venture out, they can talk together by the hour through the telephone, if they wish."

"And it won't often be too inclement to go back and forth," said Zoe, "almost always good enough for a closed carriage, if for nothing else."

"We are talking as if the place were already secured," remarked Violet, with a smiling glance at her husband.

"I think you may feel pretty sure of it if you want it, love, unless Miss Elliott should change her mind about selling," he responded in a tone too low to reach any ears but hers.

She gave him a bright, glad look that quite settled the matter so far as he was concerned. He would, if necessary, give even an exorbitant price for the place to please her.

"Have you never seen Woodburn, captain?" asked Mrs. Dinsmore.

"I have some recollection of driving past it," he replied meditatively, "but — is not the house nearly concealed from view from the road by a thick growth of trees and shrubbery?"

"Yes, you will thin them out a little, I hope, for the mansion is well worth looking at. It is a very aristocratic looking dwelling — large, substantial, and handsome architecturally."

"Papa, are you going to buy it?" asked Grace.

"It is too soon to answer that question, daughter," he said pleasantly, and Max and Lulu again exchanged glances, which this time said, "Maybe he will, after all."

Both ardently wished their father would propose taking them along. He did not. But when Dr. Conly said with a kindly glance at Grace, "There will be room in my carriage for a little friend of mine, if papa is willing to let her go with us," he at once said, "Certainly, Gracie may go if she will be ready in season and not keep the doctor waiting."

"Indeed I will, papa," she cried delightedly, and ran away to don hat and coat, for the meal was concluded and everybody was leaving the table.

Lulu followed her father, till, in the hall she found an opportunity to speak to him without being overheard.

"Papa," she asked, "what am I to do with myself today?"

"Stay in your room and learn your lessons, beginning just where you left off the other day. You will recite to me after I come back; then we will consider what you shall do for the rest of the day."

"Yes, sir. May I see Evelyn when she comes?"

"If she chooses to go to you in your room."

"Must I stay in my room all the time?" she asked dejectedly.

"While I am away. I will take you out after I return."
Then noticing her downcast look, "You shall have more
liberty when we get into our own home," he said kindly.

At that she looked up with a bright, glad smile. "Papa, it
will be so nice!"

Max had drawn near.

"Papa," he said, "won't you let Lu take a walk with me?
Mayn't we run over to Fairview, and bring Evelyn back
with us? I know she'd be glad to have company coming
over to school."

"Yes, you may go, both of you, if you like. But, Lulu,
when you get home, go at once to your room. Don't stop
in the grounds or on the veranda."

"I won't, papa," she said. "I'll go straight to my room,
and, oh, thank you for letting me go!"

CHAPTER SEVENTEENTH

Home, sweet home!

"HOW LARGE IS the estate, doctor?" asked Captain Raymond as they were on their way to Woodburn.

"I cannot say exactly," replied Arthur. "There is a bit of woodland comprising several acres, and lawn, gardens, and shrubbery cover several more. I believe that is all."

"About as much as I care for," returned the captain.

"The estate was formerly very large," Arthur went on, "some thousands of acres, and the family was a very wealthy one. But, like many others, they lost heavily by the war and were compelled to part with one portion of the estate after another, till little more than the homestead was left. And now it seems that it, too, must go."

"Are they so reduced?" the captain asked in a tone of deep sympathy.

"I think Miss Elliott does not feel compelled to part with it, and would still live on there if it were not for the loneliness of the situation, and a natural desire to be with her sister, the only remaining member of their once large family besides herself."

"Yes, yes, I see. I understand and shall feel much more comfortable in buying it than if I knew that poverty compelled her to part with it against her will."

"That shows your kindness of heart," Arthur said, turning toward his friend with an appreciative smile.

The next moment they had entered the Woodburn grounds and Captain Raymond and Grace were glancing from side to side in a very interested manner.

"The place is a good deal run down," remarked Arthur. "They have not had the means to keep it up, I suppose. But if it comes into your hands, captain, you can soon set matters right in regard to that. And I, for one, shall greatly enjoy seeing the improvement."

"And I in making it," was the cheery rejoinder, "more, I think, than taking possession of a place that was too perfect to be improved."

"Papa, I'd just love to have this for our home!" cried Gracie, flushing with pleasure as she glanced here and there, then up into his face with an eager, questioning look, "Won't you buy it, papa?" coaxingly.

"It is still too soon for that question, my child," he said, smiling down at her. "But I hope to be able to answer it before very long."

They had reached the house and were presently ushered into the presence of its owner. She was desirous to sell, the captain to buy — willing also to give not only a fair, but a liberal, price; so it took but a short time for them to come to an agreement.

He bought the land, house, furniture, everything just as it stood — was promised possession in two weeks and accorded the privilege of at once beginning any repairs or alterations he might deem desirable.

Before making the arrangements, he had inspected the whole house. He found it large, conveniently arranged, and in very tolerable repair.

The furniture had evidently been very handsome in its day and would do quite well, he thought, to begin with. Much of it might, with reupholstering and varnishing, please Violet as well as any that could be bought elsewhere. He was eager to bring her to look at it — the house and the grounds.

These last delighted himself and Grace, although lawn and gardens were far from being as trim and neat as those of Ion and Fairview. There was an air of neglect about the whole place, but that could soon be remedied.

The bit of woodland was beautiful, and through it and across lawn and gardens, ran a little stream of clear, sparkling water — a pretty feature of the landscape without being deep enough to be dangerous to the little ones.

Grace went everywhere with her father, upstairs and down,

indoors and out, quietly looking and listening, but seldom speaking unless addressed.

Once or twice she said in a low aside, "Papa, I'd like to live here if you can 'ford to buy it.

"Papa, this is such a pretty room, and the view from that window is so nice!"

He would reply only by a kind smile, or a word or two of assent. She did not understand all the talk in the library after they had finished their round, and when they left was still in some doubt as to her father's intentions.

"Papa," she asked eagerly, as soon as they were fairly on their homeward way, "have you bought it?"

"We have come to an agreement," he answered.

"Then, is it ours?"

"It will be as soon as I have got the deed and handed over the money."

"Oh, I'm so glad!" she cried, clapping her hands with delight. "And we're to be 'lowed to go there to stay in two weeks, aren't we? I thought that was what Miss Elliott said."

"Yes, can you get all your possessions packed up by that time?"

"Yes, indeed, papa. One day would be enough time for that."

"And if you should happen to forget one of the dollies, you could come back for her," remarked the doctor.

"Or replace it with a new one," said the captain.

"But I love all my dollies, papa," she returned with a wistful look up into his face. "They're my children, you know. Would you be satisfied with another new little girl 'stead of me?"

"No, indeed!" he replied, bending down to kiss her cheek. "If I had another new little girl given to me, I should want to hold fast to my little Gracie, too; and you shall keep all your dollies as long as you please."

Lulu and Max started on their walk to Fairview about the same time that Dr. Conly drove away with their father and Grace.

Their talk was principally of the new home in prospect. Lulu had only driven past Woodburn several times, but Max had been taken there once by Dr. Conly, with whom he was almost as great a favorite as his sister Grace, and had seen not only the grounds, but one or two rooms of the mansion.

Lulu was eager to hear all he had to tell about the place, and he not at all averse to describing what he had seen.

So interested were they in the topic, that they reached the entrance to the Fairview grounds almost ere they were aware of it.

"Oh, we're here!" exclaimed Lulu in some surprise. "Max, I'll stay outside while you go up to the house, for — I — I can't bear to see Aunt Elsie and the others."

Her eyes were downcast, her cheeks burning with blushes as she spoke.

"But you may as well get it over," said Max. "You'll have to see them all sometime."

"You don't care a bit, do you?" she said in a hurt tone.

"Yes, I do. I'm right sorry for you, but I can't help your having to meet them sooner or later."

"But I'm afraid I won't be welcome to Aunt Elsie. What if she should tell me to go out of the house, she didn't want such a bad girl there?"

"She isn't that kind of person," said Max. "But here comes Eva," as the little girl came tripping down the avenue to meet them.

She shook hands with Max then threw her arms round Lulu and kissed her.

"Oh, Eva! I'm 'most ashamed to look at you," murmured Lulu, half averting her blushing face. "I shouldn't think you'd want me for your friend any more."

"I do though. I love you dearly and should have gone to your room yesterday if your papa had not refused to allow it," responded Evelyn, repeating her hug. "Come in and rest, both of you. Aunt Elsie told me to ask you."

"I'm not sure that papa meant to give me permission to go into the house," said Lulu, hanging back.

"No, — come to think of it, — I don't believe he did," said Max. "Besides, it must be pretty near school time, so if you are ready, Eva, and want to walk, we'll start back directly, and be glad to take you with us.

"Yes, I prefer to walk," she said. "I'll be ready in five minutes and be glad to have your company."

Mrs. Leland was on the veranda.

"Won't they come in?" she asked Evelyn, as the child came hurrying up the steps.

"No, Auntie, Lu is not quite certain that her papa gave her permission."

"Then, I'll go to them."

Lulu's eyes were on the ground, her cheeks hot with blushes, as Mrs. Leland drew near the rustic bench on which she and Max had seated themselves.

"Good morning, my dears. I am sorry you cannot come in and sit a while," was her pleasant greeting. Then she shook hands with Max and kissed Lulu.

"I heard you were not well yesterday, Lulu. I hope you feel quite so this morning?"

"Yes, ma'am, thank you."

"I heard from Ion before breakfast and am delighted to hear that baby is still improving, as, no doubt, you are — both of you."

"Yes, indeed!" exclaimed Max.

"And I am gladder than words can tell," said Lulu, a tear rolling quickly down her cheek. "Aunt Elsie, I do love her! I think she is the nicest, sweetest baby I ever saw."

"Yes, my dear, and I have no doubt you intend to be the best of sisters to her."

"Oh, I do! I can't ever make up to her for — for hurting her so, though, I did not mean to do it."

"Of course not. You couldn't be so cruel toward any baby, but especially your own sweet little sister," was the gentle, sweet-toned reply. "I am rejoiced, especially for you, my dears, and for your mamma, that your father is going to settle down here, for I know it will add greatly to your happiness. He is such a good husband and father and you will enjoy having a home of your own."

"Yes, Aunt Elsie, we think it is the best thing that could have happened to us," replied Max.

Evelyn joined them at that moment, so they said goodbye and started on their way back to Ion.

"Eva," said Max, "have you heard about Woodburn?"

"No, what about it?"

"It's for sale and perhaps papa will buy it."

"Oh, how nice that would be!" she exclaimed. "I've been there with Aunt Elsie and it's just a lovely place! It has a rather neglected look now, but it wouldn't take long to remedy that, and then it would be quite as handsome as Ion or Fairview, or any other place about here. Aren't you happy, Lu?"

"I shall be if papa gets it, but the best thing of all is that he is to be with us all the time."

"Yes, of course," sighed Evelyn, thinking of the happy days when she had her father with her. "Lu," she said presently, "I know you are not to be sent away, but where are you to go to school?"

"To papa," replied Lulu with a glad look and smile.

Evelyn sighed again. "The only part I regret," she remarked, "is that we have to give up being together in our studies — you and I. Unless," she added the next moment, as if struck by a sudden thought, "your father would take me as a pupil, too. But I wouldn't dare to ask it."

"I would," said Max. "I dare ask papa almost anything — unless it was leave to do something wrong — and I'll undertake to sound him on the subject."

"I'm not afraid to ask him, either," said Lulu, "and he's so kind, I do believe he'll say yes, or at least that he'll do it if everybody else is agreed. Have you seen him, Eva?"

"Yes, and he had such a kind, fatherly manner toward me that I fell in love with him at once. I believe I'd be glad to have him adopt me if he was badly in want of another daughter about my age," she added with a merry look and smile.

"I believe he'd be the gainer if he could swap me off for you," said Lulu, catching her friend's tone, "but I'm very happy in feeling quite sure he would rather have me, bad as I am, just because I am his own."

"That makes all the difference in the world," said Evelyn, "and perhaps, on becoming acquainted with my faults, he might think them worse than yours."

It was not quite school time when they reached Ion, and

Evelyn proposed that they should spend the few intervening minutes in the grounds.

"I'd like to ever so much," said Lulu, "but papa bade me go directly to my own room on getting home. So goodbye," and she moved on resolutely in the direction of the house.

"Goodbye. I'll see you again when school is out, if I can," Evelyn called after her.

Lulu's thoughts were so full of other things, that she found great difficulty in fixing them upon her lessons. But saying to herself that it would be much too bad to fail in her first recitations to her father, she exerted her strong will to the utmost and succeeded. She was quite ready for him when, at length, he came in.

But looking up eagerly from her book, "Papa," she asked, "have you, oh, have you bought it?"

"Bought what?" he asked smilingly, as he sat down and drew her to his side.

"Oh, papa! You know! Woodburn, I mean."

"I think I have secured it," he said, "and that it will make a very delightful home for us all."

"Oh, I am so glad!" she cried, throwing her arms round his neck and giving him a vigorous hug. "When can we move in, papa?"

"In about two weeks, probably. Can you stand having to wait for that length of time?"

"I s'pose I'll have to," she said, laughing a little ruefully. "It'll help very much that I'll have you here and see you every day. Are you going to keep me shut up in this room all the time?"

"No, did I not tell you, you were no longer a prisoner?"

"Oh, yes, sir! But I — I don't care very much to — to be with Rosie and the rest."

"I prefer that you should not be, except when I am present," he returned gravely. "I want to keep you with me as much as possible, and would rather have you alone, or with Evelyn, Max, and Gracie only, when I am not with you."

"I like that best, too, papa," she replied humbly, "for I can't trust myself not to get into a passion with Rosie and her dog, and I suppose you can't trust me either."

"Not yet, daughter," he said gently, "but I hope the time will come when I can. Now we will attend to the lessons."

When the recitations were finished, "Papa," she said with an affectionate, admiring look up into his face, "I think you are a very nice teacher. You make everything so clear and plain and so interesting. I'm glad you're the gentleman who is to have charge of me," she added with a happy laugh.

"So am I," he said, caressing her. I am very glad, very thankful, to be able to take charge of all my children. And whatever I may lack in experience and ability as a teacher, I hope to make up in the deep interest I shall always feel in the welfare and progress of my pupils."

She then told him of Evelyn's wish, concluding with, "Won't you, dear papa? I'd like it so much, and Eva is such a good girl you wouldn't have a bit of trouble managing her. She's just as different from me as possible."

"Quite a recommendation, and if I were as sure of proving a competent teacher, I should not hesitate to grant your request. But it is a new business to me, and perhaps it would not be wise for me to undertake the tutelage of more than my own three at present. However," he added, seeing her look of disappointment, "I will take the matter into consideration."

"Oh, thank you, sir! Papa, I've just thought of two things I want to talk to you about."

"Very well, let me hear them."

"The first is about my being so naughty at Viamede," she went on, hanging her head, and blushing deeply, "in such a passion at Signor Foresti, and so obstinate and disobedient to Grandpa Dinsmore."

"I was very sorry to hear of it all," he said gravely, "but what about it?"

"Don't you have to punish me for it?" she asked, half under her breath.

"No, the punishment I gave you the other night settled all accounts up to that date."

She breathed more freely.

"Papa, would you have made me go back to that horrid man after he struck me?"

"It is not worth while to consider that question at this late day. Now, what else?" he asked.

"Papa, I spoiled one of those valuable books of engravings belonging to Grandpa Dinsmore — no, I didn't exactly spoil it myself, but I took it out on the veranda without leave, and carelessly left it where Rosie's dog could get at it. He scratched and gnawed and tore it, till it is almost ruined."

"I shall replace it at once," he said. "I am sorry you were so careless, and particularly that you took the book out there without permission. But that was not half so bad as flying into a passion, even if you hurt nothing or no one but yourself."

"But I did get into a passion, papa, at the dog and at Rosie," she acknowledged in a frightened tone, and blushing more deeply than before.

"I am deeply grieved to hear it," he said.

"And won't you have to punish me for that, and for getting the book spoiled?"

"No, didn't I tell you just now that all accounts were settled up to the other night?"

"Papa, you're very, very kind," she said, putting her arm round his neck and laying her head on his shoulder.

"I am glad that, with all your faults, my little daughter is so truthful and so open with me," he said smoothing her hair.

"Papa, I'm ever so sorry you'll have to pay so much money to replace that book," she said. "But — you often give me some pocket money, and — won't you please keep all you would give me till it counts up enough to pay for the book?"

"It is a right feeling, a feeling that pleases me, which prompts you to make that request," he said in a kind tone. And pressing his lips to her cheek he said, "Probably another time I may let you pay for such a piece of carelessness, but you need not in this instance. I feel rich enough to spare the money quite easily for that and an increase in my children's weekly allowance. What is yours now?"

"Fifty cents, papa."

"Where is your purse?"

She took it from her pocket and put it into his hand.

"Only five cents in it," he remarked with a smile when he had examined it.

Then, taking a handful of loose change from his pocket, he counted out four bright quarters and ten dimes and poured them into her purse.

"Oh, papa! So much!" she cried delightedly. "I feel ever so rich!"

He laughed at that. "Now," he said, "you shall have a dollar every week, unless I should have to withdraw it on account of some sort of bad behavior on your part. Max is to have the same. Gracie will have half a dollar till she is a little older, and you are all to keep an account of your spendings."

He took from another pocket three little blank books.

"One of these is for you, the others are for your brother and sister," he said. "See, there is a blank space for every day in the week, and whenever you lay out money, you must write down in the proper place what it was that you bought and how much it cost."

"And show it to you, papa?"

"Once in a while. Probably, whenever I hand you your allowance I shall look over your account for the week that is just past, and tell you what I think of the way you have laid out your money, in order to help you to learn to spend it judiciously."

CHAPTER EIGHTEENTH

Fortune is merry,
And in this mood will give us any thing.

THERE WAS A SOUND of small, hurrying feet in the hall without, a tap at the door; and Max's voice asked, "May I come in?"

"Yes," said his father and instantly the door was thrown wide. Evelyn came in with a quiet, lady-like step, and Max and Grace more boisterously.

The captain rose, shook hands with Eva, set her a chair, and sat down again, drawing Gracie to his arms, while Max stood at his side.

"Oh, what are those for?" he asked, catching sight of the blank books.

"This is for you, this is for Grace," the captain answered, bestowing them as he spoke. Then, he went on to repeat substantially what he had just been saying to Lulu and to replenish their purses as he had hers.

They were both delighted, both grateful.

Evelyn looked on, well pleased. "Now your allowance is just the same as mine, and I am so glad," she said to Lulu. "I have never kept an account, but I think it must be a good plan, and I mean to after this."

"There is another thing, children," said the captain. "Any money that we have is only lent to us by our heavenly Father, and it is our duty to set aside a certain portion for giving to His cause."

"How much, papa?" asked Max.

"People have different ideas about that," was the reply. "In Old Testament times, the rule was one-tenth of all, and I think most people should not give less now. Many are able to give a great deal more. I hope each of you will be glad to give as much as that."

He opened Lulu's Bible, lying on the table, and read aloud, " 'He who soweth sparingly, shall reap also sparingly, and he who soweth bountifully, shall also reap bountifully. Every man according as he purposeth in his heart, so let him give; not grudgingly, or of necessity; for God loveth a cheerful giver.' "

"I'll give a tenth of all," said Lulu. "I mean to buy a little purse on purpose to keep my tenth in, and I'll put two of these dimes in it. That will be the tenth of the two dollars you've given me, won't it, papa?"

"Yes," he said.

"And I'll do the same," said Max.

"I, too," added Gracie.

"It is just what my papa taught me to do," remarked Evelyn modestly.

"Would you children all like to take a drive with me this afternoon?" asked the captain.

There was a simultaneous and joyful assent from his own three. Then Evelyn said, "Thank you, sir. I should like it extremely, if I can get permission. Aunt Elsie expects me home for dinner, but I will go now to the telephone, and ask if I may stay and accept your invitation."

"And while you are doing that, I will go to my wife, and try to persuade her to join our party," the captain said, leaving the room.

Evelyn had no difficulty in gaining permission to stay at Ion for the rest of the day, or going anywhere Captain Raymond might propose to take her. And he found but little difficulty in persuading Violet to accompany him in a drive that would take her from her baby for an hour or two, the little one being so much better that she did not fear to leave her in charge of her mother and the nurse, thinking it might die before her return.

"The carriage will be at the door in ten or fifteen minutes after we leave the dinner table," the captain told them all and each one promised to be ready to start at once.

The children came down the stairs and out upon the veranda together, and only a little in advance of the captain and Violet.

There was a simultaneous exclamation of surprise as they saw, not the Ion family carriage, but a new and very handsome one with a pair of fine matched horses which none of them had ever seen before, drawn up at the foot of the veranda steps. And a few feet beyond, a servant held the bridle of a beautiful, spirited pony, whose long mane, gracefully arched neck, and glossy coat, struck them all with admiration.

The carriage horses were no less handsome or spirited. They were tossing their manes and pawing the ground with impatience to be off.

Violet turned a bright, inquiring look upon her husband, while all three of his children were asking in eager, excited terms, "Papa, papa, whose carriage and horses are these?"

"Ours," he said, handing Violet to a seat in the vehicle. Then, as he helped Evelyn in, "Max, my son, if you will ride that pony, there will be more room here for the rest of us."

"Oh, papa, may I?" cried the boy in tones of delight. "Did you hire it for me?"

"No, I only bought it for you. Mount and let me see how well you can manage him — how well you have improved your opportunities for learning to ride."

Max needed no second invitation, but had vaulted into the saddle before his father was done speaking.

"Now put him through his paces," was the next order.

Max wheeled about, dashed down the avenue at a rapid gallop, turned and came back at an easy canter. His father and sisters, Violet also, were watching him in proud delight — he was so handsome and sat his pony so well.

"Ah! That will do," His father said when the lad was within easy hearing distance. "These fellows," glancing at the horses attached to the carriage, "are getting too restless to stand any longer, so you may finish your exhibition at another time. I have seen enough to feel that you are quite equal to the management of your pony."

"Oh, papa, he's just splendid!" Max burst out, bending down to pat and stroke the neck of his steed, "and I can never thank you enough for such a gift."

"Enjoy him and use him kindly, that is all I ask," the captain said, entering the carriage where he had already placed his two little girls. "Drive on Scipio. Max, you may ride alongside."

"I 'spect I know where we're going," remarked Grace gleefully, and with an arch smile up into her father's face as she noticed the direction they were taking on turning out of the avenue into the high road.

"Do you?" he said. "Well, wait a little, and you will find out how good a guess you have made."

"To Woodburn, papa?" queried Lulu eagerly.

"Have patience and you will see presently," he answered with a smile.

"Mamma Vi, do you know?" she asked.

"It is your father's secret," said Violet. "I should not presume to tell you when he declines doing so."

"We shall know in a very few minutes, Lu," said Evelyn. "It is only a short drive to Woodburn."

"I was thinking about that name," said Grace. "Papa, why do they call it Woodburn? There's woods — do they burn them sometimes? They don't look as if they'd ever been burned."

"I don't think they have," he said, except such parts of them as dry twigs and fallen branches that could be picked up from the ground, or now and then a tree that was thought best cut down or that fell itself. But you know, there is a pretty little brook running across the estate, and in Scotland such a stream is called a burn. Woodburn is an appropriate name."

"Yes, papa, I think it is, and a pretty name too. Thank you for explaining it, and not laughing at my mistake."

"Even papa doesn't know nearly everything, little daughter," he said, stroking and patting the small hand she had laid on his knee, "so it would be quite out of place for him to laugh at you for asking a sensible question. We should never be ashamed to ask for information that we need. It is much wiser than to remain in ignorance for fear of being laughed at."

"And her father always gives information so kindly and patiently," remarked Violet.

"And I think he knows 'most everything," said Grace. "Oh, I did guess right, for here we are at Woodburn."

They drove and walked about the grounds, admiring, criticizing, planning improvements, then called on Miss Elliott, and, with her readily accorded permission, went over the house.

Violet and the captain selected a suite of rooms for their own occupation, and he decided which the children should use.

A bedroom opening from their own was selected for Grace, the adjoining room beyond for Lulu; and another into which both these latter opened, they were told should be their own little sitting room.

Besides these, a tiny apartment in a tower, communicating with Lulu's bedroom was given to her. The sitting room opened into the hall also, so that it was not necessary to pass through one bedroom to reach the other.

They were all bright, cheerful rooms with a pleasant view from every window. In the sitting room there were French windows opening upon a balcony.

The little girls were almost speechless with delight when told by their father that these four apartments were to be appropriated solely to their use.

Lulu caught his hand and kissed it, tears of mingled joy and penitence springing to her eyes.

He smiled down at her, and laid his other hand tenderly on her head for an instant.

Then, turning to Max, "Now, my boy," he said, "we must settle where you are to lodge. Have you any choice?"

"Is it to be more than one room for me, papa?" he asked with an arch smile. "I believe boys don't usually fare quite as well as girls in such things."

"My boy does," returned his father. "You have two or three rooms if you want them, and quite as well furnished as those of your sisters."

"Then, if you please, papa, I'll take those over Lu's, and thank you very much. But as you have already given me several things that my sisters haven't got — a gun, a watch, and that splendid pony — I think it would be quite fair that they should have better and prettier furniture in their rooms than I in mine."

"That makes no difference, Max," his father answered with a pleased laugh. "I should hardly want the girls to have guns, but watches and ponies they shall have by the time they are as old as you are now."

At that the two little girls, standing near, exchanged glances of delight. They had been unselfishly glad for Max, and now they rejoiced each for herself and for the other.

Though, in common with all the rest, deeply interested in the new home, Max was not sorry when his father and Violet decided that it was time to return to Ion. He was eager to show his pony to Grandma Elsie, Zoe, and Rosie, who had not yet seen it.

"Papa, do you require me to keep alongside of the carriage?" he asked as he remounted.

"No, if you wish you may act as our avant courier," was the smiling reply. "I quite understand that you are in haste to display your new treasure."

"Yes, sir, that was why I asked. Thank you, sir," and away the lad flew, urging his pony to a rapid gallop.

He reached Ion some minutes in advance of the carriage, found nearly all of the family who had remained at home on the veranda. He greatly enjoyed their exclamations of surprise and admiration at the sight of his steed.

As he drew rein at the foot of the steps and lifted his hat to the ladies, Zoe and Rosie came hurriedly forward to get a nearer view. The first exclaimed, "What a beautiful pony! Where did he come from, Max?"

Rosie asking, "Whose is it?"

"Mine, a present from papa," replied Max, sitting proudly erect and patting the pony's neck, "but I don't know where he came from, Aunt Zoe. You'll have to ask papa if you want to know."

"You're in luck, Maxie," she said lightly.

"Yes, indeed. I was born in luck when I was born my father's son."

"Of course you were," she returned, laughing. "Where are the others? Oh, here they come!" as she caught sight of the captain's new carriage just turning in at the avenue gates.

Those who were in it were a merry, happy party, who, all the way as they came, had been discussing plans for making the new home more convenient, comfortable, and beautiful, and for the life they were to live in it.

Woodburn was the principal theme of conversation in the evening also, the entire family being gathered in the parlor, and no visitors present.

"Tell us about your nursery, Vi," said her mother. "Where is it?"

"Next to our sleeping room, mamma, on the other side from Gracie's. You may be sure we want our little ones near us."

"But is it a pleasant room?"

"None brighter or cheerier in the house, mamma. It is of good size too, and we mean to have it furnished with every comfort and in a way to make it as attractive as possible."

"Pleasantly suggestive pictures among other things?"

"Yes, mamma. I know from our own happy experience that they have a great deal to do with educating a child."

"In both morals and art?" said the captain, looking smilingly at her. "I should think so, judging from what my wife is. And surely it is reasonable to expect a child to be, to some extent, a reflection of its surroundings — refined or vulgar, according to the style of faces — living or pictured — it is constantly gazing upon. But, however that may be, we will try to keep upon the safe side, furnishing only what must have a good influence, so far as it has any at all."

Lulu was there, sitting as close to her father as she could well get. She had a feeling that it was the only safe place for her.

"Shall I have some pictures on my walls, papa?" she asked in a low aside.

"Yes, we will go some day soon to the city and choose some fine engravings for your rooms, Max's and Gracie's — furniture, too, carpets, curtains and new paper for the walls."

"Oh, but that will be delightful!" she exclaimed. "Papa, you are just too good and kind for anything."

Max, who was near at hand, had overheard. "That's so!" he said. "I suppose you mean I am to go, too, papa?"

"Yes, Gracie also. My dear," to Violet, "when will it suit you to accompany us? Tomorrow?"

"Tomorrow is Saturday," she said reflectively. "Suppose we say Monday? I hope baby will be so much better by that time, that I shall feel easy in leaving her for a long day's shopping."

"Very well," he said, "we will go Monday morning if nothing happens to prevent."

"Lulu looks as if she did not know how to wait so long," Violet said, smiling kindly on the little girl. "Can't you take her and Gracie tomorrow and again on Monday? Surely they can select some things for their own rooms with you to help them."

"No. I want your taste as well as my own and theirs, and Lulu must learn to wait. It is a lesson she needs," he added, looking down at her with grave kindliness, and pressing affectionately the hand she had slipped into his.

She flushed and cast down her eyes.

"Yes, papa," she murmured, "I will try to be good and patient. I'm sure I ought to be when you are so very good to me."

"Now, captain, if my taste and judgment were considered equal to Vi's, and Lulu might be spared that lesson," remarked Zoe, laughingly, "I'd offer to go in her place — Vi's, I mean. I think it would be great fun to help choose pictures, carpets and furniture."

"Thank you, Zoe. That is a kind offer," said Violet. "And if mamma thinks it an enjoyable errand and will consent to supplement your taste and judgment with hers, they will be a good deal more than equal to mine," she concluded with a smiling glance at her mother.

~ 173 ~

"I am quite of Zoe's opinion as to the pleasantness of the object of the expedition, Vi," Elsie said, "and quite at the service of the captain and yourself, to go, or to take your place in watching over baby while you go. And I think you will find it necessary to spend more than one or two days in the work of selecting what you will want for the furnishing of your home."

"I dare say you are right about that, mother," said the captain, "and as it seems to be the desire of all parties that the work should be begun tomorrow, I think I will take the children and as many of you ladies as may like to accompany us."

"Papa, mayn't we drive to the city in the new carriage?" pleaded Lulu. "I'd like it ever so much better than going in the cars. And then we can drive from one store to another, without having to take the street cars or a hack."

"It shall be as the ladies who decide to go with us may wish," he said.

"I think Lulu's plan a very good one," said Grandma Elsie, kindly desirous to see the child gratified.

"And I would greatly prefer it, if I should be one of the party," said Zoe.

"As I trust you will," returned the captain gallantly. "Gracie, daughter, it is time little ones like you were in their nests. Bid goodnight and go."

The child obeyed instantly and cheerfully.

"And I must go back to my baby," Violet remarked as she rose and left the room along with the little girl.

"You may go to your room, Lulu," the captain said in a quiet aside, "but you need not say goodnight to me now. I shall step in to look at you before I go to mine."

"Yes, papa," she returned with a glad look and followed Grace's example.

"Max, what do you say to a promenade on the veranda with your father?" Captain Raymond asked, with a smiling glance at his son.

Max jumped up with alacrity. "That I'd like nothing better, sir," he said, and they went out together.

"You are pleased with your pony, Max?" the captain said inquiringly, striking a match and lighting a cigar as he spoke.

"Yes, indeed, papa!" was the enthusiastic reply. "I feel very rich owning him."

"And mean to be a kind master to him, I trust?"

"Yes, sir, oh, yes indeed! I don't intend ever to speak a cross word to him, much less give him a blow."

"He has always been used to kind treatment, I was told, and has nothing vicious in his disposition," the captain continued, puffing at his cigar and pacing the veranda with measured tread — Max keeping close at his side — "so I think he will always give you satisfaction, if you are gentle and kind, never ill-treating him in any way."

"I mean to make quite a pet of him, sir," Max said.

Then, with an arch look up into his father's face — a full moon making it light enough for each to see the other's countenance quite distinctly — "Papa, you are very generous to me, but you never offer me a cigar."

The captain stopped short in his walk and faced his son with some sternness of look and tone. "Max, you haven't learned to smoke? Tell me, have you ever smoked a cigar, or tobacco in any shape?"

"Yes, sir, but — "

"Don't do it again. I utterly and positively forbid it."

"Yes, sir. I'll obey. In fact, I have no desire to smoke again. It was just one cigar I tried and it made me so deathly sick that I've never wanted another. I wouldn't have done it, papa, if you had ever forbidden me. But — but you had never said anything to me on the subject, and I'd seen — " Max hesitated and left his sentence unfinished.

"You had seen your father smoke and, naturally, thought you might follow his example?"

"Yes, sir."

"Well, my son, I can hardly blame you for that, but there are some things a man may do with impunity, that a boy may not. Tobacco is said to be far more injurious to one who has not attained his growth than to an adult. But it is not seldom injurious to the latter also. Some seem to use it with no bad effect, but it has wrought horrible suffering for many. I am sorry I ever formed the habit and I would save you from the same regret, or something worse. Indeed, so anxious am I to do so, that I would much rather have a thousand dollars than a cigar, if I thought you would smoke it."

"Papa, I promise you I will never try the thing again — never touch tobacco in any shape," Max said earnestly.

"Thank you, my son, and I will give up the habit for your sake," returned his father, grasping the lad's hand with one of his, and, with the other, flinging his cigar far down the avenue.

"Oh, no, papa! Don't do it for my sake," said Max. "Cousin Arthur told me that when a man had smoked for years, it cost him a good deal of suffering to give it up, and I couldn't bear to see you suffer so. I'll refrain all the same, without your stopping."

"I don't doubt that you would, my dear boy, and I fully appreciate the affection for me that prompts you to talk in that way," the captain said, "but I have set a bad example quite long enough, not to my own son alone, but to others. And what ever I may have to endure in breaking off from the bad habit will be more than I deserve for contracting it. I should be very sorry, Max, to have you feel that you have a coward for a father — a man who would shrink from the course he felt right, rather than endure pain — mental or physical."

"A coward! Oh, papa! I could never think that of you!" cried the boy, flushing hotly, "and if ever any fellow should dare to hint such a thing in my hearing, I'd knock him down as quick as a flash."

The corners of the captain's lips twitched, but his tones were grave enough as he said, "I don't want you to do any fighting on my account, Max. If anybody slanders me, I shall try to live it down."

"There is another thing I want to talk to you about," he went on presently, "and that is the danger of tampering with intoxicating drinks. The only safe plan is to let them entirely alone. I am thankful to be able to say that I have not set you a bad example in that direction. My good mother taught me to 'touch not, taste not, handle not,' and I have never taken so much as a glass of wine; though there have been some times, my boy, when it required some moral courage to stand out against the persuasions, and especially the ridicule, of my companions."

Max's eyes sparkled. "I know it must, papa," he said, "and when I am tried in the same way, I'll remember my father's example, and try to act as bravely as he did."

CHAPTER NINETEENTH

Train up a child in the way he should go.

— PROVERB 22:6

"PAPA, I WANT to ask for something," was Lulu's eager salutation, as, in accordance with his promise, he stepped into her room on the way to his own, to bid her goodnight.

"Well, daughter," he said sitting down and drawing her into his arms, "there is scarcely anything that gives me more pleasure than gratifying any reasonable request from you. What is it you want?"

"Leave to invite Evelyn to go with us tomorrow, if you don't think it will make too many, papa."

"I suppose it would add greatly to your enjoyment to have her with you," he said reflectively. "Yes, you may ask her, or I will do so, early in the morning, through the telephone, if the weather is such that we can go."

"Thank you, you dear papa," she said giving him a hug and kiss. "I ought to be a very good girl, for you are always so kind to me."

She was up betimes the next morning, eagerly scanning the sky, which, to her great delight, gave every indication of fair weather for the day.

She hastened to array herself in suitable attire for her trip to the city — having consulted Grandma Elsie on the subject the night before — and had just finished when she heard her father's step in the hall.

She ran to open the door.

"Good morning, little daughter," he said with a smile, and stooping to give her a caress. "I have just been to the telephone. Evelyn will go with us and I trust you will both enjoy your day."

"Oh, I know I shall!" she cried. "It will be just delightful! Are we all to go in the carriage, papa?"

"All but Max — he prefers to ride his pony."

"I should think he would. I'm so glad you gave it to him, papa!" There was not a trace of envy or jealousy in her look or tone.

"Wouldn't you like to have one?" he asked.

"Oh, yes, indeed, papa! But," hanging her head and blushing deeply, "I don't deserve it."

"I intend to give you one as soon as you have learned to have patience under provocation, so that I shall be able to trust you to treat him kindly," he said. "How soon do you think that will be?"

"I don't know, papa. It will be a good while before I can feel at all sure of myself," she answered humbly.

"I hope it will," he said. Then, as she looked up in surprise, "The apostle says, 'When I am weak, then am I strong.' When we feel our own weakness and look to God for help, then we are strong with a strength far greater than our own; but when we grow self-confident and trust in our own strength, we are very apt to find it but weakness.

"And now I must caution you to be on your guard today against any exhibition of self will and ill temper if your wishes are overruled by those older and wiser than yourself."

"Why, papa, am I not to be allowed to choose the things for my own rooms?" she asked in a tone of deep disappointment.

"I intend that your taste shall be consulted, my child," he said, "but I cannot promise that you shall have, in every case, exactly what you most prefer. You might select carpets, curtains, and upholstery of material and colors that would wear poorly or fade very soon. Therefore, we must take Grandma Elsie into our counsels and get her to help in deciding what to take. I am sure you would like neither to have your rooms disfigured with faded, worn out furnishings or to put your father to the expense of refurbishing for you very soon."

"Oh, no, papa! No, indeed," she said.

"Besides," he went on, "don't you wish to consult my taste too? Would you not have your rooms pleasing to my eyes when I pay a visit to them, as I shall every day?"

"Oh, yes, papa! Yes, indeed! I think I shall care more for that than to have them look pretty to myself," she answered with a look of eager delight, the cloud having entirely cleared from her brow.

"Then, I think we are not likely to have any trouble," he said smoothing her hair caressingly and smiling approvingly upon her.

"Now we will go down to breakfast, and we are to set out very soon after the meal is over." He rose and took her hand in his to lead her down to the breakfast room.

"Papa," she said, looking up at him with eyes shining with filial love, "how kind you were to reason with me in that nice way, instead of saying sternly as you might have done, 'Now, Lulu, if you are naughty about the choice of things for furnishing your rooms, you sha'n't have anything pretty for them, and when we get home I'll punish you severely!'"

"Certainly, I might have done that and probably with the effect of securing your good behavior," he said, "but I think neither of us would have felt quite so happy as we do now."

"I am sure I should not," she said lifting his hand to her lips.

That little talk had a most happy effect upon Lulu, so that throughout the entire day she showed herself as docile and amiable as anyone could have desired.

Her father, on his part, was extremely indulgent toward all three of his children in every case in which he felt that it was right and wise to be so, sparing no reasonable expense to gratify their tastes and wishes. But in several matters they yielded readily to his or Grandma Elsie's better judgment — indeed, always, when asked to do so, seeming, too, well satisfied with the final decision.

They returned home a very happy set of children, except, in Lulu's case, when memory recalled the passionate outburst of the early part of the week with its dire consequences — that remembrance would be a sore spot in her heart and a bitter humiliation for many a day, probably for the rest of her life.

Rosie was on the veranda awaiting their arrival.

"Well, have you had a good time and bought great quantities of pretty things?" she asked, addressing the company in general.

It was Zoe who answered first.

"Yes, if these young Raymonds are not satisfied with the furnishings of their apartments, I, for one, shall deem them the most unreasonable and ungrateful of human kind."

"She won't have a chance to, though," said Max, "for we're delighted with everything papa has got for us. Aren't we, Lu and Gracie?"

"Yes, indeed!" they both replied. "Oh, we have ever so many beautiful things! Papa and grandma Elsie helped us choose them, so, of course, they are all just right," added Lulu, looking gratefully from one to the other.

"She takes no account of my very valuable assistance," laughed Zoe.

"Never mind, you are sure to be appreciated in one quarter," said Edward, coming up at that moment, catching her round the waist and bestowing a hearty kiss upon each cheek. "I have been lost without my wife all day."

"How good of you!" she returned merrily. "I doubt if it isn't a very good plan to run away occasionally that I may be the more highly appreciated on my return."

"Would you advise me to do likewise, and for the same reason, lady mine?" he asked, drawing her caressingly aside from the little group now busily occupied in telling and hearing about the day's purchases.

"No, sir," she said, tossing back her curls, and looking up into his face with a bewitchingly saucy smile. "You'd better not attempt it, lest there should be mutiny in the camp. When you go, I go too."

"Turn about, fair play," he said knitting his brows. "I claim the privilege of being quite as independent as you are — when you can't plead delegated authority from the doctor," and drawing her hand within his arm, he led her away to their private apartments.

Violet, hurrying down to welcome her husband home, passed them on the stairway.

"You two happy children!" she said, glancing smilingly back at them.

"Children!" echoed Edward. "Mrs. Raymond, how can you be so disrespectful to your older brother? — your senior by some two years."

"Ah! But your united ages are much less than Levis's and mine, and husband and wife make but one, don't they?" she returned gaily, as she tripped away.

Baby was almost herself again and the young mother's heart was full of gladness.

She joined the group on the veranda, her husband receiving her with a glad smile and tender caress. And standing by his side, her hand on his shoulder, his arm half supporting her slight, girlish form, she listened with lively interest to the story his children were telling so eagerly of papa's kindness and generosity to them, and the many lovely things bought to make beautiful and attractive the rooms in the new home that were to be specifically theirs.

He let them talk without restraint for some moments, then said pleasantly, "Now, my dears, it is time for you to go and make yourselves neat for the tea table. Anything more you think of that would be likely to interest Rosie and Walter, you can tell them afterwards."

The order was obeyed promptly and cheerfully, even by Lulu.

When the excitement of telling about their purchases and all the day's experiences was over the children found themselves very weary — the two little girls at least. Max wouldn't acknowledge that he was at all fatigued, but was quite willing to comply with his father's suggestion that it would be wise for him, as well as for his sisters, to go to bed early.

While Lulu was making ready for hers, her thoughts turned upon the morrow, bringing with them a new source of disquiet.

"Papa," she said pleadingly when he came in to bid her goodnight, "mayn't I stay at home tomorrow?"

"Stay at home from church? Not unless you are sick, or the weather quite too bad for you to go out. Why should you wish it?"

"Because — because — I — I'm afraid people have heard about — about how bad I was the other day. And — so I — I can't bear to go by folks out of the house that know who I am, and what happened the other day."

My child, I am sorry for you," he said, taking her on his knee, "but it is a part of the punishment you have brought upon yourself, and will have to bear it."

"But let me stay at home tomorrow, won't you?"

"No, it is a duty to go to church, as well as a privilege to be allowed to do so.

" 'Not forsaking the assembling of ourselves together, as the manner of some is,' the Bible says, so I cannot allow you to absent yourself from the services of the sanctuary when you are able to attend.

"As I have told you before, I must obey the directions I find in God's Word, and, as far as lies in my power, see that my children obey them too."

"I'd rather take a whipping than go tomorrow," she muttered half under her breath.

"I hope you are not going to be so naughty that you will have to do both," he said gravely. "You have been a very good girl today and I want you to end it as such."

"I mean to, papa. I'd be ashamed to be naughty after all you have done for me, and given me today, and I mean to be pleasant about going to church tomorrow, though it'll be ever so hard, and I'm sure you wouldn't want to go if you were me."

"If you were I," he corrected. "No, if I were you, I suppose I should feel just as you do, but the question is not what we want to do, but what God bids us do.

"Jesus said, 'If ye love Me, keep my commandments,' 'He that hath my commandments and keepeth them, he it is that loveth Me.'

"It is the dearest wish of my heart to see my children His

followers, showing their love to Him by an earnest endeavor to keep all His commandments."

"Papa, you always want to do right, don't you?" she asked. "I mean, you like it; and so it's never hard for you as it is for me?"

"No, daughter, it is sometimes very far from being easy and pleasant for me to do what I feel to be my duty; for instance, when it is to inflict pain upon you, or another of my dear children, or deny you some indulgence that you crave. I should like to grant your request of tonight, if I could feel that it would be right; but I cannot, and therefore must deny it."

Lulu acquiesced in the decision with a deep sigh and half hoped that something — a storm, or even a fit of sickness — might come to prevent her from having to go to church.

But Sunday morning was as bright and clear as the one before it, and she was in perfect health; so there was no escape from the dreadful ordeal.

She ventured upon no further entreaty, knowing it would be altogether useless, and quite as much from love to her father and a real desire to please him, as from fear of punishment, behaved herself as well as possible.

But she kept as entirely in the background as she could, not looking or speaking to anyone unless directly addressed.

No one, however, gave her any reason to suppose her involvement in the baby's accident was known; and she returned to Ion with a lighter heart than she had carried with her when she went.

She had not seen the baby yet, since the fall, and though longing to do so, having an ardent affection for the winsome creature, did not dare to ask that she might.

But as she was about to go into her own room, on reaching home, her father said, "Would you like to go with me to the nursery, Lulu, and see your little sister?"

"Oh, so much, papa, if I may!" she cried eagerly. "But," half drawing back, "perhaps she — will be afraid of me."

"I trust not," he said with emotion. "I hope she does not know that you had anything to do with her fall. Come and see."

He took her hand, and led her to the nursery. The baby was awake, sitting in her nurse's lap, and looking bright, but so much thinner and paler than before her fall that tears sprang to Lulu's eyes, and she could scarce refrain from sobbing aloud.

But the little one, catching sight of her, held out her arms with a joyful cry, "Lu!"

At that, Lulu's tears fell fast.

"May I take her, papa?" she asked sobbingly, and with an entreating look up into his face. "I won't hurt her, I wouldn't for all the world!"

"You may take her," he said, his tones a trifle tremulous. "I am quite sure you would never hurt her intentionally."

Lulu gladly availed herself of the permission, took the baby in her arms and sat down with her on her lap.

"Lu, Lu!" the little one repeated in her sweet baby voice. Lulu hugged her close, kissing her again and again, and saying softly, "You dear, sweet darling, sister loves you, indeed, indeed she does!"

The captain looked on, his heart swelling with joy and thankfulness over the evident mutual affection of the two, for there had been a time when he feared Lulu would never love the child of her step-mother as she did Max and Grace.

Violet entered the room at that moment and the little scene caused her eyes to fill with tears of gladness.

She was ready for the shopping expedition the next day. The children were allowed to go too, and again had a most enjoyable time.

After that they were told lessons must be taken up again, and Lulu passed most of her time in her own room, generally engaged in preparing her tasks for her father to hear in the evening, for he was now so busy with the improvements being carried forward at Woodburn, that very often he could not attend to her recitations till after tea.

She continued to think him the kindest and most interesting teacher she had ever had, while he found, to his surprise, that he had a liking for the occupation, aside from his fatherly interest in his pupil. Max and Grace, listening to Lulu's report, grew anxious for the time when they could share her privileges.

But their waiting time would not be very long. As soon as Miss Elliott's stipulated two weeks had expired, she would leave Woodburn, and they could take possession immediately. Their father and his young wife were quite eager as they to begin the new order of things.

CHAPTER TWENTIETH

In the New Home

THE MOVING TO Woodburn was not a formidable affair, there being little to carry from Ion besides the personal belongings of parents and children. Indeed, nearly everything, even of that kind, had been sent over beforehand.

Miss Elliott went one morning and the Raymonds drove over scarcely an hour later to find the greater part of the house in perfect order, a full staff of competent servants and an excellent dinner in course of preparation.

Max and his sisters had been directed to stay away from the place ever since the day when their rooms were assigned them, and now a glad surprise awaited them.

"Come upstairs," their father said when they had made the circuit of the lower rooms. "My dear," to Violet, "will you please come, too?"

"With all my heart," she returned merrily, and tripped lightly after him up the broad stairway — the children following.

He led them first to her apartments, and on through them into those of the little girls, greatly enjoying the exclamations of wonder and delight from her and the children.

They had all supposed the work of renovation and improvement was not to be begun till after the departure of Miss Elliott, but they found it not only begun, but finished. The new wallpapers they had chosen were already on the walls, the carpets down, the curtains up, mirrors and pictures hung, and furniture in place.

Max's rooms, visited last, were found to be in like

condition — not at all inferior to those of his sisters in any respect.

Violet was greatly pleased. The children were wild with delight. Everything was so dainty and fresh; there was such an air of elegance and refinement about the appointments of each room that all were charmed with the effect.

They were hardly yet satisfied with gazing and commenting when the summons for dinner came.

They trooped down to the dining room, the captain and Violet leading the way, and seated themselves at the table.

Here, too, all was new and handsome — the linens, china, glass and silver ware, such as would not have suffered by comparison with what they had been accustomed to at Ion and Viamede.

Lulu was beginning to express that opinion, when her father silenced her by a gesture.

All quieted down at once, while he reverently gave thanks for their food and asked God's blessing upon it.

"May I talk now, papa?" she asked a moment after he had finished.

"Yes, if you have anything to say worth our hearing."

"I'm not sure about that," she said, "but I wanted to tell you how beautiful I think the china and glass and silver are."

"Ah!" he said smiling, "I am glad they meet your approval."

"Oh, papa! Such a nice, nice home as you made for us!" exclaimed Grace in her turn. "Isn't it, Maxie?" turning to her brother.

"Yes, indeed! And we'll have to be nice, nice children to fit the home, won't we, Gracie?"

"Yes, and to fit papa and mamma," she responded, sending a merry glance from one to the other.

Both smiled upon her in return.

"We are going to have a house warming this evening, Gracie," said her father. "Do you know what that is?"

No, papa, but I think it's nice and warm now in all the rooms. Don't you?"

"It is quite comfortable, I think; but the house warming will be an assembling of our relatives and friends to celebrate our coming into it by having a pleasant, social time with us."

"Oh, that will be nice!" she exclaimed. "How many are coming, papa? I s'pose you've 'vited Grandma Elsie and all the rest of the folks from Ion and all the folks at Fairview?"

"Yes, and from the Oaks, the Pines, the Laurels, Roselands, and Ashlands. And we hope they will all come."

She gave him a wistful look.

"Well," he said with a smile, "what is it?"

"Papa, you know I 'most always have to go to bed at eight o'clock. I'd like ever so much to stay up till nine tonight, if you are willing."

"If you will take a nap after dinner, you may," he replied with an indulgent tone. "Max and Lulu may stay up later than usual if they will do likewise."

They all accepted the condition with thanks, and at the conclusion of the meal retired to their respective rooms to fulfill it.

Violet also, having not yet fully recovered from the ill effects of anxiety and nursing consequent upon the baby's injury, retired to her apartments to rest and sleep.

Captain Raymond went to the library to busy himself with some correspondence first, afterwards with books and papers. He had one of these last in his hand, a pile of them on the table before him, when, from the open doorway into the hall, Lulu's voice asked, "Papa, may I come in? Are you very busy?"

"Not too busy to be glad of my little girl's company," he said, glancing up from his paper with a pleasant smile. "Come and sit on my knee."

She availed herself of the invitation with joyful haste.

"I thought you were taking a nap," he remarked as he put his arm round her and kissed the ruby lips she held up in mute request.

"So I was, papa; but you didn't intend me to sleep all the afternoon, did you?" she asked with a gleeful laugh, nestling closer to him.

"No hardly," he returned, joining in her mirth, "so much sleep in the daytime would be apt to interfere with your night's rest. I want you all to have sufficient sleep in the twenty-four hours to keep you in health of body and mind, but should be very sorry to have you become sluggards — so fond of your beds as to waste time in drowsing there that should be spent in the exercise and training of body and mind. What have you been doing besides napping?"

"Enjoying my lovely, lovely rooms, papa, and examining the closets and wardrobe and bureau to find out just where all my things have been put."

"That was well. Do you know anything about housework — sweeping, dusting, and keeping things neat and tidy?"

"Not very much, papa."

"That is to be part of your education," he said. "I want my daughters to become thorough housekeepers, conversant with all the details of every branch of the business. Gracie is not old enough or strong enough to begin that part of her training yet, but you are. So you must take care of your rooms yourself, except when something more than sweeping, dusting, and bed making is needed."

"I'd like well enough to do it sometimes, papa," she said, looking a little crestfallen, "but I don't like to be tied down to doing it every day, because some days I shall want to be busy at something else. Besides, it is so much like being a servant."

"My little girl, that isn't a right kind of pride. Honest labor is no disgrace. And 'six days shalt thou labor, and do all thy work,' is as much a command of God as the 'in it (the Sabbath) thou shalt not do any work.' "

"Yes, papa, and I don't think I'm lazy. I like to be busy, and sometimes work for hours together at my fret sawing."

"No, I have never thought you an indolent child," he said, smoothing her hair caressingly, "but I am afraid you are willful and inclined to think yourself wiser than your elders, even your father."

"Please, papa, don't think that," she said, blushing and hanging her head. "I know you are much wiser than I am."

"Is it, then, that you doubt my affection for you?" he asked seriously.

"Why, papa, how could I, when you are so good to me, and often tell me that you love me dearly?"

"What then is the trouble? If you believe your father to be both wise and loving, and if you love him and want to please him, how can you object to his plans and wishes for you?"

"But, papa, who is to teach me how to take care of my rooms? Not Mamma Vi, I suppose! I never saw her do any such work, and — would you want me taught by one of the servants?" she queried, blushing vividly.

"No," he said. "I have a better plan than that. I have engaged Christine to be housekeeper here, and she will instruct you in all housewifely arts. She is a lady in education and manners, and you need feel it no degradation to be instructed by her."

"Oh, that will be nice! And I'll try to learn to do my work well, and to like it, too, to please you, my own, dear papa," she said, looking up lovingly into his face — her own growing very bright again.

"That is right, my dear little daughter," he returned, smiling kindly upon her.

"You asked just now," he went on, "if your Mamma Vi would teach you these things. When I asked her to become my wife, I promised that she should have no care or responsibility in the matter of training and looking after the welfare of the three children I then had, because her mother objected that she was too young for such a burden — so now that I can live at home with my children, and have no business that need interfere, I shall do my best to be father and mother both to them."

"How nice, papa!" she exclaimed joyfully. "Oh, I do think we ought to be the happiest children in the world with such a dear, kind father, and such a lovely home! But —" her face clouded and she sighed deeply.

"But what, my child?"

"I was thinking of that dreadful temper that is always

getting the better of me. But you will help me to conquer it, papa?" she added half inquiringly, half in assertion.

"I fully intend to do all in my power to that end," he said in a tender tone, "but, my beloved child, the hardest part of the battle must inevitably be your own. You must watch and pray against that, your besetting sin, never allowing yourself to be a moment off your guard."

"I mean to, papa, and you will watch me and warn me when you see that I am forgetting?"

"I shall be constantly endeavoring to do so," he answered, "trying to guard and guide all my children, looking carefully after their welfare — physical, mental, moral, and spiritual.

"To that end, I have just been examining some of the reading matter which has been provided for them in my absence. So far as I have made myself acquainted with it, I decidedly approve it, as I expected I should, having all confidence in those who chose it for you — Grandpa Dinsmore and Grandma Elsie.

"This little paper, 'The Youth's Companion,' strikes me as very entertaining and instructive, also of excellent moral tone. Do you like it?"

"Oh, yes, indeed, papa! We are all very fond of it and find a great deal of useful information in it. I wouldn't be without it for a great deal, nor Max wouldn't either. And Gracie likes the part for the little folks ever so much."

"Then, we will continue to take it," he said. "Also, this magazine, 'St. Nicholas,' if you like it, as I can hardly doubt that you do."

"Indeed we do!" she exclaimed. "We wouldn't any of us like to do without that, either. Oh, I am glad you will let us go on with both that and the paper!

"Papa, where is the schoolroom? You haven't shown us that yet."

"No, and here come Max and Gracie," he said, as the two came hurrying in together. "I will show it to you now."

"What, papa?" asked Max.

"Oh! Is there something more to see?" exclaimed Grace, running to her father and putting her hand in his. "Oh, it's

~ 192 ~

ever so nice to have such a beautiful home, and so many beautiful new things to look at!"

"It is only your schoolroom this time," her father said, closing his fingers lovingly over the little hand and smiling down into the sweet blue eyes upraised so gratefully to his.

"Oh, yes, I want to see that! I'd 'most forgotten 'bout it," she said, skipping along by his side as he led the way — Max and Lulu following.

The room he had selected for the purpose was in a wing attached to the main building at the end farthest removed from Violet's apartments, for he did not want her disturbed by any noise the children might make, or them to feel constrained to keep very quiet when not engaged in study or recitation. There was a simultaneous burst of delight from the three, as he threw open the door and ushered them in. Everything had been done to render that as attractive as any other part of the mansion. The windows reached almost from the floor to ceiling, some opening on to the veranda, one looking directly out upon the lawn and flower garden with a glimpse of the wood and the brook beyond. A handsome rug covered the center of the stained and polished floor. In an open fireplace a bright wood fire was blazing, an easy chair on each side of it and a sofa on the farther side of the room seemed to invite to repose. But the handsome writing table and three pretty rosewood desks were suggestive of work to be done ere the occupants of the room might feel entitled to rest. The walls were tinted a delicate gray, an excellent background for the pictures that adorned them here and there. Most of these were marine views — that over the fireplace, a very large and fine one of a storm at sea.

On the mantel shelf were heaped sea mosses, shells and coral; but the tiles below it represented Scripture scenes. Blinds and curtains shaded the windows; and the broad, low sills were cushioned, making pleasant places to sit in.

"It will be just a pleasure to study in such a place as this," cried Max, rubbing his hands with satisfaction and smiling all over his face.

"Indeed it will! Especially with such a teacher as we are to have," chimed in Lulu.

"Oh, I'm just in ever such a hurry to begin!" said Grace. "Papa, which is my desk?"

"They are exactly alike," he said. "I thought of having yours made a trifle lower than the others, but concluded to give you a footrest instead, as you will soon grow tall enough to want it the height it now is. Max and Lulu, shall we give your little sister the first choice, as she is the youngest?"

"Yes, indeed, papa! Yes, indeed!" they both answered with hearty good will, Max adding, "And Lu must have the next, if you please, papa."

That matter being speedily settled, the next question was when school was to begin. They were all three asking it.

"You may have your choice — we will put it to vote — whether we will begin tomorrow morning or not till Monday," replied their father. "Tomorrow, you will remember, is Thursday. We will begin school regularly at nine o'clock each morning, and it is to last four hours, not including five or ten minutes at the end of every hour for rest."

"That'll be ever so nice!" was Lulu's comment.

"That's so," said Max. "I see you are not going to be hard on a fellow, papa."

"Wait till you are sure," said his father. "There's to be no idling, no half attention to study, in those hours. You are to give your whole minds to your lessons, and I shall be very strict in exacting perfect recitations."

"Do you mean, sir, that we are to repeat the answers in the book word for word?"

"No, not at all. I shall very much prefer to have you give the sense in your own words. Then I shall know that you understand the meaning of the text, and are not repeating sounds merely like a parrot — that you have not been going over the words without trying to take in the ideas they are meant to express."

"But suppose we can't catch the writer's meaning?"

"If you fail to do so after giving your best efforts to the task, your teacher will always be ready to explain to the best of his ability," was the smiling rejoinder. "But remember, all of you, that I intend you to use your own brains with as little assistance from other people's as possible. Mind as well as body grows strong by exercise."

"But we haven't decided when we are to begin," said Lulu.

"I vote for tomorrow," said Max, "afternoons will give us time enough to do anything else we want to."

"Yes, I second the motion," she said.

"And I third it," added Grace. "Now, papa, you are laughing at me, and so is Max. Wasn't that the right way to say it?"

"It was 'most as right as Lu's," said Max.

"And both will do well enough," said their father.

"I was going to ask if I might have Eva here to visit me tomorrow, papa," said Lulu, "but she'll be busy with lessons in the morning too. May I ask her to come in the afternoon?"

"Yes, you can ask her this evening. She will be here with the rest.

"Now I have something else to show you. Come with me."

He took Gracie's hand again, and led them to a small, detached building, only a few yards distant — a one-story frame, so prettily designed that it was quite an ornament to the grounds.

The children exclaimed in surprise, for, though it had been there on their former visit to Woodburn, it was so greatly changed that they failed to recognize it.

"It wasn't here before, papa, was it?" asked Grace. "I'm sure I didn't see it."

"Yes, it was here," he said as he ushered them in, "but I have altered and fitted up expressly for my children's use. You see, it is a little away from the house so that the noise of saws and hammers will not be likely to prove an annoyance to your mamma and visitors. See, this is a workroom furnished with fret and scroll saws, and every sort of tool that I know of which would be likely to prove useful to you, Max and Lulu."

"Papa, thank you! How good and kind you are to us!" they both exclaimed, glancing about them, then up into his face with sparkling eyes.

"You must have spent a great deal of money on us, sir," added Max thoughtfully.

"Yes, indeed," chimed in Lulu with a slight look of uneasiness. "Papa, I do hope you won't have to go without anything you want because you've used up so much on these and other things for us."

"No, my dears, and if you are only good and obedient, and make the best use of what I have provided, I shall never regret anything of what I have done for you.

"See here, Gracie."

He opened an inner door as he spoke and showed a playroom as completely fitted for its intended use as the room they were in. It was about the same size as the workroom, the two occupying the whole of the small building.

A pretty carpet covered the floor; a few pictures hung on the delicately tinted walls. There were chairs and a sofa of suitable size for the comfort of the intended occupants, and smaller ones on which Gracie's numerous dolls were seated. A cupboard with glass dolls showed sets of toy china dishes and all the accessories for dinner and tea table. There were also a bureau, washstand, and table corresponding in size with the rest of the furniture. The captain, pulling open the drawers of the bureau, showed them well stocked with materials of various kinds suitable for making into new garments for the dolls and with all the necessary implements — needles, thread, thimbles, scissors, etc.

The two little girls were almost breathless with astonishment and delight.

"Papa!" cried Gracie, "you haven't left one single thing for Santa Claus to bring us on Christmas!"

"Haven't I?" he returned, laughing and pinching her round, rosy cheek. "Ah, well! Wouldn't you as soon have them as presents from your own papa?"

"Oh, yes, papa! I know he's just pretend, and it would be you or some of the folks that love me," she said, laying her cheek against his hand. "But I like to pretend it, 'cause it's such fun."

"There are a good many weeks yet to Christmas time," remarked Lulu, "and perhaps our Santa Claus folks will think up something else for you, Gracie."

"Perhaps they may," said the captain, "if she is good. Good children are not apt to be forgotten or neglected, and I hope mine are all going to be such."

"I'm quite sure we all intend to try hard, papa," Max said, "not hoping to gain more presents by it, but because you've been so good to us already."

"Indeed we do!" added his sisters.

CHAPTER TWENTY-FIRST

Then all was jolity,
Feasting and mirth,
light wantonness and laughter.

"IT SEEMS NICE and warm here," remarked Lulu, "but," glancing about, "I don't see any fire."

Her father pointed to a register. "There is a cellar underneath and a furnace in it," he said. "I thought that the safest way to heat these rooms for the use of very little people. I do not want to expose you to any danger of setting yourselves on fire."

"It's getting a little dark," remarked grace.

"Yes," he said. "We will go in now. It is time for you to be dressed for the evening."

"Papa, who is to tell us what to wear — you or Mamma Vi?" asked Lulu as they pursued their way back to the house.

"You may wear your cream colored cashmere with the cherry trimmings; Gracie, hers with the blue," he replied.

"That's just what I wanted you to say, papa! I like those dresses," remarked Lulu with satisfaction.

"That is well, and Gracie, of course, is pleased for she never objects to anything papa or mamma wishes her to do," he said with a loving glance down into the little girl's face.

" 'Course not, papa, 'cause I know you and mamma always know best," she said, her blue eyes smiling up into his.

"And I mean to try to be like her in that, papa," Lulu said with unwonted humility.

"I hope so. I have no fault to find with your behavior of late," he returned kindly.

They passed into the house and in the hall met Christine and Alma.

"Ah! You have come, my good girls?" the captain said to them with a pleased look. "Jane," he said to the girl who had admitted them, "show them to their rooms."

Christine had come to assume her duties as housekeeper at Woodburn. Alma was to make her home there while still continuing to sew for the families at Ion and Fairview — an arrangement which suited the sisters admirably.

"Thanks, sir. It ees one grand place you haf here," said Christine. "We shall be very pleased to haf so nice a home."

"I hope it will prove a happy one to you both," he returned kindly. Then, as they followed Jane to the rear of the mansion he said, "Now, children, make haste with your dressing."

"Yes, sir," they replied, hurrying up the broad stairway with willing feet.

At its head they met Agnes, their mamma's maid.

"I'se to help yo' dress, Miss Lu and Miss Gracie," she said. "Miss Wi'let tole me so, and I'se laid out yo' things on yo' beds."

"What things? What dress for me?" asked Lulu sharply.

"De cream colored cashmere, what Miss Wi'let correct me to."

Lulu laughed. "Directed, you mean, Agnes. You may tie my sash when I'm ready. I can do all the rest myself," she said, passing on into her bedroom while Grace skipped merrily into hers.

"Mamma's very good to send you, Agnes," she said, "and you may please dress me as fast as you can, 'cause papa told us to make haste."

Grace was a favorite with Agnes as with all the servants at Ion.

"Ya'as, I'll dress yo' up fine, Miss Gracie, and make yo' look putty as a pink," she said, beginning her task.

"Lots ob folks comin' tonight, honey, and grand doin's gwine on in de kitchen and de dinin' room. Dere's a long table sot out in de dinin' room and heaps and heaps ob splendiferous china dishes wid fruits and flowahs painted onto 'em, and silverware bright as de sun, and glass dishes dat sparkle like Miss Elsie's di'mon's. And in de kitchen dey's cookin' turkeys and chickens and wild game ob warious kinds, and oysters in warious styles, 'sides all de pastry and cakes and fruits and ices, and — oh, I cayn't begin to tell yo' all de good things the captain has perwided! Dere wasn't never nuffin' grander at Ion or Wiamede or de Oaks or any ob de grand places belongin' to our fam'lies."

Grace was a highly interested listener.

"Oh," she said, "I want to see the table when it's all set and the good things on it! I wonder if papa will let me eat any of them."

"Maybe," said Agnes, "but you know, Miss Grace, yo's sickly — leastways, not bery strong — and de doctah doan' let you eat rich things."

"No," returned the little girl, sighing slightly, "but I do have a good many nice things. And I'd rather eat plain victuals than be weak and sick. Wouldn't you, Agnes?"

"Yass, I reckon. Dere, you's done finished, Miss Gracie, and looks sweet as a rosebud."

"So she does," said Lulu, coming hurrying in from her room, arrayed in her pretty cashmere and with a wide, rich sash-ribbon in her hand. "Now, Agnes, if you will please tie my sash, I'll be 'done finished' too."

"Oh, Lu!" exclaimed Grace in loving admiration, "I'm sure you must look twice as sweet and pretty as I do."

Their father opened the door, and stepped in just in time to hear her words, and, glancing smilingly from one to the other, said, "To papa's eyes, both his dear little girls look sweet and lovable. Agnes, their appearance does you credit. Now, my darlings, we will go down to tea, for there is the bell."

"Have the folks come, papa?" asked Grace, putting her hand into his.

"No, daughter, they will probably not begin to come for an hour or so."

"Then, are we going to have two suppers?"

"Yes, one for ourselves — the children especially — at the usual hour, and a later one for the company. That last will be too late, and too heavy for your weak digestion."

"But not for Max's and mine, will it, papa?" questioned Lulu.

"Yes, I fear so."

"But we are strong and healthy."

"And I wish to keep you so," he said pleasantly, "but you may rest assured that I shall not deny you any enjoyment I think it safe to grant you. Now sit down and be quiet till the blessing has been asked," — for they had reached the dining room and found Violet and Max there waiting for them.

Lulu had overheard a good deal of the glowing account of the coming feast to which Agnes had treated Grace. And, when at liberty to speak again, asked, in a rather disconcerted tone, if she and Max were not to have any share in the good supper being prepared for the expected guests.

Instead of answering directly, the captain turned to his son and asked, "Max, what do you think of this supper?"

"It's good enough for a king, sir," returned the lad heartily, glancing over the table as he spoke. "There's the nicest of bread and butter, plenty of rich milk and cream, canned peaches and plums, and splendid gingerbread. Why, Lu, what more could you ask?"

Lulu only blushed and hung her head in reply.

"I think it is a meal to be thankful for," remarked Violet cheerily, "but, my dear, you will let them share in some of the lighter refreshments provided for our guests, won't you?"

"Yes, I intend they shall," replied her husband. "Even Gracie can, I think, eat some ice cream with safety."

"Thank you, papa. I'll be satisfied with that, if you don't think it is best for me to have anything else," said Lulu recovering her spirits.

They had scarcely left the table when the guests began to arrive, those form Ion and Fairview coming first.

"Mamma, dearest mamma! Welcome, a thousand times welcome to our home!" exclaimed Violet, embracing her mother with ardent affection.

"I wish it were yours also, mother," the captain said. "There could be no more welcome inmate."

There were cordial, affectionate greetings for each of the others also. Then, when outdoor garments had been laid aside, all were conducted over the house, to be shown the improvements already made, and told of those still in contemplation.

It was a great delight to Lulu and grace to exhibit their pretty rooms to Evelyn and Rosie, and hear their expressions of surprise and admiration. The pleasure was repeated several times, as the little folks from the Laurels, the Oaks, and the Pines arrived, and in succession went the same round.

"I am pleased with all I have seen, Vi; but this room is especially charming to me," Grandma Elsie said, when Violet led her a second time into the nursery, the rest of the Ion party having passed on down to the parlors. "Baby should be a merry, happy child if pleasant, cheerful surroundings can make her so."

"I trust she will, mamma," returned the young mother, leading the way to the dainty crib where the little one lay sweetly sleeping.

Elsie bent over the little form, gazing at the sweet baby face with eyes brimful of motherly love and tenderness.

"The lovely, precious darling!" she murmured softly. "I am so rejoiced, so thankful, to see her looking almost herself again!"

"As we are," said Violet, in low, tremulous tones. "Her father is extremely fond of her, mamma, as he is of all his children. I think he has no favorite among them, but loves each one devotedly."

"As I do mine," Elsie responded, a bright, sweet smile lighting up her face. "I love you, My Vi, and all your brothers and sisters very dearly — each with a love differing somewhat in kind from that given to the others, but not at all in intensity."

They lingered a moment longer, watching the young sleeper. Then, with a parting injunction to the nurse to be very careful of her — not leaving her alone for an instant, they went downstairs again and rejoined the rest of the company.

Everybody had come, the last party of children just descended from the inspection of the rooms of Max and his sisters.

"Now, we have seen positively everything?" asked Rosie Travilla.

"Why, no!" cried Max, as with sudden recollection. Then hurrying to his father, who was talking on the other side of the room to Dr. Conly and Mr. Horace Dinsmore of the Oaks, he stood waiting respectfully for an opportunity to speak.

The gentlemen paused in their conversation and the captain asked, "What is it, my son?"

"We haven't shown the workroom or the playroom, papa."

"Ah, sure enough!" We must have them lighted first. Send Scipio out to put a lamp in each. Then the ladies' wraps will have to be brought down, for they would be in danger of taking cold going even that short distance without."

"I'll attend to it all, sir," Max rejoined with cheerful alacrity, and he hastened away to do so.

In a few minutes all was in readiness.

Max, announcing the fact to his father and the company in general, said dubiously, "I'm afraid we can't go all at once. The rooms aren't big enough to take in so many."

"So we will go in divisions," said Mr. Dinsmore. "There are thirty of us — not counting the Woodburn family proper. We will make five divisions, six in each, in addition to the guide and exhibitor. Does everybody consent?"

"Yes, yes," was heard on every side.

Then ensued a merry time forming the divisions and

deciding the order of precedence, for everyone was in a mirthful mood."

It was all settled at last. The visits of inspection were made. Everybody agreed in praising all they saw and congratulating Max and his sisters on the good fortune that had befallen them.

The rest of the evening passed off very pleasantly. The feast was enjoyed — every dish being pronounced a success. The Woodburn children were satisfied with the share of it allowed them — all the more, perhaps, that a like care was exercised by the parents and guardians of the other young folks in respect to their indulgence of appetite.

Grace bade goodnight and went to her nest at nine o'clock, a cheerful, happy child; but, as the party broke up at ten, Max and Lulu were allowed to remain up to see them off.

Lulu had taken an early opportunity to give the invitation for the next day to Evelyn and it was joyfully accepted — Uncle Lester giving ready permission.

"You'll come as soon as lessons are over at Ion, won't you?" asked Lulu in parting.

"Yes, you may be sure I'll come the first minute I can," Eva answered merrily. "I expect to have a lovely time with you in those lovely rooms and I've had a lovely time tonight. Goodbye," giving her friend a hearty embrace.

"Well, children," the captain said at breakfast the next morning, "remember, I expect everyone of you to be in the schoolroom at five minutes before nine and to begin studying exactly at the hour."

"Everything to be done with naval precision, I suppose," remarked Violet, giving him a bright, half-saucy smile, "that being, I understand, about on a par with military."

"Yes," he said, smiling in return, "that is to be the rule in this house for everyone but my wife — she is to follow her own sweet will in all things."

"Ah!" she responded merrily, "I fear you do not realize what a rash promise you are making, or, rather, how rash you are in according such a privilege."

"It is hardly that," he answered, "acknowledging a right would be my way of expressing it."

They had left the table and the breakfast room and were alone at the moment, the children having scattered to their work or play.

"How good you are to me, my dear husband!" she said, looking up fondly into is face as they stood together before the parlor fire.

"Not a whit better than I ought to be, my darling," he responded, bending to kiss the sweet, upturned face. "I have taken you from a tender mother and a most luxurious home, and it must be my care to see that you lose nothing by the transplantation — sweet and delicate flower that you are!"

"In my place, Zoe would call you an old flatterer," she returned with a light laugh, but a telltale moisture gathered in her eyes.

"And what do you call me, my Violet?" he asked, putting his arm about her and drawing her close to his side.

"The kindest, best, dearest of husbands, the noblest of men!"

"Ah, my dear! Who is the flatterer now?" he laughed. "I'm afraid you and I might be accused of forming a mutual admiration society."

"Well, what if we do? Isn't it the very best sort of society for husband and wife to form? Levis, am I to have no duties in this house — none of the cares and labors that the mistress of an establishment is usually expected to assume?"

"You shall have no care of housekeeping that I can save you from," he said. "I understand that, with Christine as my head assistant — though you, of course, are mistress, with the right to give orders and directions whenever you will — to housekeeper, servants, children, even to your husband if you see fit," he concluded with a humorous look and smile.

"The idea of ordering you whom I have promised to obey," she returned merrily. "But I'm afraid you are going to spoil me. Am I to have nothing to do?"

"You are to do exactly what you please," he said. "The

care and training of our little one, aside from all the assistance to be had from servants, will furnish you with no small amount of employment.'

"But you will help me with that?"

"Certainly, love. I intend to be as good and faithful a father to her as I know how to be, but you are her mother, and will do a mother's part by her, I know. Then, there are wifely duties which you would not wish to delegate to anyone else."

"No, never!" she cried. "Oh, my dear husband, it is the greatest pleasure in life to do anything I can to add to your comfort and happiness!"

"I know it, sweet wife. Ah!" glancing at his watch, "I must tear myself away now from your dear society and attend to the duties of employer and teacher. I have some directions to give both employees and children."

Grace ran and opened the schoolroom door at the sound of her father's approaching footsteps.

"See, papa," she said, "we are all here, waiting for you to come and tell us what lessons to learn."

"Yes, you are good, punctual children," he replied, glancing at the pretty little clock on the mantel, "for it still wants five minutes to nine."

"Papa, I know what lessons to learn, of course," remarked Lulu, "but the others are waiting for you to tell them."

"Yes. I shall examine Max first," the captain said, seating himself at his writing table. "Bring your books here, my son."

"Are you dreadfully frightened, Maxie? Very much afraid of your new teacher?" Lulu asked laughingly as her brother obeyed the order.

"I don't expect to faint with fright," he returned, "for I've a notion he's pretty fond of me."

"Of you and of all my pupils," the captain said. "Lulu, you may take out your books and begin to study."

When the tasks had been assigned to each he said, "Now children, I am going to leave you for a while. I can do so without fear that you will take advantage of my absence to idle away your time, for I know that you are honorable and trustworthy, also obedient. I have seldom known any one of you to disobey an order from me."

"Thank you, papa," Max said, answering for both himself and sisters and coloring with pleasure as he spoke. "We'll try to deserve your praise and confidence. But are we to consider ourselves forbidden to speak at all to each other while you are gone?"

"No, not entirely, but do not engage in unnecessary talk to the neglect of your studies."

So saying, he went out and left them.

Returning exactly at the expiration of the first hour of study, he found them all busily at work.

He commended them their industry and gave permission for five minutes' rest.

They were prompt to avail themselves of it, and gathered about him full of gleeful chat, the girls seating themselves one on each knee, Max standing close at his side.

School was a decided success that day, and neither teacher nor pupil saw any reason to regret the establishment of the new order of things.

Evelyn came soon after they were dismissed, spent the afternoon and evening, and, when she left, averred that it had been the most delightful visit she had ever paid.

CHAPTER TWENTY-SECOND
Life at Woodburn

LULU'S TEMPER was not conquered, but she was more successful than formerly in combating it. The terrible lesson she had had in the injury to her baby sister, consequent upon her outburst of passion, could not be easily forgotten. The bitter recollection was often a great restraint for her, and her father's loving watchfulness saved her many a time, when, without it, she would have fallen. He kept her with him almost constantly when at home — and he was rarely absent — scarcely allowed her to go anywhere off the estate without him, and seemed never for a moment to forget her and her special temptation. The slightest elevation in the tones of her voice was sure to catch his ear, and a warning look generally proved sufficient to put her on her guard, and check the rising storm of anger.

There were several reasons why it was — as she often asserted — easier to be good with him than with Mr. Dinsmore. He was more patient and sympathizing, less ready to speak with stern authority, though he could be stern enough when he deemed it necessary. Besides, he was her father, whom she greatly reverenced and dearly loved, and who had, as she expressed it, a right to rule her and to punish her when she deserved it.

One morning, after several very happy weeks at Woodburn, the quiet of the schoolroom, which had been profound for many minutes, was broken by a slight exclamation of impatience from Lulu.

Her father, glancing up from the letter he was writing, saw an ominous frown on her brow, as she bent over her slate, setting down figures upon it and quickly erasing them again, with a sort of feverish haste, shrugging her shoulders fretfully, and pushing her arithmetic peevishly aside with the free hand.

"Lulu, my daughter," he said in a quiet tone, "put on your hat and coat and take a five-minutes' run on the driveway."

"Just now, papa?" she asked, looking up in surprise.

"Yes, just now. When you think you have been out the specified number of minutes, you may come back, but I shall not find fault with you if you are not quite punctual, as you will not have a timepiece with you."

"Thank you, sir," she said, obeying with alacrity.

She came in again presently with cheeks glowing and eyes sparkling, not a cloud on her brow.

"Ah! I see you feel better," her father remarked, smiling kindly upon her, "and I have finished my letter, so have time to talk with you. Max and Gracie, you may take your turn at a run in the fresh air now."

Donning their outdoor garments, while Lulu took hers off and put them in their proper place, they hurried away.

"Bring your slate and book here, daughter," was the next order, in the kindest of tones, "and let me see what was troubling you so."

"It's these vulgar fractions, papa," she said, giving herself an impatient shake. "I don't wonder they call them vulgar, for they're so hateful! I can't understand the rule, and I can't get the examples right. I wish you wouldn't make me learn them."

"Daughter, daughter!" he said in grave, reproving accents, "don't give way to an impatient temper. It will only make matters worse."

"But, papa," she said, bringing the book and slate as directed, "won't you please let me skip these vulgar fractions?"

"I thought," he said, "that my Lulu was a brave, persevering little girl, not ready to be overcome by a slight difficulty."

"Oh! But it isn't a slight one, papa. It's big and hard!" she pleaded.

"I will go over the rule with you, and try to make it clear," he returned, still speaking in a pleasant tone. "Then we will see what we can do with these troublesome examples."

She sighed almost hopelessly but gave her attention fully to his explanation, and presently cried out joyfully, "Oh, I do understand it now, papa! And I believe I can get the sums right."

"I think you can," he said. "Stand here by my side and let me see you try."

She succeeded and was full of joy.

"There is nothing like trying, my little girl," he said, smiling at her exultation and delight.

She came to him again after lessons were done, and Max and grace had left the room once more.

"May I talk a little to you, papa?" she asked.

"Yes, more than a little, if you wish," he replied, laying aside the book he had taken up. "What is it?"

"Papa, I want to thank you for sending me out to take a run, and then helping me so nicely and kindly with my arithmetic."

"You are very welcome, my darling," he said, drawing her to a seat upon his knee.

"If you hadn't done it, papa, or if you had spoken sternly to me as Grandpa Dinsmore would have done in your place, I'd have been in a great passion in a minute. I was feeling like just picking up my slate and dashing it to pieces against the corner of the desk."

"How grieved I should have been had you done so!" he said, "very, very sorry for your wrong doing and that I should have to keep my word in regard to the punishment to be meted out for such conduct."

"Yes, papa," she murmured, hanging her head and blushing deeply.

"Would breaking the slate have helped you?" he asked with grave seriousness.

"Oh, no, papa! You cannot suppose I'm so foolish as to think it would."

"Was it the fault of the slate that you had such difficulty with your examples?"

"Why, no, papa, of course not."

"Then, was it not extremely foolish, as well as wrong, to want to break it just because of your want of success with your ciphering?"

"Yes, sir," she reluctantly admitted.

He went on, "Anger is a great folly. The Bible says, 'Be not hasty in thy spirit to be angry; for anger resteth in the bosom of fools.' It seems to be the sort of foolishness that, more than any other, is bound in the heart of this child of mine. It seems, too, that nothing but 'the rod of correction' will drive it out."

She gave him a frightened look.

"No," he said, "you need not be alarmed — as you did not indulge your passionate impulse, I have no punishment to inflict.

"My dear, dear child, try, try to conquer the propensity! Watch and pray against this besetting sin."

"I will, papa," she murmured with a half despairing sigh.

Some weeks later — it was on an afternoon early in December — Lulu and Grace were in their own little sitting room busied in the manufacture of some small gifts for papa and Maxie, who were, of course, to be kept in profound ignorance on the subject till the time of presentation. Therefore, the young workers sat with locked doors.

When presently Maxie's boyish footsteps were heard rapidly approaching, their materials were hastily gathered up, thrust into a closet close at hand and the key turned upon them. Then Lulu ran and opened the door.

"Hello!" cried Max in a perfectly good-humored tone, "what do you lock a fellow out for? It looks as if you're up to some mischief. I just came to tell you there's company in the parlor and they've asked for you — both of you."

"Who are they?" asked Lulu, glancing at her reflection in a mirror opposite, to make sure that dress and hair were in order.

She was neat and orderly by nature and her father very particular about the appearance of his children. He did not care to have them expensively attired, but always neat and tidy.

"The Oaks young folks," replied Max, " — Horace and Frank and their two sisters, Maud and Sydney."

"Come, Gracie," said Lulu, turning to her little sister, "we both look nice and we'll go right down."

The children all felt rather flattered by the call because the Oaks young people were older than themselves. Horace, Frank and Maud were all older than Max, and Sydney was between him and Lulu in age.

With the Dinsmore girls, the Raymonds were quite well acquainted, having seen them frequently at Ion, and sometimes met them elsewhere; but the boys, who had been away at school, were comparative strangers.

Violet was in the parlor chatting pleasantly with her young cousins, the call being intended for her also, and her cheerful presence set her little step-daughters more at their ease than they would otherwise have been.

They had not been long in the room ere they learned that the special object of the visit was to invite them and Max to the Oaks to spend the greater part of Christmas week.

"It is to be a young people's party, you must all understand," said Maud, who seemed to be the chief speaker, "and so the captain and Cousin Vi are not invited — not that Cousin Vi is not young, you know, for she is that — but there are to be no married folks asked.

"There is to be the usual Christmas Eve party at Ion for all the family connection, Christmas tree and all that, and the grand dinner party on Christmas Day. Then all the boys and girls of the connection are invited to the Oaks to stay till the next Saturday evening.

"We hope, Cousin Vi, that Max and his sisters may come?"

"If it depended upon me," returned Violet pleasantly, "I presume I should say yes, but of course it will have to be as their father says."

"Oh, yes, certainly! Is he in?"

"No, and I fear he will not be for an hour or two, but if you will stay to tea, you will be pretty sure to see him."

The invitation was declined with thanks for they had other calls to make and must be going. They sat for some minutes longer — the whole four joining in an animated description of various diversions planned for the entertainment of their expected guests, and repeated again and again that they hoped max and his sisters would be permitted to come.

"I do wish papa may let us go!" cried Lulu, the moment the visitors had departed. "I'm sure it will be perfectly delightful!"

"So do I," said Max. "Mamma Vi, do you think papa will consent?"

"I really cannot say, Max," she answered doubtfully. "Do you want to go, too, Gracie?" she queried drawing the child to her side and softly smoothing her hair.

"Yes, mamma, if — if I could have you or papa with me. I don't want to go very much 'less one of you goes too."

"And you are such a delicate little darling that I hardly think your papa will feel willing to have you go without either of us along to take care of you."

"I can take perfectly good care of Gracie, Mamma Vi," asserted Lulu with dignity.

"Here comes papa," cried Max as a step was heard in the hall.

Then the door opened and the captain came in.

"We've had an invitation, papa, and hope you will let us accept it," Max said, coming eagerly forward.

"Oh, papa! Please, please do!" cried Lulu, running to him and taking hold of his hand.

"Let me hear about it," he said, sitting down and allowing Lulu to take possession of one knee, Gracie of the other, "but speak one at a time. Max, you are the eldest — we will let you have the first turn."

Violet sat quietly listening and watching her husband's face while the eager children told their tale and expressed their wishes.

He looked grave and thoughtful, and before he spoke she had a tolerably correct idea what he was about to say.

"I am glad my little Gracie does not care to go," he said, caressing the child as he spoke, "because she is too feeble and too young to be so long among comparative strangers, without papa or mamma to take care of her. I am sorry Lulu does want to accept the invitation, as there is an insuperable objection to letting her do so."

Lulu's countenance had assumed an expression of woeful disappointment not unmingled with anger and willfulness.

"I want to go, papa, and I do think you might let me go," she said with an ominous frown. "I'm not sickly and I'm a good deal older than Gracie."

"You cannot go, Lucilla," he said gravely and with some sternness of tone. "Max," in answer to the eagerly questioning look in the lad's eyes, "if you are particularly desirous to go, you have my permission."

"Thank you, sir," said the boy heartily.

"Papa, why can't I go?" grumbled Lulu.

"I think a moment's reflection will tell you why," he answered. "I will talk with you about it at another time. And now not another word on the subject till I mention it to you first."

Lulu was silenced for the time, but after tea, going into the library and finding her father sitting there alone, she went up to him, and in her most coaxing tones said, "Oh, papa! Won't you please let me go? I'll be — "

"Lulu," he interrupted sternly, "go immediately to your room and your bed."

"Papa, it isn't my bedtime for two hours yet," she said in a half pleading tone, "and I want to read this new 'Companion' that has just come."

"Don't let me have to repeat my order," was the stern rejoinder, and she obeyed, trembling and in haste.

She felt sorely disappointed, angry, and rebellious; but, as her father had said, a few moments' reflection showed her the reason of his refusal to allow her to accept the invitation to the Oaks. And, as she glanced round her rooms at the pretty things his indulgent kindness had supplied, her anger changed to penitence and love.

"Of course, papa was right," she sighed to herself as she moved about, getting ready for bed, "and it wasn't because he doesn't love to see me happy. I wish, oh, how I wish I'd been good about it!"

She was not at all drowsy, and it seemed a long, long time that she had been lying there awake, when at last she heard her father's step in the hall. Then he opened the door and came in.

He had a lighted lamp in his hand. He set it on the mantel and drew near the bed.

"You are awake, I see," he said.

"Yes, papa, and I'm sorry I was naughty."

"You understand why I sent you to bed? And why I refused to grant your request?"

"Yes, sir, you can't trust me to pay that visit because of my bad temper, and you sent me to bed for disobeying you by asking again after you told me to say no more about it."

"Yes, you must learn to be more obedient, less willful. Did you obey me about going immediately to bed?" he asked, drawing up a chair and seating himself close beside her."

"Yes, papa — just as quickly as I could get ready.'

"I hope you did not neglect to kneel down and ask forgiveness of God?" he said inquiringly, in a gentle, tender tone, bending over her, and smoothing her hair as he spoke. "You do not need to be told that when you are rebellious and disobedient to your earthly father, you are so toward your heavenly Father also, because He bids you 'honor thy father and thy mother.' "

"Yes, papa, I know. I did ask Him, and won't you forgive me, too?"

"Yes," he said, giving her a kiss. "I am sorry to have to deprive you of the pleasure of accepting that invitation, but I cannot yet trust you anywhere away from me, and it was to spare your feelings that I did not state my reason before your mamma and brother and sister."

"Oh! I'm sorry I was naughty about it, papa," she said, again putting her hand into his."

He held it in a kindly pressure while he went on talking to her.

"I intend you shall go to Ion to the Christmas Eve party and the dinner party the next day, as I shall be there too."

"Thank you, dear papa. I'd like to go ever so much, but I don't deserve to," she said humbly, "or to have any Christmas gifts. If I were you and had such a bad child, I wouldn't give her a single thing."

"I hope she is going to be a better girl in the future," he said kissing her goodnight.

It was a joyful surprise to Lulu when, at the breakfast table the next morning, her father said, "Children, your mamma and I are going to drive into the city and will take you along, and, as I suppose you would like to do some Christmas shopping, I shall advance your next week's allowance — perhaps furnish something over," he added with a kindly smile.

All three young faces had grown very bright and there was a chorus of thanks.

"We expect to start a few minutes after prayers," the captain went on, "and so there will be no school today."

"We like school, papa," said Grace. "I never liked it half so well before."

"Nor I." "Nor I," cried the other two.

"But you are glad of a holiday once in a while, nevertheless?" their father said with a pleased look.

"Oh, yes, indeed, papa! 'Specially when it is to go somewhere with you," replied Grace, and again the others gave hearty assent.

When family worship was over, the captain handed a little roll of bank notes to each, saying, "Now run away and get yourselves ready for your ride. Put on your warmest clothing for the wind is sharp."

They hurried out into the hall. Then Lulu hesitated, turned about and ran back.

"Papa," she said, rushing up to him, where he sat beside a table with some papers before him, and throwing her arm round his neck, "dear papa! You are just too good and kind to me! Oh, I don't mean to be disobedient, willful, or passionate ever again!"

"I am rejoiced to hear you say that, my dear little daughter," he replied, putting his arm round her, hugging her close, and kissing her tenderly, "and I do not think I shall regret anything I have done for you or either of the others. It is, to me, the greatest pleasure in life to do whatever I can to make my children happy."

"I am so, so sorry I was naughty and disobedient last night," she murmured, laying her cheek to his.

"Dear child," he said, "it is fully and freely forgiven. Now run up to your room and dress."

Grace called to Lulu as she came up the stairs, "Oh, Lu! Come in here a minute, into my room. Look, look, on the bed! See how many papa has given me — ten nice new one dollars."

Lulu counted them as they lay spread out in a row.

"Yes, ten," she said. "Oh, Gracie! Isn't it nice? Isn't papa kind?"

" 'Course he is — kindest man ever was made," said Grace. "Now see how many you have."

Lulu hastily spread out her roll and counted the bills. "Nine ones and one two," she announced.

"Just as many as mine," said Grace, "and I've got this besides," holding up a bright new silver half-dollar. "So mine's the most this time, isn't it?"

"No, because one of my bills counts two. That makes mine fifty cents the most. Papa has given us each ten dollars besides our regular allowance."

CHAPTER TWENTY-THIRD

At Christmas play, and make good cheer,
For Christmas comes but once a year.

—TUSSER

THE MORNING of the twenty-fourth found Grace almost too ill with a heavy cold to be out of bed, and it was quite evident that she would not be able to go to the Christmas Eve party at Ion, or the dinner on Christmas Day.

The captain was just finishing his morning dressing when Lulu knocked at his dressing room door. She had come with the news of Grace's illness and he followed her at once to the bedside of the sick child.

"My poor darling," he said, bending over her in tender concern, "you seem quite feverish. I think you must stay in bed and we will send for your doctor."

"And can't I go tonight, papa?" she asked, the tears starting to her eyes.

"I'm afraid not, darling; but don't fret, papa will try to find some way to make it up to you."

"I'll stay with her, papa, and read her stories, and do everything I can to help her enjoy herself," cried Lulu eagerly. "I may, mayn't I?"

"You may, if you choose," he said, "but I thought you were very anxious to go."

"I was, but I'm not now," she said. "I'd rather stay with Gracie. I shouldn't be one bit happy there without her."

"Oh, Lu! I'd love to have you! But I don't want you to lose all that fun just for me,' Grace said with a wistful, loving look into her sister's eyes.

~ 218 ~

"It wouldn't be fun without you, my Gracie," was the quick rejoinder.

"I am glad indeed that my little daughters love each other so dearly," the captain said, kissing first one and then the other. "Well, we will see what can be done. If it were not for disappointment to your mamma, I should stay at home with you, my darlings. As it is, I shall spend at least a part of the evening with you."

He left them and sought Violet in her dressing room.

"My dear, what has happened? I am sure you look anxious and troubled!" she exclaimed the instant she caught sight of his face.

"I confess that I am a little troubled about Grace," he replied. "She seems to have taken a very heavy cold. I shall send at once for the doctor. And, of course, she has to be disappointed in her expectations for this evening."

"Then, let us all stay at home," returned Violet promptly. "I could not enjoy myself, leaving the poor darling at home sick. Besides," glancing from the window, "do you see? It is snowing fast and I should not like to expose baby to the storm. So I propose that we change our plans entirely and have a private Christmas of our own," she went on in a lively tone. "What do you say to it, my dear?"

They discussed the idea for some minutes, presently growing quite enthusiastic over it.

Their plans were nearly matured when the breakfast bell rang, and shortly after leaving the table they began to carry them out.

Max was taken into their confidence and allowed to assist. A proud and happy boy was he, going about with an air of mystery as one to whom secret and important business is entrusted.

The little girls, shut up in their own apartments — Grace reclining on a couch, Lulu with her as constant companion, and making every exertion for her entertainment, while papa, mamma, and Maxie came running in now and then to ask how she was — knew nothing of messages sent back and forth through the telephone, of packages of various shapes and sizes brought into the house, of mysterious goings and comings, and much time spent by papa, mamma, Maxie, Christine, and others in a certain large room, hitherto but little used.

Grace frequently fell asleep. Then Lulu would darken the room, go into the adjoining one, leaving the door ajar, so that she could hear the slightest movement her little sick sister might make on waking, and amuse herself with a book or her own thoughts.

Their meals were brought to them, and set out in their sitting room upon a little round table covered with a snowy damask cloth whereon were arranged a set of dainty china dishes of a size just suited to the occasion, and toothsome viands such as papa deemed they might eat and enjoy without danger to their health.

It was very nice, they thought — almost nicer, just for a change, than going to the larger table downstairs with the rest of the family.

Soon after they had their supper, their father came in, bringing the doctor with him, for his second visit of the day.

"Ah! She is a good deal better," Dr. Conly said, when he had examined his little patient. "Hardly well enough yet to go to Ion," he added with a humorous look and smile, "but I think, if well wrapped up, she may venture a trip downstairs in papa's arms and even stay a little while, if she finds the change to the parlor a pleasant one."

"Should you like it, papa's dear pet?" the captain asked, leaning over her.

"Yes, sir, if you and my doctor think it will be good for me," was the reply in a submissive and rather languid tone, "and if my Lulu is to come, too," she added with a loving look at her sister.

"Oh, yes, indeed! We would not think of going without Lulu!" their father said smiling affectionately upon her also.

So a large shawl was brought and carefully wrapped about Gracie's slender little figure, and she made the short journey in her father's strong arms, the doctor and Lulu going before, hand in hand, chatting and laughing merrily.

Max heard them and threw open the parlor door just as they reached it.

Then what a surprise for the little girls! A large, handsome Christmas tree loaded with beautiful things, burst upon their astonished sight and was greeted by them with exclamations of wonder and delight.

"Oh! Oh! Oh! It's the very prettiest Christmas tree we ever saw! And we didn't know we were to have any at all! And how many, many lovely things are on it! Papa, papa, how good and kind you are to us!"

He looked as if he enjoyed their surprise and delight quite as much as they did the tree.

"Other folks have been kind to you, too, my darlings," he said seating himself with Gracie still in his arms, "as you will see presently, when the gifts are distributed."

"Who, papa?" asked Gracie, laying her head on his shoulder and gazing with delighted eyes, beginning to single out one beautiful object from another as she sent her glances up and down, here and there.

"Grandma Elsie, and everybody else in the Ion family, I believe — the Oaks and Laurels and Fairview friends, and Roselands people, too, to say nothing of mamma and Maxie."

"They're ever so good and kind! They always are," she said in grateful tones. "Oh!" for the first time perceiving that Violet stood near her with the baby in her arms, "mamma and baby, too! And how pleased baby looks at the tree!" for the little one was stretching her arms toward it, and cooing and smiling, her pretty blue eyes shining with delight.

When all, children and servants — for the latter had been called in to enjoy the sight also — had looked to their fill, the gifts were distributed.

They were numerous — nearly everybody having given to nearly everybody else — and many of those received by the parents and children were very handsome. But their father's gift — a tiny watch to each, to help them to be punctual with all their duties, he said — was what gave the greatest amount of pleasure to Lulu and Grace.

Both they and their brother went to bed that night and woke the next morning very happy children.

The weather being still too severe for the little ones to be taken out, the captain and Violet went to Ion only for a call, and returned early in the day, bringing a portion of the party that usually gathered there, to dine with them at Woodburn.

Among these, to Lulu's extreme satisfaction, was Evelyn. She stayed till after tea, and all the afternoon there was much passing to and fro of the different members of the large family connection.

Evelyn was to be at the Oaks for the next few days with the other young people, and regretted greatly that Lulu was not to go too.

But Lulu's rebellious feeling about it was a thing of the past. She told Evelyn frankly her father's reason for refusing his consent, adding that she felt that he was right, and that he was so dear, so kind and indulgent in everything that he thought best to allow, that she was now entirely satisfied to stay at home — particularly as Gracie was not well and needed her nursing.

Grace went early to bed and to sleep. Max and Evelyn had gone to the Oaks. There were only grown people in the parlors now, and Lulu did not care to be there, even if she had not wanted to be near her sleeping sister.

There was an open, glowing fire in their little sitting room, a high fender of polished brass obviating all danger from it to the children's skirts. Lulu seated herself in an easy chair beside it and fell into a reverie unusually deep and prolonged for her.

She called to mind all the Christmases she could remember — not very many — the last two spent very pleasantly with her new mamma's relatives, the two previous ones passed not half so agreeably in the poor apology for a home that had been hers and Gracie's before their father's second marriage.

But what a change for the better that had brought! What forlorn little things she and Gracie were then! And what favored children now! What a sweet, sweet home of their own, with their father in it! As she had said to Eva that afternoon, "such a dear, kind father — interested in everything that concerned his children; so thoughtful about providing pleasures for them, as well as needful food, shelter, and clothing; about their health, too, and the improvement of their minds; reading with them, even in other than school hours; talking with them of what they read, and explaining so clearly and patiently anything they did not quite understand; but, above all, striving to lead them to Christ, and train them for His service in this world and the next."

He had read with them that morning the story of the Savior's birth, and spoken feelingly to them of God's wonderful love shown in the "unspeakable gift" of His dear Son.

"Certainly, there could not be in all the world a better, dearer father than theirs. How strange that she could ever grieve him by being naughty, rebellious, passionate! Oh, if she could only be good — always a comfort and blessing to him! She would try, she would, with all her might!"

Just then the door opened softly, and he came in, came noiselessly to her side, lifted her in his arms, and sat down with her on his knee.

"What has my little girl been thinking of sitting here all by herself?" he asked, pressing his lips to her cheek.

She told him in a few words, finishing with her longing desire to be to him a better child, a comfort and blessing.

"Indeed I ought to be, papa," she said, "and you are such a dear, kind father! You have given me — and all of us — such a lovely home and such a happy, happy Christmas — the very happiest we have ever known!"

"And it is God our heavenly Father who has put it in my power to do all that I have done for you and for all my darlings," he said with emotion, drawing her closer and holding her tenderly to his heart, "and, oh, my dear child, if I could know that you had begun this day to truly love and serve Him, it would be to me the happiest Christmas that I have ever known."

The End

Learn more in this fun Biographical Novel about

Martha Finley

the beloved author of The Elsie Books!

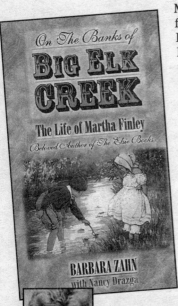

Martha Finley wrote the famous Elsie Books in Elkton Maryland, where Barbara Zahn, author of this biographical novel currently resides. Motivated by her own love for The Elsie Books, Barbara draws us into to this fictional but factual presentation of Miss Finley's unusual & devout life. Peppered with personality from this small town and true to the times, this lively & dramatic heartwarming story satiates the appetite of the most avid Elsie Dinsmore fan.

Barbara Zahn read her first Elsie book at age ten and is a collector of original editions. She lives not far from Martha Finley's original home in Elkton Maryland, where Martha Finley is now remembered and laid to rest.

Another quality paperback from Hibbard Publications.
Available from your favorite retail bookstore.

Collect all 28 books in

THE ELSIE BOOKS

Series by Martha Finley

*Hibbard Publications is proud to bring you this
growing line of great Elsie Dinsmore books.*

Elsie Dinsmore: Book 1
Elsie's Holiday: Book 2
Elsie's Girlhood: Book 3
Elsie's Womanhood: Book 4
Elsie's Motherhood: Book 5
Elsie's Children: Book 6
Elsie's Widowhood: Book 7
Grandmother Elsie: Book 8
Elsie's New Relations: Book 9
Elsie at Nantucket: Book 10
The Two Elsies: Book 11
Elsie's Kith & Kin: Book 12
Elsie's Friends at Woodburn: Book 13
Christmas with Grandma Elsie: Book 14
Elsie and the Raymonds: Book 15
Elsie Yachting with the Raymonds: Book 16
Elsie's Vacation: Book 17
Elsie at Viamede: Book 18
Elsie at Ion: Book 19
Elsie at the World's Fair: Book 20
Elsie's Journey on Inland Waters: Book 21
Elsie at Home: Book 22
Elsie on the Hudson: Book 23
Elsie in the South: Book 24
Elsie's Young Folks: Book 25
Elsie's Winter Trip: Book 26
Elsie and Her Loved Ones: Book 27
Elsie and Her Namesake: Book 28

Available from your favorite retail bookstore.